CAUTION CAUTION C
TION CAUTION

PAWS vs. CLAWS

UTION CAUTION
CAUTION CAUTION

PAWS VS. CLAWS

A QUEENIE AND ARTHUR NOVEL

SPENCER QUINN

SCHOLASTIC INC.

Copyright © 2019 by Pas de Deux Corp

This book was originally published in hardcover by Scholastic Press in 2019.

All rights reserved. Published by Scholastic Inc., *Publishers since 1920*. SCHOLASTIC and associated logos are trademarks and/or registered trademarks of Scholastic Inc.

The publisher does not have any control over and does not assume any responsibility for author or third-party websites or their content.

This book is a work of fiction. Names, characters, places, and incidents are either the product of the author's imagination or are used fictitiously, and any resemblance to actual persons, living or dead, business establishments, events, or locales is entirely coincidental.

ISBN 978-1-338-24581-3

10 9 8 7 6 5 4 3 2 1   20 21 22 23 24

Printed in the U.S.A.   40
This edition first printing 2020

Book design by Maeve Norton

THIS BOOK IS DEDICATED TO FOUR
YOUNG READERS—VIVIAN, TORI, GABI,
AND NORAH—AND A FIFTH ONE WHO
WILL BE APPEARING RIGHT AROUND
PUB DATE.

ONE

QUEENIE

BAD NEWS, PUSSYCAT," SAID BERTHA. "No cream today."

No cream today? Had I heard right? Well, that's not a real question. Of course I'd heard right. My hearing is as good as it gets. Everything about me is as good as it gets. My looks, for example, are off the charts. I'm a thing of beauty, from my gold-flecked button nose to the tip of my snowy tail. And my eyes! I'll make this simple: When you gaze into them, you never want to stop. That's happened to me so often—in fact, every time I come upon a mirror.

There are no mirrors in our kitchen here at the Blackberry Hill Inn. I prefer rooms with mirrors, but I make an exception for the kitchen. Every morning when I wake up I take an elegant little stretch—very different from the clumsy stretches of a certain other party who inhabits this place and whom you'll probably meet later, nothing I can do about it—and I glide down off the top of the grandfather clock in the front hall and make my way here, where Bertha, the cook, is standing by to serve me fresh cream in a pretty china saucer, white with a gold border. This saucer is known to everyone as Queenie's saucer. I'm Queenie, in case you haven't guessed. I hope I'm not going too fast, although if I am, don't expect me to do anything about it.

I stood motionless in the doorway, waiting for . . . what, exactly? For some explanation? For Bertha to come to her senses? No! I was waiting for my cream, period. This was basic: I, Queenie, start my day with fresh cream served in a special saucer named after me, Queenie. End of story.

Bertha looked at me. I looked at Bertha. Bertha's a big, strong woman with a roundish, not unpleasant face. She's quite presentable for a human, and we've always gotten along well, right up until now.

"What's with you?" she said.

Seriously? I didn't move a muscle. Perhaps a whisker or two quivered in the slight breeze drifting in from the hall. My whiskers are lovely, kind of a finishing touch to the whole stunning package, and quite intelligent in their own way. I wouldn't have minded watching them quiver for a bit, but . . . no mirror. My mood—so cheery on awakening, the memory of a brief nighttime trip down to the basement and a chance encounter with a mouse fresh in my mind— was darkening fast.

"Don't blame me," Bertha said. "It's not my fault."

So? What did that have to do with anything? Did I care about the whos or whys or—

At that moment Mom walked in, entering through the door that led to our family quarters upstairs.

"Morning, Bertha," Mom said. She glanced around. "Were you talking to someone?"

Bertha pointed at me with her chin. Some humans have a cool move or two—I don't mind admitting that—and the chin point is a personal favorite.

Mom laughed. "I do that all the time."

If that was a joke, I didn't get it. So Mom talks to me all the time? What's funny about that? We're very close. She tells me all sorts of things she tells nobody else. That's how I know, for example, that the Blackberry Hill Inn, which belongs to us—us being me; Mom; and the twins, Harmony and Bro, now on some sort of school vacation— and I suppose that one other party mentioned earlier, although he's the classic free-riding type, contributing nothing while eating us out of house and . . . but where was I? Right, the inn. The inn's not doing so well, Mom told me the other night, when it was just the two of us sitting by the fire in the small parlor. A bunch of money coming our way is still tied up in court, with more knots added by the day, Mom says. "We need guests, Queenie, and lots of 'em. But you know the problem."

I did. It was the end of winter, a time of year known as mud season in these parts. All the snow melts, somehow turning into mud. Through the kitchen window I could see the remains of the tall, shining snowman Harmony and Bro had built, now short and squat and marked with many yellow zigzags, thanks to certain bathroom habits of that other party. I myself don't go outside much at any time, but never in mud season. Mud spatters on my coat? What could be worse? Rain started up outside, pounding on the roof and slanting down the window.

"I think Queenie's mad at me," Bertha said.

"Oh?" said Mom.

"There's no cream today."

"How come?"

"No idea. I set the empties on the back step when I leave for the day, and Walter has always made the delivery by the time I get here in the morning—two gallons of whole milk and a pint of cream."

"Who's Walter?" Mom said.

"Mr. Doone's hired man," said Bertha. "More like a hired kid—he can't be more than seventeen or eighteen."

Mom opened the side door. One small glass bottle and two big ones, all empty, stood on the back step. Were we getting anywhere? If so, very very slowly. Mom closed the door.

4

"Maybe the cows are taking the day off," she said.

Bertha laughed, so this must have been another joke. Mom laughed, too. Sometimes Mom laughs at her own jokes. She looks very pretty when she laughs; actually she looks pretty all the time. Her eyes are really quite beautiful, big and dark and full of thoughts. Not beautiful like mine—just throwing that in so you don't form a wrong opinion. You're welcome, but don't count on me to keep looking out for you.

"The fact is, there's only one cow," Bertha said. "And she never takes a day off."

"Mr. Doone has only one cow?" said Mom.

"But she's an Emsworth."

"Emsworth?" Mom said. "Is that a breed of cow? I've never heard of it."

Bertha shook her head. "Not a breed. This cow is the great-great—I don't know how many greats—granddaughter of Lady Emsworth, the most prizewinning cow that ever lived in the Green Mountains. She's called Sweet Lady Em, on account of the sweetness of her milk." Bertha glanced my way. "And her cream," she added.

Yes, my cream. That was the issue. Thanks for remembering. Where was my cream? Had this Sweet Lady Em character—evidently a cow having something to do with the delivery of my cream—messed up? I had very little experience with cows—in fact, only one, and that experience was not good. This was back in the days when I used to do much more outdoor roaming. That ended when we had a visit from an unpleasant old lady from a group with a strange name—the Society for the Protection of Birds, or something of that nature. The protection of birds? That made no sense to me. Birds are very capable of protecting themselves—by quickly taking off and soaring into the sky, for example. You've got to be even quicker to have the slightest chance of actually catching one, which I'm happy to say I've done on many many . . .

But back to my one and only experience with a cow. At the time, I happened to be following a mousy scent trail that led through a tiny hole in the wall of a barn not far from Blackberry Creek, which I've never crossed, creeks being wet. Tiny holes are no problem for me. I just sort of flowed through it and came softly down inside the barn, where I got my first look at this mouse of mine, a fattish little fellow burrowing into some straw on the floor. We seemed to be in a stall, sharing the space with a yellowish-colored cow busy chewing on something that smelled atrocious, chewing and chewing but never swallowing. Not my problem. I had no problems. Fattish mice are never much of a challenge. You don't even need to be the best pouncer in the world, although it just so happens that I am.

I pounced. What fun! Very quiet fun—a look of terror in micey eyes is completely silent—and at the same time good-natured, one of us batting the other around from paw to paw, and the other getting batted, no harm, no foul. No telling how it would end—which makes it even more fun! My mouse buddy and I were so busy having fun that we lost track of the cow, who must have changed position slightly because all of a sudden I felt an extremely heavy hoof settle down on my tail. I tried to scramble away and got nowhere. This was a nightmare. Meanwhile the mouse shot me one brief glance, then scurried up the wall and disappeared somewhere above, as though it got to decide when our little game was over. How maddening! Also maddening was this heavy hoof. I curled around and bit into it in decisive fashion. My teeth are needle-sharp, by the way, maybe should have gotten that fact in earlier. The cow lowered her head slightly and gazed down at me, still chewing in that annoying way but otherwise showing nothing—like pain, for example, from my needle-sharp teeth.

I tried hissing. I have a loud, harsh hiss that even scares me sometimes. She went on chewing. Her cud? Is that what it's called? I believe so. And then came the very worst moment of the whole episode. The cow slobbered some of that cud directly down on me! On my sublime and glowing coat! I know how terrible you're feeling for me right now, and I appreciate it. I'm sure nothing remotely so awful has ever happened to you.

But back to me. For no reason I could see, the cow slowly raised her hoof and shifted toward the other side of the stall. I bolted out of that barn and made my way home to the inn, where I mounted the grandfather clock, remaining there until the cuddy smell had vanished completely—several days, if I remember right.

And now cows were out to get me again. Where was my cream? I wanted my cream! Cream! Cream! Cream!

"Is her hair standing on end?" Mom said.

"Looks that way," said Bertha.

"I wonder if something's wrong with her."

"Something's wrong with her, all right. She wants her cream."

"You think?"

"I know."

Mom gazed down at me. "What a funny little character!"

"That's one way of putting it," Bertha said.

"Come on, Bertha. I know you love her."

"Hrrmmph," said Bertha. That's a sound she makes to show she loves me, just in case you were wondering. Mom's always right about the big things.

Meanwhile she'd opened the door to our quarters and was calling up the stairs.

"Bro? Are you awake?"

"No."

"I want you to walk over to the Doones' place, see if they're on the way with the milk."

"And cream," Bertha said.

Yes, she loves me, loves me very much. Very nice, although not surprising.

"What about Harmony?" Bro yelled down. Bro and Harmony are twins, but not the identical kind. I've heard that explained to so many humans so many times that it makes me crazy. When I'm crazy my fur stands on end. Like now. I was having a very bad day and it had hardly begun.

"I picked you," Mom said.

"Why?"

"Luck of the draw. And take Arthur. He could use the exercise."

TWO

ARThUR

I DREAMED I WAS AT A COOKOUT. I LOVE cookouts so this dream couldn't have been any better. Bro was at the grill flipping burgers. Burgers flipped by Harmony stay flipped. Burgers flipped by Bro have a way of getting loose from time to time. That's something I've noticed all by my very own self. You may hear that old Arthur doesn't have a lot going on upstairs. Don't you believe it! I'm upstairs every night, sleeping under Bro's bed. That way I have two roofs over my head, one the bed and the other the actual roof. What could be snugger than that? So there I was caught up in a very snug dream, a burger in my near future, when from over in the meadow I heard the mooing of a cow. Was this mooing part of the dream? Or part of whatever happens in the world when I'm all caught up in a dream? Whoa! That was a deep thought. I prefer the other kind, not so deep. With all this confusion going on, my lovely cookout dream faded away until there was nothing left but the smell of grilling burgers. I came very close to waking up, settling into a nice doze at the very last moment. Arthur dodges a bullet! Which had actually sort of happened once with real gunfire, a big event for all of us at the inn, although the details grow sketchier every day. One thing I know how to do is keep a clear mind. A clear mind is ready for anything!

Just above me on the bed, Bro made a soft sort of dozing murmur. Mom always says it helps to be really good at doing at least one thing in this life. No worries. We're champion dozers, me and Bro. I heard a few more moos, but distant now, almost at the edge of what I could hear, so maybe beyond what your ears—rather small compared to mine—can do. Distant mooing turned out to go very well with dozing, and so did the sound of rain, pitter-pattering on the window. This day was off to a great start.

And it could have gone on and on just like this, as far as I was concerned, but then, from somewhere below, came the voice of Mom.

"Bro? Are you awake?"

From the bed above came a low groan. Then Bro raised his voice and said, "No."

Whew! Lucky for him. If he'd been awake, how could he have avoided whatever Mom wanted him to do? I couldn't think what that might be, but it was sure to be worse than what we had going on right now. I really loved Bro at that moment, hard to explain why. Except that I always love him, of course.

One little problem. Mom didn't seem to have gotten the message. "I want you to walk over to the Doones' place," she was saying, "see if they're on the way with the milk."

Then came Bertha's voice. "And cream."

I had no interest in milk or cream, but some mornings Bertha fries up sausages. Suddenly I was wide awake, sniffing the air and listening for the hiss and bubble of sausages in the pan. Meanwhile there was some back-and-forth about Harmony, not easy to follow, and then from out of nowhere I came into the conversation, and in the worst possible way.

"And take Arthur. He could use the exercise."

Downstairs in the kitchen, there was no pan on the stove, no Bertha, no sausages. We had Mom, dressed in jeans and a sweater; Bro, in his pj's; and me, wearing my plaid collar. I also have a collar that lights up in the nighttime, and a Christmas collar with bells, but they both make me a little jumpy. Not jumpy enough to get me actually jumping, actual jumping being quite tiring, as I'm sure you know. Mom went into a long explanation about milk and cream and the Doones' farm. Bro scratched himself under his arm and said, "Huh?" I hadn't been even the slightest bit itchy, but all of a sudden I was itchier than I'd ever been! Life is so full of surprises! I scratched behind one ear with one back paw, and then tackled the other ear with the other back paw, moving on to the—

"Arthur!" said Mom. "Get a grip!"

I froze, one paw—or maybe more than one—in midair. Mom doesn't look scary, but she can be scary just the same. I gave myself a real good shake, putting everything in the past. Meanwhile Mom seemed to be going over the whole milk story once more.

"All right, all right," Bro said. "I got it."

And the next thing I knew, we were in the front hall, Bro putting on boots and a yellow raincoat and me trying not to glance back toward the reception area—specifically at the grandfather clock. But then I did—I just couldn't help it. And of course there she was, lounging way up on top, gazing down at me with one of those cool golden looks, a look with a clear message: *I'm above you in every way.* I gave her a look right back, better believe it, a look designed to let her know what was what, and in no uncertain terms. She yawned an enormous yawn.

"Arthur!" Bro said. "What's with the growling? Cool it!"

Growling? I listened for growling, heard none.

Bro opened the front door. "Let's get this over with." We went outside.

Hey! It was raining! That took me by surprise. But then I remembered it was mud season. Mud season! My favorite season of the whole year, although I couldn't think of the names of any of the others. And there was no time for thinking because down at the end of our long circular drive I spotted a nice big mud puddle, so inviting. I took off in that direction, maybe not at my top speed but much much faster than standing still. On the way, I made one little detour over to our snowman. We'd had so much fun building him, me, Bro, and Harmony. You make a snowman by rolling up balls of snow—a huge one, a not-so-huge one, and a small one, and then stack them up, also taking big bites out of them every chance you get. Harmony and Bro handled the rolling and stacking and I took care of the biting. That's called teamwork, and we're a real good team, the twins and me.

But now—poor guy!—our snowman wasn't looking his best. He'd gotten short and slumpy, and his face was blank. I raised my leg and marked him. Just part of my job here at the inn—didn't Bertha often say, "Somebody let Arthur out so he can do his business"? Your mind can wander a bit while you're out marking things—which you probably know already—so when I was done I couldn't remember what I'd been doing before that. And then it came to me: mud puddle!

"Arthur! No!"

When you're on the move, your ears flap around, stands to reason. And I was closing in on top speed, meaning I'd be reaching that mud puddle sometime soonish, certainly before lunch. But back to my ears. Flapping ears make a flap-flap-flapping sound in your head, surprisingly loud. And if someone says something while you've got that flap-flap-flapping going on, you may not hear that something right. Take "Arthur! No!" for example. Maybe that was it, but how can you be sure? What if it was "Arthur! Go for it! Go for it, my man!" Confusing, right? I ended up doing the best I could with the information available.

"Oh my god."

We followed the cart path that led past our toolshed and the rusted-out old sports car—possibly called a Triumph—that Dad hadn't finished fixing up before he went away. Dad had left not long after I got here, but not because of me. Was it because of Lilah Fairbanks, the interior decorator Mom hired to fix things up nice and fancy? All I know is that I haven't seen Dad or Lilah Fairbanks in a long time and the decor is back to how it was. Much nicer, in my opinion. Bro took a sidelong look at the Triumph as we went by. He kind of slumped a little in his raincoat. Why? I had no idea, but I didn't like seeing him that way. It reminded me of the slumping snowman. Bro was no slumper. He was Bro! Actually, he's not Bro. Bro's what everyone calls him, but his real name is . . . something else. It might come to me. Is it possible Mom named Harmony and Dad named Bro with whatever the real name was? Wow! My mind was having a brilliant day and it had only just begun.

Meanwhile we had this other situation, the slumping one. I have a lot of jobs—way too many to go into now, a good thing because it's not so easy to remember them all—but one of my most important jobs is to stamp out slumping here at the Blackberry Hill Inn. My first go-to anti-slumping move is all about pressing myself against the slumper's leg, nice and hard so they know I'm there.

"Arthur! For god's sake!"

Bro backed away. Was there some problem? His raincoat snaps seemed to have come unsnapped, and his pj's had suddenly gotten all muddy for some reason. Had Bro been rolling around with me in the mud puddle? What a great kid! Who wouldn't love Bro? And the fact that he was rocking that raincoat-and-pj's combo just made him all the greater in my book. I pressed against his leg again, maybe a little more vigorously this time.

"Arthur! You're . . . whatever that word is. 'In' something or other. Harm would know." More quietly he added,

"Of course Harm would know." He got a faraway look in his eyes. At the same time, his hand came down—sort of all on its own—and gave me a nice scratch on the top of my head, right on that spot that's so hard for me to reach.

We walked on. The rain slanted down, dripped off Bro's chin. After a while he said, "Incorrigible! That's the word. You're incorrigible, Arthur."

Incorrigible? A new one on me. But it sounded real good! Arthur the Incorrigible! I picked up my pace a bit.

But not for long. Picking up the pace can be very tiring. I might have lagged behind a little, a realization that came to me when I noticed Bro up ahead, waiting by the old weather-beaten fence at the end of our meadow. On the other side there were woods and then, if I remembered right, the Doones' farm. I'd only been there once, on a strange summer day when I'd sort of wandered off and ended up lost. Not lost, exactly, because after Mr. Doone called Mom and she drove me back home, Harmony said, "No way he was lost— all he has to do is follow his own scent back home." Wow! If only I'd thought of that at the time!

Instead I was thinking about it now, on the cart path still some distance from the fence. I raised up my nose and sniffed the air. And sure enough, there was my smell, a nice mixture of wet wool, mud, something not too different from earwax, and a touch of something else hard to describe. Let's call it pure Arthur. And what was this? A hint of cow smell? Cow smell is somewhat like horse smell, although milkier. What was going on? No way I had any cow smell in me. Even just the idea was—

"Arthur! We haven't got all day!"

We didn't? Don't we always have all day, each and every day? That's how I roll. But I'd never want to disappoint Bro. I geared up to a quick trot, almost, and caught up to him. He stepped over a broken fence rail and headed toward the woods. I came very close to leaping right over that broken rail myself, only ramping that leap over down to a crawl under at the very last second. I'm something of an athlete, perhaps a fact I should have mentioned earlier.

"Come on, Arthur," Bro said. "Heel. That means walk beside me. I've told you a million times."

Heel meant walk beside Bro? How interesting! I drew up beside him and did some big-time heeling. A narrow, muddy trail led us squish squish into the woods. We were among the first trees when someone appeared up ahead, rounding a bend and coming toward us.

He saw us and stopped, a kid, like Bro, but bigger. This was Jimmy Doone, maybe not a friend of Bro's, but someone we knew. Was he in Harmony's class at school? I might have heard something about that. It's also possible that Harmony's class was a year ahead of Bro's class; I might have heard something about that, too. Meanwhile Bro and Jimmy were having a conversation.

"Bro?"

"Jimmy?"

"Hey."

"Hey."

"What's up?"

"Not much."

Jimmy came closer. He wore jeans, a T-shirt, and laceless sneakers. No raincoat, no hat, no boots, so he was soaked right through.

"What happened to you?" Bro said.

"Nothin'," said Jimmy.

"Like, your eye," Bro said. "It looks bad."

Whoa! I saw the same thing. One of Jimmy's eyes was swollen almost totally shut, the skin all purple and even bleeding a bit.

"Uh," Jimmy said. "Ran into a door."

"Huh?"

"You heard me," Jimmy said. He turned his face away.

"Um," Bro said.

Jimmy said nothing, just gazed into the distance.

"We kinda . . ." Bro went silent, then tried again. "My mom sent us for, uh, the milk."

Jimmy wheeled around on him. "Ain't gonna be no stupid milk!"

THREE
ARTHUR

BRO AND JIMMY GAZED AT EACH other. Jimmy's gaze was real angry. At first Bro's gaze was surprised, then sort of puzzled, and finally on the way to anger, too. What was going on? I was afraid a fistfight might be next. Jimmy was a big kid and a lot taller, but Bro was very sturdy. I'd only seen Bro in a fight once. He'd popped a bully named Foster a good one, bang on the nose. That was a nice moment in my life, although I wasn't in a hurry to see more. I rolled over and played dead.

They both turned my way. I tried wagging my tail, only to find it was trapped under me and couldn't move. Playing dead is not as easy as you might think. Meanwhile the anger was leaking out of both of them. I could feel it, a thick, twisted thing that rose and drifted away.

"What's his name again?" Jimmy said.

"Arthur," said Bro.

"What's he doing?"

"Playing dead."

"Does he know any other tricks?"

"Nope."

Okay. Maybe that was true. I'd tried to master shake-a-paw, but it had proven a little too complicated. No worries: Playing dead was a much better trick. Lying there on the muddy path just inside the woods, cold rain beating down on my face, I felt pretty pleased with myself.

"So, uh," Bro said, "what's with this milk thing?"

Jimmy looked down at the ground. "It's not my fault."

"Huh? Who said it was?"

Jimmy's voice rose, cracking a little at the end. "That jerk Walter. And my dad believes him. Like always."

"Who's Walter?" said Bro.

"A high-school dropout my dad hired," Jimmy said. He raised his head. Rain washed away the blood from around his swollen eye. "But this time he's wrong. I always lock the door, every night. It's my last chore. I look forward to it."

"What door?"

"The barn door."

"Someone broke into your barn?"

"They must've. But Walter says the door was unlocked and hanging open when he went to do the milking this morning."

"Maybe someone broke in and left the door that way," Bro said.

"That's what I told him. But my dad took a look and said no one broke in—'no one broke in, you moron,' were the exact words. On account of no sign of any tampering."

"Tampering?"

"Like messing with the lock, marks from a crowbar, a screwdriver, anything like that. So I forgot to lock the door, like, logically." Jimmy's open eye got fierce. "But I didn't forget. I have this whole routine, Bro. I've got routines for everything." That one open eye suddenly teared up. Jimmy wiped away the tears with the back of his hand, in an impatient way, like the eye had let him down.

Bro looked away from Jimmy. His gaze found me. I seemed to still be playing dead. Among the many good things about it, playing dead's a restful trick. Bro blinked a couple of times, that human blink for when they don't quite believe what they're seeing. I got that totally. How could anyone be so good at playing dead? That's what Bro had to be thinking. I tried to wag my tail. It wouldn't wag. I remembered I was lying on it and decided to try again later.

Bro turned to Jimmy. "You've got routines for everything?"

Jimmy nodded. "That's how I deal with . . ."

"Deal with what?"

Jimmy shook his head. "Nothing."

"Okay," Bro said.

Then came a long silence, except for the rain.

"So, uh," Bro said at last, "is something missing from the barn?"

"Bro? What's with you?"

"Huh?"

"I already told you—there's no milk."

"The cows got away?"

Jimmy's voice rose. "Someone must've . . . must've helped." He calmed down a little. "And there's only one cow."

"Yeah?"

"Sweet Lady Em. She's very valuable—our most valuable possession. Hey! Maybe you saw her on your way here."

"What does she look like?"

"A cow," Jimmy said. "Did you see a cow—any kind of cow?"

"Nope," said Bro. "But I'll help you find her."

Jimmy looked surprised. "Yeah?"

"Sure." Bro turned my way. "Knock it off, Arthur. Time to rock and roll." Rock and roll? A new one on me. But I understood the knock-it-off part. I'd never want to disappoint Bro, so I stopped what I was doing, namely playing dead, and just lay there.

"Arthur! That means you have to get up."

Ah. How interesting! Rock and roll meant getting up? I'd learned a new thing! Kind of fun, although I wouldn't want to make a habit of it.

"So get up."

Right. I got my paws under me and pushed, my usual method for getting up. It works just about every time. Next I gave myself a good shake, sort of making a rainstorm of my own. Wow! What a day I was having! Was a snack in the cards, preferably very soon? I was getting hungry. Then it hit me that I hadn't even had breakfast. Uh-oh. Maybe things weren't as rosy as I'd thought.

"What kind of dog is he?" Jimmy asked.

"Just a mutt," said Bro.

Mutt? I'd heard that before, and always like this, as though mutt wasn't the very best type of dog. But of course it was, so this had to be one of those mysteries you just have to live with in this life.

"I've always wanted a dog," Jimmy said.

"You don't have one?"

Jimmy shook his head.

"How come?"

"He hates dogs."

"Walter?"

"I meant my dad," Jimmy said. "But probably Walter, too. They think alike."

■ ■ ■

We set off in search of a cow named Sweet Lady Em, if I'd been following things right. First we headed back, wandering this way and that over our meadow—a hilly, rolling kind of meadow, more tiring than the flat kind, my preference when it comes to meadows. There were no cows in sight, although I did pick up some cow scent. Had I already picked it up, not long after Bro and I started out? Maybe yes, maybe no. Was cow scent important somehow? I was still wondering about that when we came to a dirt road lined with low, mud-splattered snowbanks.

"Is Arthur good at tracking things?" Jimmy said.

"Once he found a kimono in the trash," said Bro.

"Huh?"

"Like a kind of robe. From Japan. It was my mom's. Arthur dug it out and brought it to her. Turned out she'd thrown it away."

"How come?"

"Didn't like it anymore."

"How come?" Jimmy asked again.

I didn't remember hearing anybody so interested in how comes before. I gave Jimmy a quick a sniff, picked up a certain boy-plus-smelly-socks scent I was already familiar with from Bro. I didn't really know Jimmy, but I was starting to like him. I'd only seen him a few times, once at the outdoor rink, watching the U-12 all-stars. Harmony and Bro both played on the team, and I loved going to their games, and if only that incident of me and the puck— inedible, by the way—hadn't happened, Mom would have taken me to a lot more games this season. But now it was over, so no worries. Was baseball next? I thought so. I couldn't wait. Baseball is my favorite sport, the baseballs themselves fascinating, especially their insides.

"I don't know," Bro was saying. "My, uh, dad brought it back from a business trip or something."

Was this still about the kimono? I remembered its silky feel, fun to chew on, but otherwise I was lost.

"They're divorced?" Jimmy said.

"Uh-huh," said Bro.

"Mine, too.

"You live with your dad?"

"Oh, yeah."

The rain let up a bit. It got quiet in the meadow. I shifted over and sat on Bro's foot, not sure why.

"Let's find Sweet Lady Em," Bro said. He patted my back. "Find the cow, Arthur."

No problem! I loved Bro and would do anything for him, as long as a snack break was coming soon. Now would have been nice, but I smelled no snacks on either of them. Something about a cow, was it? I raised my nose, smelled no hint of cow. Too bad. When you sniff for something and come up empty, you have to go elsewhere and try again. Going elsewhere means moving, never my first choice.

I rose. The first problem you have to deal with when moving is this: Where to? For no reason, I decided to scramble over the snowbank and onto the road, a dirt road, if I haven't mentioned that already, and therefore very muddy, this being mud season, as I may also have mentioned. Next I took a quick sip from a puddle—not the tastiest water I'd ever tried, but no complaints—and sniffed the air. Cow? No cow? I wasn't sure, but some sort of car had been by this spot and not long ago. Cars leave a smell no one could miss, not even you with your tiny nose. Sorry about the tiny nose remark. I take it back.

Meanwhile I was setting off down the road, following the car smell.

"Arthur?" Bro said. "You smell something?"

They ran along beside me. Well, maybe not running, but certainly not walking their slowest. We went up a hill and had almost reached the crest when a man appeared, walking our way. Jimmy came to a sudden stop.

"You know this guy?" Bro said.

Jimmy nodded. "Walter."

Walter? Hadn't I just heard about him? I dug deep into my memory, a mostly empty space and not very big. But was there something about Walter? Uh-oh. Not fond of me and my kind, perhaps? How could that even be? It made no sense.

I took a close look at Walter as he approached. His hands were busy with small green pieces of paper. Money? Wow! Money was little green pieces of paper! I'd made a mental leap, maybe my very first.

Walter looked up, saw us, and stuffed the money in his pocket. He had a thin mustache and a bit of scruffy hair on his chin, but the rest of his face seemed more kid than man. The body was all man, big and strong. He walked up to us, in no hurry, and smiled. "Any luck, Jimmy?"

Jimmy glared at him with his good eye. "What's it look like?"

Walter's gaze went to Bro. "Who's this?"

"My friend Bro," said Jimmy.

"Bro, huh?" Walter said. "You really a friend of Jimmy's? 'Cause this is the first I heard of him having any friends."

"Yeah," Bro said. "I'm his friend."

"Then, as a friend, you should tell him to get that barn door good and locked every night," Walter said.

Jimmy kept glaring at Walter. "I locked the door," he said.

"We want to go through that again?" said Walter.

Jimmy looked down.

"Didn't think so," Walter said.

I decided that I didn't like Walter. The next thing I knew, I was growling, a deep growl with some fierceness in it. I hadn't heard my growl in some time. It gave me the chills. Wow! I was having a pretty good day.

Walter jumped back. "Hey! Is that fleabag fixin' to bite me?"

"He's not a fleabag," Bro said. "And he likes most everybody. Just about."

"What's that supposed to mean?" said Walter.

Bro didn't answer but tilted up his chin, keeping his eyes on Walter and not looking away. Walter's face reddened. Was he about to come closer? I upped my growl. Walter shot me a nasty glance, then circled around us, heading in the direction we'd come from.

"Good luck, kiddies," he said. "And no point in searching down this road. I already checked it out."

Walter went away, walking that in-no-hurry walk of his. Jimmy and Bro watched him go.

"What's with him?" Bro said.

"He's a jerk."

"So how come he works for you?"

Jimmy's voice rose. "He doesn't work for me."

"Your dad—you know what I meant."

"Sorry, Bro."

"Nothing to be sorry about," Bro said.

Jimmy gave Bro a quick look, like . . . like he was seeing Bro in a new way. "Walter's the son of an old buddy of my dad's from up in Maine."

"And he needed a job?"

"Partly," Jimmy said. "But mostly my dad's buddy thought working on a farm would be good for him, maybe straighten him out."

"Straighten him out from what?"

"Dropping out of high school, getting speeding tickets, stuff like that." Down the road, Walter went around a bend and out of sight.

"And your dad likes him?" Bro said.

"Oh, yeah," said Jimmy.

Meanwhile I was still picking up car smells, wafting to us over the crest of the hill. I followed those smells, following smells being one of my specialties.

"He's smelling something, no doubt about it," Bro said.

"But Walter's already been that way," Jimmy said.

"Arthur's nose is better than Walter's," said Bro.

That Bro! Who wouldn't love him?

Jimmy laughed, a short little laugh, not particularly happy. They followed me to the top of the hill. And there in the distance stood my car, stopped in the middle of the road beside an old stone wall. Not my car, of course, and not actually a car, as I saw when we got closer, but a muddy white van with a roof rack. The rear end was jacked up and two shaven-head dudes seemed to be changing a tire. One of the shaven-head dudes was huge and the other wasn't. The huge one was doing the changing and the small one was watching, a steaming paper cup in one hand and a cigar in his mouth. They both looked up at the same time, real quick, and saw us. The small one took a sip from his cup. The huge one spun his tire iron in his hand and went back to changing the tire. But their eyes stayed on us the whole time.

We walked up to them. They both had bushy beards, wet with rain, and neck tattoos, visible above the collars of their raincoats. What else? They smelled like wet mops. Their watchful eyes shifted, taking in the swollen side of Jimmy's face.

"Hi," Jimmy said. "You guys see a cow?"

"Us guys see a cow?" said the huge one.

"It got loose," Bro said.

The huge one tightened a nut, grunted, and said, "See any loose cows, Roscoe?"

"Sure," said Roscoe, blowing out a little cloud of cigar smoke. "Jumpin' over the moon."

The huge one laughed, then rose and looked down at us. "Sorry, gentlemen. No cows today." He lowered the rear end of the van—one of those extra-tall vans—and strapped the jack and spare on the roof. Roscoe crumpled his cup, tossed it over the stone wall, opened the driver's side door. He took one last drag from the cigar, then flicked the stub into the bushes. They got in the van and drove away, rounding the next curve and vanishing from sight.

I went into the bushes, found the cigar stub, and gazed down at it. Ordinarily I'd be tempted to snap up some object that had just been in a human mouth, but this time I did not. I'd snapped up a cigar butt once and told myself never again. And after a few more tries, I'd made never-again happen! Don't forget I'm a real quick learner.

Jimmy peered across the empty fields on the far side of the road. He pounded his fist into his other hand. "Where is she?"

"How about calling her?" Bro said.

"Calling her?" said Jimmy.

Bro raised his voice. "Lady Em! Lady Em! Lady Em!"

Silence, except for the rain, coming down hard again.

"One thing's for sure," Jimmy said. "You don't know squat about cows."

Cows? They'd slipped my mind, but now that they were back in play, I realized that cow smell was in the air, and lots of it. I trotted around in a little circle. That's how you pick up a scent trail, but in every direction I went, the smell got weaker. I didn't understand how that could be.

"Why's he barking?" Jimmy said.

"Probably hungry," said Bro.

Hungry? That wasn't it at all. And then it was.

FOUR
QUEENIE

WOULD I CALL MYSELF THE MOODY type? Never! Moody types are negative. No one wants to be around negativity. Everyone wants to be around me. Therefore I'm not the moody type.

That doesn't mean I can't be in a bad mood from time to time. For example, I was in a bad mood right now, this very morning. Surely you know why: I wanted my cream, fresh cream served by Bertha in my own special saucer. My cream! This instant!

What was wrong with everyone today? From my spot on the grandfather clock I could hear Bertha humming to herself in the kitchen. Humming to herself like things were hunky-dory, when they were as far as possible from hunky or dory. Bertha's coat hung on the coatrack by the front door, her blue scarf trailing from one pocket, blue being Bertha's favorite color if I remembered right, and I always do. I was contemplating a quick trip over to the coatrack and taking possession of the blue scarf with a view to doing who knows what when Bertha walked out of the kitchen, put on her coat, and wrapped the blue scarf around her neck! Like she'd been reading my mind! What an uncomfortable thought—my mind is mine and mine alone. All the more reason I had to have that blue scarf. What could be more logical?

Meanwhile I could hear Mom talking upstairs. "Harmy? Can you cover the desk for half an hour? I have to go to the bank."

"Sure," said Harmony. "I won't even bill you."

"Ha-ha," said Mom.

A few moments later she appeared in the hall, grabbing her bag and an umbrella. As she opened the front door, she glanced back at me. "You okay, Pretty-Face?"

An amazing question. Me okay? How could that be possible? I had no cream. People were reading my mind. That blue scarf was rightfully mine. Does any of that sound okay to you?

Mom went out and closed the door. Harmony came into the hall from the kitchen, eating yogurt from a plastic container. I've tasted yogurt from time to time and it's all right, but doesn't compare to you-know-what. On the other hand, as humans like to say—and if they had one or two more hands, you can be sure they'd think a lot differently, and probably better—even though my mood was bad, it's always a pleasure to see Harmony. It's because of how she stands so straight, and her glowing skin, and her big brown eyes, full of golden glints and every bit as sharp as Mom's. Yes, a thing of beauty. Although not quite in my class. It's my duty to point that out, keep you from getting confused. That part about humans and their hands was probably more than enough for you in the confusion department.

Harmony went behind the desk, spooning yogurt into her mouth and flipping through the big black book. The big black book is where the guest reservations get written down. Whatever Harmony saw there seemed to be making her worried. Without looking, she tossed the empty yogurt cup over her shoulder, in the direction of the wastebasket. Bro's forever tossing things at wastebaskets and trash cans, but they never go in on the first shot. I hadn't seen Harmony do any similar tossing before, but the yogurt cup went plunk into the wastebasket, dead center. The next thing I knew, I'd eased my way down from the grandfather clock— my grandfather clock, as I'm sure you know by now—and crossed over to the desk, my movements silent, even to me. I hopped up into Harmony's lap.

"There you are," she said, stroking my back, her gaze still on the big black book. She turned the pages. They were all blank. "What are we going to do, Queenie?"

Do? About what? Everything had suddenly gone perfect. My job was to sit right where I was. Harmony's job was to stroke me. Life can be simple. Don't mess it up by overthinking. If I had the power I'd have stopped time there and then. Why didn't I have that power, by the way? Perhaps it would come to me. I was thinking of how to speed that development along when the front door opened and a tall woman dressed in black rain gear walked in. She shrugged off her backpack, lowered her hood, and shook out her hair, long and blond, the silvery kind of blond, almost white.

Harmony set me on the desk and rose. "Welcome to the Blackberry Hill Inn," she said. "Can I help you?"

The woman came up to the desk, gazed down at Harmony. Some grown-ups brighten up at the sight of a kid, especially a kid like Harmony. And some grown-ups do not. The tall woman was in this second group. "A room for one night," she said. "Possibly two."

Human voices are way too big a subject to go into here. Mom's voice is the best I've heard: strong, but almost like music. This woman's voice was just as strong or stronger, but the musical part was completely missing.

"Let me check," said Harmony. She ran her finger down a blank page in the big black book. "Hmm. The Violet Room seems to be available. It costs the most but—"

"That'll be fine." The tall woman dropped a couple of cards onto the blank page. Those would be the credit card and the driver's license, if I understood our check-in routine, which I probably did although it's of no interest to me.

"Don't you want to see it first?" Harmony said.

"No," said the woman.

Bro and Harmony both have this way of raising their heads so their chins stick out. I'm not sure what it means, but Harmony did it now. "The Violet Room is our nicest," said Harmony.

The tall woman glanced around the front hall. A lovely front hall, may I say, although she didn't look impressed. Harmony did some paperwork, then handed back the cards, plus a room key.

"Turn left at the top of the stairs and it's the last room down the hall," Harmony said. "I can take you, if you like, Ms., uh, Pryor."

"Actually," said Ms. Pryor. She drummed her fingers on the desk, then looked again at Harmony, a very careful look this time. "What's your name?"

"Harmony."

"How interesting," said Ms. Pryor. "Do your parents own this place?"

"My mom," Harmony said.

"And what's her name?"

"Yvette." Harmony glanced at the door. "She'll be home soon."

"And the last name?"

"Reddy."

"Making you Harmony Reddy," Ms. Pryor said.

"Yes."

"Almost a found poem. Has anyone ever mentioned that?"

"No," said Harmony. "What's a found poem?"

"Doesn't matter," Ms. Pryor said. "You seem like a smart person. What grade are you in?"

"Sixth."

"Today's not a school day?"

"Vacation week."

Ms. Pryor drummed her fingers on the desk again. "Are you familiar with Blackberry Creek?"

"Sure." Harmony pointed out a side window. "You can almost see it from here."

Ms. Pryor didn't look. "I've heard there's a big waterfall."

Harmony nodded. "Catastrophe Falls."

"That's quite a name."

"It's all about some canoeing expedition long ago."

"What happened?"

"They went over the falls and died," Harmony said.

"Who?"

"The canoeing expedition."

Ms. Pryor's voice sharpened a bit. "But who were they?"

"I don't really know the details," Harmony said. She turned to the brochure rack, flipped through a brochure or two. Harmony's eyes were on the flipping pages. Ms. Pryor's eyes were on Harmony. "Nothing here," Harmony said. She looked up, caught Ms. Pryor's intense gaze. Ms. Pryor softened it real quick. What was going on with her? For a second or two I almost forgot about my cream.

Harmony replaced the brochures. "It's probably because you can't actually get to Catastrophe Falls."

"I don't understand," said Ms. Pryor.

"It's on private land. But there's a lookout on the other side of the creek, just off old Route 99. You can see the falls from there."

"That sounds good," said Ms. Pryor. "What's the cost?"

"Of what?" Harmony said.

Ms. Pryor's eyes narrowed. "Of you taking me to the lookout, of course."

"Oh, no cost," Harmony said.

"Perfect," said Ms. Pryor. "Then let's go."

"Now?"

"He who hesitates is lost."

"I'm sorry?"

"It's just a saying—never mind." Ms. Pryor gave Harmony a quick look. "You'll be wanting rain gear."

"The thing is," said Harmony, "I'm alone on the desk right now and there's nobody—"

The front door opened and Elrod came in. Elrod's the handyman. He's a very big guy with a thick beard and a ponytail, a look you see a lot in these parts. For a long time I thought that he was called the handyman because he was good with his hands, but it turns out he is not. Right now he had a ladder over one shoulder and a large square of plywood under the other arm. Then there was his tool belt, loaded up with all sorts of things, including a steaming cup of coffee. Big Fred, Bertha's boyfriend and head of the volunteer fire department, says, "What can go wrong, will go wrong." That's certainly true with Elrod, although the how part of the going wrong is always unpredictable. In this case it started with the coffee cup just brushing against the doorknob, spilling coffee down the side of Elrod's leg.

"Ouch," said Elrod, twisting around to see what had happened, a movement that started a whole noisy chain of events involving ladder, plywood, hatstand, and a Chinese urn that Mom was fond of and kept full of umbrellas for rainy days, just like this one.

My ears are very sensitive. I leaped off the desk silently, of course—and slipped away from the front hall and into the downstairs bathroom. The downstairs bathroom is for guests only, but it's a peaceful place and I needed peace. I also needed to scratch something, this instant. There was nothing really scratchable in the bathroom so I made do with the baseboard under the sink. An interesting part of my mind took over for a while, the part that likes to . . . how to put this in a nice way? The part that likes to damage things slowly and carefully? Something like that.

After some time, feeling a lot better, I returned to the front hall. There'd been some changes in my absence. Now Harmony and Ms. Pryor were at the front door, both dressed in rain gear, and Elrod was behind the desk. Elrod behind the desk? How was that going to work?

I looked at Harmony. She looked at me. "And why don't we take Queenie? She hasn't been outside in ages."

Outside? An appalling idea. My hair stood on end. Harmony came over and scooped me up. The scratch-loving part of my mind stirred, trying to come to life, but this was Harmony. I let myself be scooped up.

FIVE

QUEENIE

THAT OTHER PARTY OFTEN GOES ON walks, many of them unleashed for some reason. He's had many misadventures off the leash, so why doesn't Mom rein him in? It's a mystery. I myself am never leashed, of course, the mere idea unimaginable, even sickening. When I'm sickened I tend to upchuck, although in a very delicate way that couldn't possibly disturb anybody, rather different from the lakes of puke the other party is capable of coughing up.

But back to outdoor walks. Instead of a leash, I'm put in a special backpack with a see-through mesh part, and then Harmony hoists the backpack onto her chest. I ride in front, not in back, as I made clear the first day the backpack appeared at the Blackberry Hill Inn. What I'd prefer when it comes to walks—and what sometimes still happens late at night, using a tiny escape hatch I've discovered down in the basement—is freedom! Daylight freedom! One problem with nighttime freedom is the scarcity of birds, although there are some. Including owls, by the way. I had a surprise encounter with an owl late one night, one of the very few surprises of my life. I'm a hunter, not prey. The owl seemed to miss that distinction.

"Does he like it in there?" said Ms. Pryor as we went outside, a cold raindrop already finding a gap in the mesh and landing on my nose in the most annoying way.

"Queenie's a she," Harmony said. "And yeah, she does."

He? Ms. Pryor had called me a he? I decided to have nothing to do with her, not now, not ever.

We followed one of the old cart paths across our meadow, all mud and puddles and slush. Rain fell hard, slowed down to a drizzle, ramped back up to hard. I made myself very small and turned my eyes on Harmony's face, lovely golden eyes that said, *Take me home.*

But Harmony did not look down at me, and we did not turn for home. Instead she got busy pointing things out for Ms. Pryor, like, "That's the new barn."

Ms. Pryor gave the new barn—standing before some tall Christmas-type trees not far from the inn—a careful look. "What's in it?"

"Right now?" said Harmony. "Some chickens and a pig named El Jefe. But if business gets bet—" She stopped and started again. "But I'm hoping for a horse on our next birthday."

"Our?" said Ms. Pryor.

"I'm a twin."

And then came some back-and-forth about Bro. My mind remained on El Jefe. I'd only been in the new barn once, and very briefly, Mom—and what a fast runner she'd turned out to be!—soon arriving to . . . perhaps not remove me, but rather to invite me to return home at my earliest convenience. I have a clear memory of her counting the chickens out loud, and then El Jefe came snuffling over in my direction, snout and odor both enormous.

"Easy there, El Jefe," Mom had said. She gave his head a nice scratch. And then she'd carried me home—without first washing her hands! I'd smelled of El Jefe for two terrible days.

Meanwhile we'd climbed to the crest of a not-very-steep hill. In one direction stood some dense woods. In the opposite direction, quite far away, stood the old barn, lopsided and weather-beaten. And straight ahead was Blackberry Creek, still partly iced over.

"What's that?" said Ms. Pryor, pointing to the old barn.

"The old barn," Harmony said.

"Anything in it?"

"Empty," said Harmony. "It's a wreck. We've never used it."

Well, not completely empty. There were mice, for example, although fewer and fewer all the time.

"So no one goes down there?" Ms. Pryor said.

"Except for this home builder guy one time," Harmony said. "He thought he could maybe use the boards for fancy kitchens, but they were the wrong kind."

She started down to the edge of the creek, meaning I started down there, too. Iced over, yes, but not completely, and between the ice patches flowed water, fast and frothy. Rocks poked up through the water here and there, some flat-topped, some not.

"You okay to step across on the rocks?" Harmony said.

I most certainly was not, but it turned out Harmony was talking to Ms. Pryor, not me.

"Why wouldn't I be?" said Ms. Pryor.

Harmony and I crossed first, Harmony taking her time and using only the flat-toppers, and me with my claws sticking through the mesh. Ms. Pryor ran across, stepping on any old rock, making the whole thing look easy. I'd made up my mind to ignore her, but she was turning out to be hard to ignore.

The other side of the creek was much rougher than our meadow. "This is state land," Harmony said as we started onto a forest path, climbing up, up, and away from the creek, its sound fading and fading. Another sound soon started up, this one a sort of soft booming. There was less mud on the forest path and more snow—the crunchy kind, not deep. The branches overhead blocked most of the rain.

My mood improved very very slightly. After a while the booming grew louder and we came to a clearing. Far below, a barbed-wire fence ran along the near side of the creek. On the other side of the fence lay a strip of cleared land, and then a section of creek, wider than where we'd crossed, almost like a river, and flowing much faster. I could see it picking up speed, bubbling and rolling right up to a sharp drop-off, where it tumbled straight down, a long long way.

"Catastrophe Falls," said Harmony.

Boom boom boom went Catastrophe Falls. Ms. Pryor gazed down at all that falling water, hurtling endlessly over the edge. Although Ms. Pryor didn't remind me of Bro in any other way, the look in her eye was just like the look in his when he spotted what he wanted for Christmas in the window of Mr. Hinault's bike shop in town. She slipped a camera out of her jacket pocket and took a few photos.

"If you move over that way, I could maybe get one of you with the falls in the background," Harmony said.

Ms. Pryor blinked and turned to her. "Excuse me?" she said.

"You know," Harmony said. "A souvenir."

For a moment, Ms. Pryor looked impatient, like Harmony had interrupted something important. Then her face smoothed over, very fast. She smiled: Her teeth were the whitest human teeth I'd ever seen. "Sure," she said. "Why not?"

Ms. Pryor handed her phone to Harmony. Right away it began blasting a siren sound, not as loud as an ambulance but pretty loud for such a small thing. Ms. Pryor snatched it back, went tap tap, and the phone fell silent.

"What happened?" Harmony said.

"It didn't recognize your touch," said Ms. Pryor.

"Your phone knows your touch?"

Ms. Pryor nodded. "It's actually one of our products," she said. "In development."

"You're in the tech business?"

"Partly." She held out the phone. After a slight hesitation, like it might pull some new trick, Harmony took the phone. It didn't try anything this time, but I was hoping Harmony would rear back and hurl the thing into Catastrophe Falls. My ears are sensitive, don't forget. Hurl the phone, Harmony, hurl it!

But she did not. Ms. Pryor sat on a log at the edge of the clearing and showed her very white teeth again. Harmony took the picture, turned the phone so Ms. Pryor could see the screen. Ms. Pryor didn't seem interested. She tucked the phone in her pocket.

At that moment, a log came bobbing along in Blackberry Creek. Ms. Pryor was interested in that. She watched the log as it picked up speed and plunged over the falls. Whoosh went the log, like it was getting sucked away by the vacuum cleaner—also no favorite of mine—and of course there was always that boom boom boom. By now I'd had enough of the falls and of this entire wet and noisy expedition.

But Ms. Pryor had not. Her eyes stayed on the log as it got tossed in the air at the base of the falls, then disappeared and reappeared downstream a few times before vanishing around a bend.

"Power," said Ms. Pryor very softly, possibly to herself.

"Did you say power?" Harmony said.

Ms. Pryor frowned. "Just thinking out loud."

"The power of nature?" said Harmony. "My mom talks about that a lot."

"Does she have any idea of the power of these falls?"

"How do you mean?" said Harmony.

"It's quantifiable," Ms. Pryor said.

"What does that mean?"

"You can express it in numbers. Most things can be expressed in numbers. One day—sooner rather than later—everything will be."

"Everything will be expressed in numbers?"

"That should be clear to anyone with a brain by now."

"But—"

Ms. Pryor waved off whatever Harmony was about to say. "Is there a way down? I want to get closer."

"I don't know," Harmony said. "I've never been down there."

"Then it will be an adventure."

Was I in the mood for adventure? Not one little bit. No one seemed interested in my opinion. Ms. Pryor walked along the edge of the lookout and into some trees. We followed. Ms. Pryor's gait caught my attention. It was powerful, but at the same time smooth and light-footed. Was there something . . . catlike about her? What an unpleasant thought! I had no desire for any humans to be catlike. If they wanted to be doglike—and many of them seemed to—then fine. But me and my kind would be in charge of the cat part of the world, thank you very much.

We walked through the trees for a while before Ms. Pryor turned and started down toward the creek. There was no path that I could see—by myself I wouldn't need a path, of course—but Ms. Pryor latched onto branches on the steep parts, and Harmony did the same. We were almost at the bottom when one of those branches sprang back and flung icy water right through the mesh and onto my face! Oh, how horrible! And there was nothing I could do. Why was I here? What was life all about? Where was my cream?

When we came down onto flat land, I still had no answers. We walked along beside the barbed-wire fence, the creek very near now on the other side of the fence and flowing faster and faster. Boom boom boom went the falls, and then we were at the drop-off. The noise! Catastrophe Falls was like a living thing, a huge and noisy living thing. I gazed up at Harmony, my golden eyes sending one message and one message only: *Take me home!*

Harmony wasn't watching me. Instead her gaze was on the falls, like she couldn't look anywhere else. Ms. Pryor's eyes flickered toward Harmony, then real quick—almost cat-quick, something I'd have to think about later—she turned, slipped some sort of small tool from a pocket, and cut right through a couple strands of the barbed wire.

"Oh, look, Harmony," she said. "A big gap in the fence." She stepped through.

Harmony turned. "Ms. Pryor?"

"Won't be a second," said Ms. Pryor, taking out her phone. "Just want a nice close-up. And an unmaintained fence isn't meant to be taken seriously."

Was that true? Maybe, because Harmony followed Ms. Pryor through the gap, meaning I followed, too. Ms. Pryor stood right at the edge of the creek, within a few steps of the falls. I couldn't bear to look! The falls wanted to grab us and pull us in! I'd never been more sure of anything in my life.

"Ms. Pryor? I don't think this is a good idea. Mr. Doone— he's the owner of this land—is pretty strict about—"

"Oh, I'd never want to offend anyone," Ms. Pryor said. "Let's go." But at that moment, her phone slipped from her hand and fell on the ground at Harmony's feet. Harmony stooped to get it, twisting a little, meaning that I, in my mesh pocket, was looking sideways. And I saw something happen, real quick, that Harmony, her attention on the dropped phone, did not. Ms. Pryor whipped out a strange object from inside her jacket, an object like a tiny red ball with a tiny white flag on top. She pressed the tip of the tiny flagpole and a tiny light flashed. Then she flicked the thing into the creek, a bouncing red dot in all that churning blue and white, headed for the falls.

Harmony straightened and handed over the phone.

Ms. Pryor gave her a nod. "You're a competent young woman."

"Thanks," said Harmony.

Was this the time for a lot of polite chitchat? My face was still soaking wet. Snow was starting to mix in with the rain. Did my happiness matter? What a terrible situation! Then, just when I was sure that things couldn't get any worse, they did. A big red-faced man with a shotgun under one arm walked out of the woods and said, "Hold it right there."

The red dot shot over the falls and disappeared.

SIX
ARTHUR

W HY DOES HE DO THAT?" JIMMY SAID.

"No idea," Bro told him.

They were looking down at me. Above their heads was the low, dark sky, with funny bluish wet lines coming straight down. All at once I realized what they were: raindrops! That was what raindrops looked like when you were lying on your back and wriggling around in a mud puddle, which was exactly what I happened to be doing. Wow! I was at my very smartest! Wet lines were raindrops! What would I think of next? I went still, waiting for the next thought, but when it didn't seem to be coming anytime soon, I went back to wriggling.

"He's done this in six puddles so far," said Jimmy.

"You counted?"

"I count everything."

Bro shot Jimmy a quick glance. "Harmony says you're good in school."

Jimmy shrugged.

"Aren't you in the same class?"

"Uh-huh."

"She says you're smart."

Jimmy shook his head. "But she is."

"Yeah," said Bro. "She's a year ahead of me."

"So?" Jimmy said. He picked up a round stone, hefted it in his hand. Whoa! Was fetch a possibility? I like fetch, as long as I don't have to run too far and we keep it down to one or two fetches, three tops.

"It kind of sucks," Bro said.

"There's worse things," said Jimmy. He hefted the stone again, then kind of effortlessly flung it into the sky. Up and up it flew, over a tall tree, higher and higher, hanging so high for a moment, a tiny dot, and finally falling down and out of sight. Was I supposed to fetch it? I went still and tried to make myself unnoticeable.

"Wow!" said Bro. "You've got a great arm!"

"Yeah?" Jimmy said. There was a gleam in the sliver of eye between his swollen eyelids.

"How come you don't play baseball?"

"I played for a couple of years."

"Yeah, but how come you stopped? You didn't like it?"

The gleam faded from his eye. "Just no time."

"How come?"

Jimmy's voice rose. "How come? School. Chores. That's how come."

"I got school and chores," Bro said. "But I still play baseball. Tryouts are this afternoon, rain or shine. You should come."

Jimmy gave Bro a look. Hey! I knew that look! It said, *What am I going to do with you?* Then his gaze lowered down to me.

"Know how funny you are with your paws up like that and your tongue sticking out?" he said.

What was that? I was wondering who Jimmy might be talking to when all of a sudden he started laughing. Bro glanced at him in surprise, then he started laughing, too. Something must have been funny. I had no idea what, but I loved seeing happy kids. I sprang up—and if not actually springing, at least getting up pretty quick—and gave myself a good shake. For some reason muddy water started flying all over the place. Some got on Bro and Jimmy. It made them laugh harder.

When the laughter died away, Jimmy said, "Come on, Arthur. Find me that stupid cow."

Finding a cow? Was that it? Easy peasy! Cows have a strong cowy smell and my nose is . . . is a genius. A genius when it comes to smelling! I'd never realized that before, but now I knew. I was a genius!

"How come he's wagging his tail like that?" said Jimmy.

"Must be happy about something," Bro said.

"Like what?"

"Hard to say."

"If he's not careful it's gonna fall right off."

Uh-oh. Were they talking about my tail? Falling off? Life without a tail? That was unimaginable. Therefore I couldn't have heard right. I went over the conversation in my mind and found that most of it was already gone, leaving my mind pretty much empty. I'm lucky that way. A mind cluttered with all sorts of info would be too tired to do much thinking. My mind is always ready to think and think hard. In fact, I felt a new thought coming this very moment . . . coming coming coming, boom! Here it was: Things are good. Wow! What a thought, one of my very best.

"Is he trying to tell us he's picking up cow scent?" Jimmy said.

"Could be," said Bro. "Take us to her, Arthur."

Cow scent? Was that important? Too bad I wasn't smelling anything cowish, not the slightest whiff. But I'd never want to disappoint Bro, and Jimmy seemed like a real nice kid, so I turned and set off in the first direction I set off in, even ramping up to what I'm sure was a brisk trot.

"Hey!" said Jimmy. "He's onto something!"

Did you hear that? I, Arthur, was onto something. What a proud moment in my life! I kicked it into top gear.

Glancing back, I saw that the boys had to walk pretty darn fast to keep up.

"Is he part bloodhound?" Jimmy said.

"Probably," said Bro. "The vet said he's got more breeds in him than any dog she's ever seen."

"King of the mongrels, huh?" Jimmy said.

Bro gave Jimmy a look, the same sort of look, surprised and impressed, that he sometimes gives Harmony. "Yeah," he said. "King of the mongrels."

The king of the mongrels—meaning me, Arthur!—led his men through the woods and up a long steep hill, a climb that made the king huff and puff a bit. Once or twice he paused to mark something that caught his interest, especially anything that had been recently marked by a fox. The king was no fan of foxes. Foxes are sneaky. The king is not sneaky.

"Why does he keep doing that?" Jimmy said.

"Marking his territory," said Bro.

"But it's not his territory. It's been in my dad's family for a hundred years."

"Um," said Bro. "Your dad's and yours, right?"

Jimmy gave Bro a look, not at all friendly. "What's your point?"

Bro shrugged and didn't answer.

Jimmy raised his voice. "I asked you a question."

Bro tilted up his chin and his eyes got slightly hooded. There are times when Bro looks a little bit dangerous, just one of the many interesting things about him. "What happened to your eye, Jimmy?" he said.

"Huh? I told you. I ran into a tree branch."

"I thought it was a door," Bro said. They glared at each other for what seemed like a pretty long time. At last Bro said, "Did Walter hit you?"

Jimmy took a deep deep breath and let it out with a low sound, almost like a groan. Then he nodded. "I didn't leave that door unlocked," he said.

"I know that," said Bro.

"I told him he was lying. He lied to my dad about me. So I said he was the liar. And he was like, what are you gonna do about it."

"This was in front of your dad?" Bro said.

Jimmy shook his head. "Later. Back of the barn, after my dad said he believed Walter."

"So it was just the two of you?"

"Yeah," Jimmy said. "Back at the barn when we were getting ready to go look for Lady Em, me and Walter. I took a swing at him, Bro. I was so mad. Tried to paste him right on the nose, but I missed by a mile, ended up hitting his shoulder. Then . . . then he punched me back." Jimmy's hand rose, touched the skin around his eye, very gently.

"What did your dad say?" said Bro.

"How do you mean?"

"When he saw your eye?"

"I didn't show him."

"Huh? You didn't tell him Walter hit you?"

"I swung first. That makes it a fair fight."

"Jimmy! He's, like, seventeen. You're eleven."

"My dad hates whiners."

"But that wouldn't be whining."

"It would be to him. You fight your own battles or you're a weak sister."

"Weak sister?"

"That's one of his favorite expressions."

"He should meet Harmony," Bro said.

Jimmy laughed, a not very happy laugh, maybe not happy at all. I went over and pressed against his leg. He gave me a pat.

"He's a good dog, huh?" Jimmy said.

"For sure," said Bro.

A good dog? Meaning me? I had a real big thought, not my kind of thing at all, but here goes: Being a good dog was even better than being king! Wow! Amazing! What did it even mean?

Meanwhile we were still on the move. Soon we reached the top of the hill, me leading from behind, which turned out to be less tiring. We stepped into a clearing.

"Arthur?" Bro said. "Any cow smell?"

Cow smell! I'd completely forgotten. Probably not important, since there was no cow smell. I did smell water and followed that smell across the clearing. There, not far below, flowed a creek that smelled just like Blackberry Creek. So maybe it was Blackberry Creek, although I'd never seen it flowing so fast or make such a boom-booming noise.

"Are we near Catastrophe Falls?" Bro said.

"Uh-huh," said Jimmy. "Should be able to see them if we just step this way."

We stepped that way. All of a sudden I saw something very strange, kind of . . . kind of like a cliff of water. A cliff of water! What a thought! A little too much, really. I hoped thoughts like that weren't about to start filling my head. There'd be no space for . . . for whatever went on in there already.

"Hey!" Bro said. "Is that Harmony?"

Maybe because of how that cliff of falling water had grabbed my attention, I hadn't seen what was happening on the other side of the creek. Now that I did see, I'm not sure I understood. Yes, there was Harmony, all right, and wearing the backpack with the mesh pocket, the backpack that becomes a front pack when a certain someone's inside. Harmony and a tall woman stood near a barbed-wire fence not too far from the creek. Confronting them was a man, not as tall as the woman but very broad and strong-looking. The most important thing about this man was probably his shotgun, pointing down but not totally straight down. Also he was shouting something at Harmony and the woman. I couldn't make out the words on account of the boom-boom-boom, and I didn't know what was going on. I just knew one thing: That combo of shouting and shotgun was very bothersome. Am I the kind of dude who gets bothered easily? No. But the shouting and the shotgun, with Harmony so close by? That made a big impression on me. There are times in life for thinking. Those haven't always turned out to be my best times. Then there are times for no thinking. That's when I really shine! The next thing I knew I was in midair, launching myself into Blackberry Creek.

I love swimming and I'm pretty good at it. Swimming is very simple, just a matter of running in the water. The difference is that when I'm running in the water I weigh nothing at all—Arthur the jock!—but when I'm running on land I weigh . . . perhaps a little more. So there I was swimming my way across Blackberry Creek, nose up in the air in proper swimming style. The water might have felt a bit icy to you, but you don't have my nice warm coat. I swam and swam, perfectly comfortable. Did I hear voices calling,

"Oh, no! Arthur! Arthur!"? Possibly, but it was hard to tell with that boom-boom-boom constantly going on, perhaps even getting louder. Maybe they were shouting, "Go, Arthur, Go! Arthur! Arthur! Greatest swimmer in the whole state!" For a moment, I almost even remembered the name of our state. Wow, just wow. But before the name would come, I began to notice something a bit odd, namely that even though I was a champion swimmer, I didn't appear to be getting across the creek. Instead I seemed to be headed in a slightly different direction, more going with the flow, if you see what I mean. Then it hit me that going with the flow meant I was headed to that booming cliff of water. Was that good or bad? Quite possibly bad, but I wasn't sure until I heard Harmony scream, "He's going over the falls!" I'd never heard Harmony scream like that. I wanted to make her feel better, of course, so I changed direction, turning against the flow. Problem solved!

Except maybe not. The flow turned out to be a surprisingly strong swimmer in its own right, and it wanted to go the other way. I did not want to go the other way, not if going the other way meant being swept over the falls. What would that be like? I really didn't know but it was a long long distance to the bottom. My heart started going fast, boom boom inside my chest. And always there was that huge boom boom boom of Catastrophe Falls, so loud it seemed to shake the air. I noticed that I was shaking, too, but was this a time for shaking? No! It was a time for swimming my very best.

Which was what I did! I swam and swam, all legs moving their fastest, my paws pushing their hardest, pushing me back upstream and away from that boom boom boom. But strangely enough that boom boom boom kept getting louder when it should have been getting softer. How could that be? I glanced sideways and saw Bro and Jimmy at the edge of the creek, waving their arms and shouting, and also—oh, no!—I saw that although I was swimming forward, I was actually moving backward.

Boom boom boom went my heart. BOOM BOOM BOOM went Catastrophe Falls.

SEVEN

QUEENIE

ONE THING YOU LEARN WHEN YOU hang out with humans: They get themselves in complicated and messy situations, over and over. Dogs are very similar, by the way, which explains a lot. We in the cat world—and this should go without mentioning—are different. We don't care for mess, and when we encounter a complicated situation, we simplify it as soon as possible. Have you ever seen a cat pounce, for example? Then you know what I mean. Complicated to simple in a flash! Most of the time you don't even see the blood.

Perhaps I should have kept that last bit to myself. The point is that a little way upstream from what appeared to be a rather impressive waterfall, we had goings-on of an extremely complicated and messy kind. On my side of the creek we had me, Harmony, Ms. Pryor, and this angry red-faced man with the shotgun. He had the sort of voice that would be irritating even if he hadn't been shouting, but he was shouting, so it was even worse.

"You're on private property!" was something he shouted more than once. There was also "Whaddaya think a fence means?" and "Who do you think you are?"

That was when Harmony spoke up. "Harmony Reddy, Mr. Doone," she said. "I'm really sorry about this. I was only—"

"Hold it right there! How come you know my name?"

"But—but we've met. Jimmy and my—"

"Don't you go draggin' that no-good—"

"—brother are friends. We're from the inn, the Blackberry Hill Inn."

And I have no idea where we were headed from there—personally, I was interested in the question about the meaning of fences, fences having no meaning at all as far as I was concerned—because at that moment whole new developments started up on the other side of the creek.

Three figures suddenly stepped into a clearing just across from us, all of them familiar to me. First was Bro, very wet and mud-spattered. Second was a tall kid I'd seen through the kitchen window early on a morning or two, getting out of the passenger's side of a truck and delivering my cream, a kid possibly named Jimmy, also wet and muddy. Did he have my cream now? Was there some way of delivering it to me across the creek? I had my doubts. For one thing, cream came in bottles. I saw no bottles.

Thinking of my cream, I almost left out the third figure, the wettest and muddiest of all. This figure seemed very interested in our little group over on my side of the creek, caught up in our rather unpleasant conversation with Mr. Doone. What did this third party make of it? I had no idea. His mind worked in ways I've never understood. Right now, for whatever reason, it must have said something like, "Arthur! Dive into the creek!"

Which was what he did. It was the sort of dive you'd have to call enthusiastic, the unusually floppy ears of the diver spread wide in a strangely wingish manner, the oddly enormous paws stretched way out, like they couldn't wait to get into the creek. This was something I had never done and would never do, even if there'd been no falls waiting just a short distance downstream.

Around then was when Harmony screamed, "He's going over the falls!"

A loud scream. I could feel its vibrations through her chest, pressing against the backpack. Harmony: on the money, as usual, because even with a little confusion about which way he should point his nose, it was clear that his swimming ability was no match for the power of the creek, no matter what he did. My own heartbeat sped up a little at that moment. Why would that have been? No time to figure it out, because right then was when Bro took a few quick steps and did exactly what he shouldn't have done, never ever ever. Yes. Without a pause, without a glance back, he dove straight into the creek! Had I seen anything so terrible in my whole life? This was going to upset me. I hate being upset. His ball cap flew high in the air, got caught in some sort of current up there, and came down on land, where it lay all alone. That made me even more upset for some reason.

"Oh my god," Harmony said, and began taking off the backpack. I'm talking about the backpack with me in it. This was unsettling, and more unsettling things were happening in the creek. What I noticed first was the difference in swimming styles. Arthur swam with only his eyes and nose above water, and regardless of what he was trying to do, ended up going where Blackberry Creek wanted him to go. Bro rose high in the water, even though his clothes must have been weighing him down, his arms flashing through the air and sweeping through the water. Maybe he could have even swum safely across the creek to our side, especially if he'd been swimming in a straight line. But he wasn't swimming in a straight line, on account of the fact that he was headed for Arthur, and Arthur, despite whatever his plan might have been, was on his way to the falls, and soon.

Everything sped up after that, even the BOOM BOOM

BOOM of the falls, an annoying sound to begin with. I'm not sure I caught every single detail, the most amazing one probably the look on Bro's face. I saw no fear there at all, just a sort of firm-jawed determination, every stroke so smooth his movements seemed calm. At the same time, he looked so young, the way he'd looked when I'd first arrived at the inn, an interesting story we'll save for later.

What else? There was Arthur, nose pointed upstream and body headed downstream, the expression in his eyes the usual combo of blankness and confusion until all at once it changed over to something I'd never seen from him: pure terror. Oh, poor Arthur. An odd thought for me to have, but I just couldn't help it. He began barking, a high-pitched bark that didn't even sound like him, his normal bark having a low rumble that I admit is not the most unpleasant sound I've ever heard. Bro must have heard those terrified barks, even over the BOOM BOOM BOOM, because he raised his head and cried, "Hang on, Arthur! I'm coming!"

Arthur turned his own head and saw Bro. All sorts of— what would you call them? Emotions, maybe? Good enough. All sorts of emotions rose in Arthur's eyes. Below the surface his paws must have been working very hard, because tiny wavelets appeared in the water, wavelets moving against the current. The distance between Bro and

Arthur shrank and shrank—both of them at the same time still getting dragged downstream—and at last Bro reached out with one hand and grabbed Arthur. This turned out to be a tricky maneuver, because Arthur made an effort to do some grabbing of his own, an effort that ended with both of them sinking quickly beneath the surface and out of sight.

And the very next moment I landed bump on the ground. Inside the backpack, you understand, and not a hard bump, more like the backpack had been quickly lowered. The top of the mesh pocket opened and I glided out, only to see Harmony running down the creek bank at the very edge. Just then Bro and Arthur popped up to the surface, Bro sputtering and coughing, and Arthur looking like he was trying to climb on top of Bro's head. At the same time, some current in the creek seemed to be pushing them closer to our side, although still basically down toward the falls.

"Bro! Bro!" Harmony shouted, running alongside the flowing water, now churning and throwing off spray.

Bro's head turned. He saw Harmony. She reached out, stretching her arm as far as possible. With one arm around Arthur, Bro reached out to Harmony, also stretching to the limit. Their fingertips touched. Their hands locked. Harmony slowed down, tried to plant her feet. But the ground was soaking wet and her feet slid out from under her, and Blackberry Creek jerked her right off the land.

Now they were all in the water, all clinging to each other, Harmony closest to the bank and Arthur the farthest away. The creek was racing now, faster and faster. Over on the other side, Jimmy was running downstream toward the falls and yelling something into a cell phone. On my side Mr. Doone and Ms. Pryor were just standing with their mouths open. I myself took off toward the falls.

And there was the drop-off, so close, thundering away, spray flying high, so much water gathering into a huge gleaming roll and tumbling down. The three of them were zooming now, a tight little ball of life. But what was this? At the very edge of the watery cliff, a downed tree stuck out a short way into the creek, one end on land, the other caught on a rock sticking just above the surface.

Harmony! Harmony!

Yes, Harmony. At the last possible moment, or even slightly after, Harmony saw the tree, reached for it, grabbed hold of a branch, held on. Bro swung in a sort of curve at the top of the falls—and Arthur actually went over, for one long second in midair, Bro's hand tight around his collar—and then Harmony pulled Bro in, and Bro pulled Arthur in. They crawled up on the fallen tree, where I seemed to be waiting for them, briefly unaware that I was soaked to the skin. I just hate being soaked to the skin.

BOOM BOOM BOOM went the falls, the only sound in the world. There's a lot to be said for staying indoors.

Did the inside of the police station count as indoors? Warm and dry, yes, but in no way cozy or comfy. I like my indoors cozy. I also like comfy. Plus cream. What was so hard to understand?

We seemed to have a lot going on in an office that was much too small. But that didn't make it cozy, not one bit. Standing behind his desk was Deputy Sheriff Carstairs, a tall man with a rather large nose. Until recently we'd had a sheriff named Hunzinger, but he'd retired or been run out of town, I didn't know or care which. I knew the deputy—his daughter, Emma, was a good friend of Harmony's. I'd even been to their house. They have a pet gerbil, name of Jerry, who spends his time in a cage with tiny—what would you call it? Gym equipment? Yes, tiny gym equipment that Jerry likes to play on. Is it the kind of cage I could figure out how to open, given time? Yes. Have I been given time? No.

Deputy Sheriff Carstairs rubbed his hands together like he was trying to whip up some enthusiasm, but none of the humans in the room—Harmony and Bro, both wrapped in blankets; Mom, standing between them, an arm over each of their shoulders; Ms. Pryor; Jimmy; and Mr. Doone— looked at all enthusiastic. Are you thinking I left out one other participant? Would you call someone sleeping on the floor under the desk a participant? Case closed.

"Looks to me," said Deputy Carstairs, "that what we have here is one of those all's well that ends well situations." He turned to Jimmy. "But you did the right thing calling it in, no question." He took a closer look at Jimmy's face. "Did you get hurt out there or somethin'?"

Jimmy, standing by the wall opposite the desk, glanced at Bro, then looked down and said, "Yeah, um, I . . . ran into a branch. Like, a tree branch."

"Might want to stop by the ER on your way home, get it checked out," said Carstairs.

Jimmy glanced at Bro again. They exchanged a look, a look that Carstairs caught and seemed to find interesting. "I'm okay," Jimmy said.

"Well, then," the deputy said, after a long pause, "why don't we wrap this up and all of us get back to—"

"Huh?" said Mr. Doone, who hadn't spoken till that moment. "What're you talkin' about, all's well that ends well?"

"It's an expression, Gorman," Carstairs said. "Kind of like no harm, no foul."

"No foul?" Mr. Doone's voice rose. Some loud voices have a sharp edge to them. Mr. Doone's was one of those. I gazed at him through the mesh—perhaps I should have mentioned that I was in the backpack with Harmony again. I could feel that my golden eyes were hot and glowing. An impressive look: I'd seen it in the mirror many times.

But Mr. Doone didn't seem to notice. "No foul?" he said again. "How about trespassing? Since when's that not a foul?"

"Strictly speaking, of course," Carstairs began, "folks shouldn't—"

"That's right!" said Mr. Doone. "Folks shouldn't, period. But they went ahead and did it. That one there—" He stabbed a finger at Ms. Pryor. "And that one there." And he stabbed again, now at Harmony. Or maybe even me and Harmony. I felt my eyes heating up even more.

"Well," said Carstairs. "I'm sure Ms., uh—"

"Pryor," Ms. Pryor said.

"—and Harmony here will be happy to promise they'll never trespass on your land again."

"What good are promises in this world?" Mr. Doone said.

Which was the first time he'd made any sense to me. For example, fresh cream every morning: Wasn't that a kind of promise? But what good was it?

Meanwhile through the backpack I felt Harmony getting

restless, like she was about to speak. But before she could, Mom looked Mr. Doone directly in the eye and said, "My daughter's promises are as good as gold."

Harmony relaxed, and right away. But that was not all. I also felt something deep in her, something fine, something solid. This was an interesting moment in my life, almost sharing in human feeling. Interesting, true, but also somewhat tiring. I saw no need for a repeat anytime soon.

At that moment, Mr. Doone surprised me a bit. He lowered his voice and said, "If you say so, Mrs. Reddy."

"You can count on my promise as well," Ms. Pryor said, "but if that's not good enough I'm happy to pay you for the trouble I've caused."

"Don't want your money," Mr. Doone said.

"Does one hundred dollars sound fair?"

"Make it two."

Ms. Pryor took out some money, peeled off a couple of bills, and gave them to Mr. Doone.

"And how about shaking hands?" said Deputy Carstairs.

Ms. Pryor held out her hand. Mr. Doone kept his at his side.

"Come on, Gorman," Carstairs said. "Think how bad this could have been."

"Huh?"

"Gorman! The falls! Those kids!"

Slowly Mr. Doone raised his hand, a hand as big as the deputy's, but much more muscular. He and Ms. Pryor shook, each meeting the other's gaze. Mr. Doone's eyes were unfriendly; Ms. Pryor's way more so.

Everyone started filing out. There, in the doorway, was where Jimmy and Mr. Doone came close together. Mr. Doone stared at Jimmy's eye, shook his head, and in a low voice said, "It never ends with you." They walked out in single file, Jimmy trailing well behind.

My last thought on all these events? *Take me home!*

EIGHT

ARTHUR

I WAS VERY SLEEPY. ALSO VERY HUNGRY. I've often been both of those things, but never at the same time. Can you sleep and eat at once? I lay by the fire in the small parlor, a crackling fire that felt very nice, and waited for my mind to come up with an answer. A bowl of fresh kibble sat quite near, possibly within reach if I stretched my head out. But I don't eat lying down. I eat standing up. And I don't sleep standing up. I sleep lying down. Life can be so confusing.

Meanwhile over on the corduroy couch, Mom, Harmony, and Bro were drinking hot chocolate. They sat close together, Mom in the middle. I wanted to be there, too, close as close can be. If only the couch had been more reachable. I thought of barking, a bark or two that said, "Come pick me up! Carry me over to the couch!" But barking requires lots of energy. Try it sometime.

Mom took a sip, then set her mug on the coffee table.

"Well," she said. "Who wants to start?"

"Start what?" said Bro.

"Explaining," Harmony said.

"Bingo," said Mom.

"Harm wants to start," Bro said.

"You first."

"No, you."

"Kids?" said Mom.

"You're the oldest," Harmony said.

"Hey!" said Bro. "Four minutes."

"The most peaceful four minutes in human history."

"What does that even mean? How come—?"

"Kids?"

"Two hundred and forty blissful seconds," Harmony said.

"Harmony!" said Mom.

"Okay, okay," Harmony said. "After you went to the bank, Ms. Pryor arrived. I got her registered and she wanted to see the falls, and since Elrod was here to work the desk, I thought it was okay."

Then came a lot of back-and-forth about Elrod, Blackberry Creek, and the falls. It sounded kind of interesting, but way too complicated. My eyelids got very heavy. How strange that eyelids—tiny, thin things, really—can all of a sudden weigh so much! The fire crackled. The voices of Mom and Harmony made lovely little waves in the air, hard to describe, so I won't even try.

■ ■ ■

"And that's really the whole thing, Mom," Bro said.

I opened my eyes. They were still sitting on the couch, all three mugs now finished with and on the coffee table.

Mom took a deep deep breath and let it out slowly. Then she pulled the kids close and just held them like that. "I don't even know where to start," she said.

"No worries," Bro said. "We won't do it again."

"Which part?" said Mom.

The kids gazed at her for a moment. Harmony started laughing. Then Bro and Mom, too. They laughed and laughed, all of them, laughing and laughing until they cried. Uh-oh. Was something wrong? I couldn't think what it might be, and all at once was too hungry to think about anything at all. And just my luck! There within easy reach was my bowl! And full of kibble. I rose, considered giving myself a good head-clearing shake, decided to postpone it until after breakfast or lunch or whatever this meal happened to be. I moved over to the bowl and started chowing down.

And right away felt eyes on me. I prefer not to be watched when I'm eating, but I wasn't about to make a big deal about it. What could I do? Leave my kibble uneaten? What a crazy idea! Like I wasn't being my own friend.

I chomped away, perhaps more noisily than usual, but

not so noisily that I didn't hear Mom say, "Hard to believe Arthur really did that."

I glanced their way. Yes, the center of attention for sure. What was so interesting? Was it possible they wanted a taste of my kibble? That had never happened. Then I remembered that Bro had actually tasted my kibble, once when it was just him and me, and once when it was him and me at the start, and then Mom, and that was that. I lowered my head to the bowl and ate faster.

"He was kind of heroic, Mom," Harmony said.

I paused in mid-chew, waiting to hear who they were talking about, but they didn't say.

"Was Mr. Doone threatening you?" Mom said.

"I don't know if I'd put it that way," Harmony said. "He was yelling pretty good."

"And he had a rifle."

"A shotgun," Harmony said.

"Did he aim it at anybody?"

"No. He kept it pointed at the ground the whole time. And he's got a permit—he showed it to Mr. Carstairs."

"Still," Mom said.

"Still what?" said Bro.

Mom turned to him. "Not that I know him very well, of course—which is part of the problem. After all, he's been our neighbor since we bought this place and we do business with him, yet he's pretty much a stranger. But you must have an opinion."

"Me?" said Bro.

"You're friends with Jimmy; you've spent time over there."

"Not like close friends," Bro said.

"But my point is you've seen Mr. Doone in action."

Bro's eyebrows rose. "Action? What kind of action?"

"You tell me."

Mom gazed at Bro. He looked down. Meanwhile I'd worked my way to the bottom of the bowl—good boy, Arthur!—and was licking up the last of the kibble dust, one of those special treats.

"Well," Bro said, "I think Mr. Doone's pretty upset about Sweet Lady Em."

"Go on."

"Like, her disappearance."

"Go on," Mom said again.

"He thinks she just wandered off."

"Then I'm sure she'll be found soon."

I caught a tiny golden glow from high up in the bookcase across the room. Two tiny glows, actually. And there she was, perched on a paperback and looking down on everything. As usual! How bothersome! Then came some more cow talk. The golden glow brightened and brightened in the most annoying way.

"Arthur!" Harmony said. "Knock it off!"

Me? Knock what off? I cocked my head and thought I heard the faded ending of what might have been a bark or two, perhaps from that dog who lived at the gas station, surprisingly noisy for such a little guy.

"I don't know, Mom," Bro was saying. "Maybe instead of wandering off, it was more like—"

I never found out where Bro was heading with this because at that moment a tall woman walked into the room. I'd seen her by the creek and at the police station, but my memories of both those occasions were a bit hazy. Ms. Something-or-Other? Close enough. That's how I roll, by the way: Close enough is good enough! Why make yourself unhappy?

Ms. Something-or-Other saw Mom and the kids on the couch and spread her hands.

"My, my, what a lovely scene."

Ms. Something-or-Other took off her rain hat and shook out her hair, quite long and silvery blond.

She came forward. Bro and Harmony shifted away from Mom, so now they weren't sitting so close. I might have moved a bit as well, if I'd been standing. But although I'd been standing very recently, by my kibble bowl, I found that I was now lying down again by the fire. When had that happened? I didn't know. Did knowing when matter? I didn't know that, either. I considered stretching out one of my front legs, and decided against it. The fire made more of those crackling noises I like.

Mom rose as Ms. Something-or-Other approached the couch. Ms. Something-or-Other held out her hand.

"Yvette, I believe? We haven't properly met. I'm Ottoline Pryor."

They shook hands, Ms. . . . Pryor, was it? . . . holding on to Mom's for what seemed like a bit of extra time.

"First," she said, "I need to apologize for my role in this whole affair. I'm afraid I let the nature-loving part of me take over—I just had to see those falls!"

Mom freed her hand. She wasn't as tall as Ms. Pryor, but Mom stands straight and you can't help noticing her. At least, I can't. I love noticing Mom. Her hair wasn't as long as Ms. Pryor's and also not so fair, but it was glossier. Glossy is good when it comes to hair. My own coat is glossy. I've heard that said more than once, or maybe just the once, after a mineral oil incident there's no time for right now.

"Apology accepted," Mom said.

Ms. Pryor's smile faded. She got it back in place real quick, but why had it faded in the first place? Mom hadn't said, "Apology not accepted." So hadn't Ms. Pryor gotten what she wanted? I was confused, but I had no chance to figure things out, because Ms. Pryor was already going on to something else.

"Second," she said, "your kids are amazing! You and your husband have done a wonderful job."

"Thank you," Mom said. "We're divorced."

Ms. Pryor laughed. "Join the club!"

Mom smiled a very small smile.

Ms. Pryor eased up on the laughing, a good thing since she had something shrill going on at the top end of her laughter, if that makes any sense. Shrillness hurts my ears. For some reason I glanced up at the bookcase. Those golden eyes were glowing hot.

"And third," Ms. Pryor went on, "I just love your inn. I'd appreciate a tour whenever you have the chance."

At that moment a ray of sunshine came streaming through the window, even though I could hear a light pitter-patter on the roof. We get all kinds of weather, best appreciated from where I happened to be, in front of the fire.

"How about now?" Mom said.

Mom followed Ms. Pryor out of the room. I was watching closely, somewhat tempted to go with them. If I hadn't been watching closely I might have missed my shadowy friend—what am I saying? Enemy! That's better. My shadowy enemy, gliding down from the bookcase and trailing Mom out the door.

■ ■ ■

Harmony and Bro sat on the couch, both of them staring into the fire.

"What's up?" Harmony said.

"Huh?" said Bro.

"You heard me."

"Why should anything be up?"

"That's what I'm waiting to find out."

"Huh?"

"You heard me."

They kept staring at the fire. As for what was going on, I had no idea.

"I'm waiting," Harmony said.

"For what?"

"Bro?

"Yo."

"Look at me."

"Why?"

"Bro!"

Bro turned and looked at Harmony.

"What's up?" he said.

"Spill it."

"Spill what?"

"Whatever's on your mind."

"There's nothin' on my mind."

"Bro. Please. I can read your mind, or just about. You know that."

"Then you're reading a blank."

"Nope. It's about Jimmy, isn't it?"

"How come you can read my mind?"

"Probably the twin thing. Spill it."

"We're not real twins."

"Why do we have to go over and over this? We're not identical twins but we're twins."

"Like any other brother and sister."

Harmony shook her head. "I don't think so. We were together for nine months, twenty-four seven, side by side from the get-go. That has to make a difference."

"Huh?"

"In the womb, Bro."

"What's the womb again?"

"Bro!"

"Okay, okay," Bro said. "It's about Jimmy."

"His face?"

"Yeah."

"Didn't he say he ran into a tree branch?"

"Also a door."

"What?"

"Doesn't matter. He told me what really happened. Walter punched him."

"Who's Walter?"

Bro started in on a long explanation about Walter. Since I already knew about Walter, I had no problem tuning out. I have no problem tuning out in any case, one of my greatest strengths.

When I tuned back in, Bro was saying, "Jimmy's a good kid."

"And a human being," said Harmony. "So what are we going to do?"

"I don't know."

"Tell Mom?"

"Jimmy would hate that," Bro said.

They sat in silence for a while. The fire went pop pop pop, and some sparks flew out from beside the screen. Bro got up and swept them back in with the little fireplace broom.

"You should speak to Jimmy first," Harmony said.

"And say what?"

"We'll have to think about that."

"Maybe he'll come to the tryouts."

"The tryouts?"

"Baseball."

"Baseball! I almost forgot." Harmony jumped up. "Let's go oil the gloves."

"Why?"

"Bro! It's a new season! Move!"

86

NINE

QUEENIE

I'M THE TYPE WHO STAYS CALM, INSIDE and out. Do I ask for much? No, I do not. I take care of myself, clean up after myself, add nothing to the noise and mess of the world, unlike another party I could mention but will not, because . . . because that's how I am, not a whiner. I'm reminded of a movie Bro and I once watched, all about a lone warrior who rides into a tough town, takes care of the bad guys, and then rides away, pretty much silent the whole time. If you ever have trouble picturing me, just think of the lone warrior.

But remember one thing: Even a lone warrior can be troubled at times, for example, by some irresponsible cow with a ridiculous name who seemed to have wandered off somewhere, thus depriving me of my morning . . . well, you know where I'm going with this, no sense in beating you over the head with it. But wouldn't it be nice, if only once in one's life, to be able to beat—well, perhaps a thought best kept to myself. I'm only pointing out the challenges that sometimes arise, challenges that make it hard to stay calm, this so-called Sweet Lady Em character being a prime example. Another problem I had was Ms. Pryor's irritating laugh, especially the shrill part at the top end. Laughter is normally one of best sounds humans make—I'm also partial to the cello—so why not Ms. Pryor's laughter?

You may be wondering why, if her laughter annoyed me so much, did I follow her and Mom out of the small parlor, one of the comfiest and coziest rooms in the inn? Let's put it this way: If Ms. Pryor had gone alone, I would have stayed. But she didn't go alone. She went with Mom. Therefore the lone warrior trailed behind, the strong—if not very big—and silent type. The lone warrior had Mom's back.

". . . and here's the front hall," Mom was saying, "which you already know."

"Lovely," said Ms. Pryor.

"It's actually one of the newest parts of the inn," Mom said, "an add-on dating from the 1960s. Nothing like that could be done now—we were landmarked a few years back."

Ms. Pryor ran her finger lightly on the little round stained-glass window beside the front door. "There are always work-arounds for that kind of thing," she said in that soft sort of voice people use when they're talking as much to themselves as to the other person.

Mom looked surprised. "Are you a lawyer, Ms. Pryor?"

"Ottoline, please," said Ms. Pryor. "And no. Well, actually, yes, I have a degree in law. But I'm not a practicing lawyer. What's in there?" She pointed toward the double doors just on the other side of my grandfather clock.

"The breakfast room," Mom said, leading Ottoline inside. I followed, right at Ottoline's heels, unnoticed. "This is the oldest part—except for the east end of the cellar. It was built just after the Revolutionary War. Those ceiling beams are original."

"Very nice," Ottoline said. "And how interesting that you've left the floor so uneven."

"Uh, thanks," said Mom, crossing the room and entering the big lounge. Not much went on in the big lounge. We'd tried a few weddings, but at the last one, the mother of the bride and the mother of the groom, meeting for the first time, found that they were wearing the same dress. Things had gone downhill after that, for reasons I didn't understand, although I have a very clear memory of a certain party getting a little too excited and doing something he really shouldn't have done involving the wedding cake. In short, we were taking a break from weddings.

Ottoline walked around the room, touching a silver candlestick and a china teapot, then standing before a big painting of . . . of Catastrophe Falls? Certainly of a waterfall, with our kind of dark green forest on both sides. I'd seen the painting many times, but hadn't really looked at it. *Careful, Queenie*, said a voice in my head. My own inside voice, known only to me. All I can tell you is it's low and lovely, a lot like a cello, in fact. But what was I supposed to be careful about?

"The whole place has a wonderful vibe, Yvette." Ottoline turned to Mom. "You must get offers."

"Offers?"

"From people who want to buy it."

"Not offers, exactly, but there has been some recent interest—a Boston law firm acting for a buyer they didn't name."

"No offer?" Ottoline said. "I'm not sure I understand."

"It didn't get that far," said Mom. "I told the lawyer that the inn is not for sale."

Ottoline smiled. Her teeth were very white, quite small, and . . . looked kind of sharp. Almost like mine. How strange! And uncomfortable. "Everything's for sale," she said. "At the right price."

Mom shook her head. "Not this place."

Ottoline's smile broadened. "Of course you're attached to it. That's the emotional part. But even emotions can be expressed in dollars and cents."

"You really believe that?"

"Certainly. History proves it time after time. But getting back to particulars, suppose you got an offer big enough so you could rebuild the whole inn precisely as it is on a similar plot of land, just not here?"

"In that case," said Mom, "the person making the offer could do the exact same thing himself—or herself—and leave me out of it."

Ottoline rocked back, very slightly. Then she laughed, not loudly, but the shrill part pretty much took over. I was close to her ankles at that moment and considered—and rejected—doing something dramatic. I knew from the movie that the lone warrior does swing into action at times, but this particular time didn't feel right. We in the cat world are very good at sensing that kind of thing, far far better than those in the dog world, and also probably better than you. Sorry if you're offended, but isn't it better to know the truth?

"Very good, Yvette," Ottoline said. "I'll have to remember that."

"Thanks," said Mom. Now she smiled, too. Mom's smile is always nice, of course, although this wasn't her nicest. "Anything else you'd like to see?"

"You mentioned the oldest part of the house, in the cellar."

"Right this way," said Mom.

We walked along the long hall past the kitchen and headed down the back stairs, Mom first, then Ottoline, and me last. The back staircase is my usual route to the cellar, although the fastest way—which I discovered completely by accident, chasing a mousy acquaintance who turned out to know the house better than I did!—was down the old laundry chute, no longer used and rather tricky. Tricky for both of us, and in the end trickier for him. Poor fellow!

We went through all the newer parts of the basement— furnace room, storeroom, sports equipment room, laundry room, broken-furniture room, wine cellar with no wine in it, and came to the old, dirt-floored part.

"Okay with a few cobwebs?" Mom said.

"Up to a point," said Ottoline.

Mom switched on a light, catching a momentary expression on Ottoline's face, the face of someone not okay with cobwebs. I myself avoid cobwebs without even thinking about it. There are many things I know how to do because I just know.

Mom pointed up to the ceiling, all shadows and exposed rafters, cracked with age. "If you look closely, you'll see a date burned into that beam."

Ottoline stood on tiptoes. "1799," she said. "Ah! I get it. The place has been in your family the whole time."

"Oh, no," Mom said.

"But you're from here, going way back."

"Not that, either, although my ex-husband is. We bought the inn thirteen years ago."

Ottoline glanced at her. "And now it belongs just to you?"

"More or less," Mom said.

"I hear you," said Ottoline. "The financial details of my own divorce are still being ironed out, and it's been three years."

Mom nodded but said nothing. I remembered Dad, of course, a handsome guy who did a lot of pacing when he was alone, and for some reason he thought he was alone even when I was right in the same room. Then came Lilah Fairbanks, the interior decorator Mom hired to make some changes. "She sure did that," Mom said to me one day, long after the divorce. I didn't miss Dad.

"All powered with coal until quite recently," Mom said, moving past the huge old rusted-out boiler and over to the coal chute by the window. This window, the only one in the old cellar, was small and high up on the wall, at the level of the ground outside. Elrod had explained the whole thing to Bro—about how the coal got delivered through the window and down the chute, back in the old days. Not long ago, a mousy playmate of mine had run up the coal chute and clear outside, escaping through a hole in one of the windowpanes. Frustrating, yes, but I'd soon discovered that I could squeeze through that hole myself! Which had already led to one or two nighttime adventures, and promised many more.

"We put up solar panels on the south part of the roof and were hoping . . ." Mom's voice trailed off in the way it did when she's suddenly noticed something, usually something not quite right. Uh-oh? Had she noticed that broken pane? That would lead to Elrod, followed by a day or two of trial and error, mostly error, but in the end my special window would be fixed, an extremely bad result.

But it turned out Mom had seen something else. She knelt and began examining the foundation wall. Was there a crack in it, way down near the floor? Yes. Very hard to spot in the shadows, but Mom had spotted it.

Ottoline stood right behind her. "Your job never ends, does it?" she said.

"Comes with the territory," Mom said, running her finger along the crack. "No complaints."

Ottoline glanced up. Some old tools hung from the rafters—one of those two-man saws, a giant auger, a scythe. Elrod had pointed them all out to Bro, whose eyes had gone glassy, the way they do when Bro tunes out. But I'd been tuning in, so I knew that the scythe, for example, was for cutting tall grass, a long-handled thing with a curved, pointed blade.

"That's the spirit," Ottoline said. "And even if you do complain, nobody— Oops!"

And all at once Ottoline was falling, like she'd taken a step and lost her balance, although she'd been standing still. Then, in normal falling-human style, she flailed her arms around wildly, hoping to grab something steady. Instead one of her hands struck the handle of the scythe, knocking it off its hook. The scythe spun slowly in the air and started falling, blade first.

I screamed. I'd never screamed in my life. The sound was huge and terrifying, terrifying to me, too. Mom twisted around in my direction real quick. The scythe plunged down, right through the space where her head had just been, landing point first, blade sticking deep in the dirt floor, the whole nasty thing quivering, almost like it was alive.

"Oh my god!" Mom said, her hand to her chest. She glanced around wildly, saw Ottoline slowly picking herself up off the floor.

"I-I'm so sorry," Ottoline said. "I lost my—the cat! I must have stepped on the cat and lost my balance. I didn't even know she was here. Did I hurt her? I must have—that scream! But are you all right, Yvette? I'm so, so sorry."

Mom knelt on the floor. Her face had lost all its color, making her eyes very dark. She looked up at Ottoline, now on her feet, wringing her hands like humans do when they're worried out of their minds. Then Mom glanced my way. I happened to be very close to Ottoline's feet. Why couldn't I have been somewhere else? Up on the coal chute, for example?

Mom took a deep breath. "Well, as Deputy Carstairs said down at the station, no harm, no foul."

"I feel terrible," Ottoline said.

"Please don't." Mom got to her feet. "Accidents happen."

But! But! But! Had I ever been so frustrated in my entire life? Half of me wanted to scream again. The other half was too frightened of the sound.

TEN
ARTHUR

N OW, ARTHUR," SAID MRS. SALMING, "you be good."

Well, of course! I was working on a nice big bone she'd cooked up just for me, and being as good as good gets, with no plans to be anything else. I sat with Mrs. Salming in the first row of the bleachers at the baseball field. Baseball was my favorite sport and Mrs. Salming and I were ballpark buddies. Mr. Salming, a tall, broad-shouldered dude who didn't say much, was the coach. He was also the hockey coach and the mailman, the only mailman in town who wore shorts all year round. Right now he was standing on home plate with a bunch of kids around him, including Harmony, up front, and Bro, way at the back. The infield was kind of muddy and there were puddles on the outfield grass, but the sun was shining now and I couldn't wait for Mr. Salming to say, "Play ball!" I like hockey, too, but not as much as baseball. Anyone who's chewed both pucks and baseballs would have the same opinion. Mr. Salming had a whole big bag of baseballs at his feet. The moment one got loose, I'd race out there and—

I felt Mrs. Salming's hand tighten on my leash.

"Arthur? You with the program?"

Oh, certainly. No one could be more with the program than me, whatever that meant exactly. I sat up my very tallest and paid my very closest attention to what was happening on the field. Was the bone hanging out the side of my mouth? Possibly. There are some things you just have to live with.

"Welcome to baseball in Vermont," Mr. Salming said. "Is there a better baseball state in the whole union?"

A scrawny kid standing next to Harmony raised his hand.

"Oh, not Maxie Millipat," said Mrs. Salming quietly.

"No answer necessary, Max," Mr. Salming said. "It was just one of those rhetorical questions."

Maxie waved his hand around. "But, Coach! I have an answer!"

Mr. Salming sighed. "Go on."

"Just about every state is better, Coach. Carlton Fisk is our only Hall of Famer, and he's actually from New Hampshire."

"Appreciate the input, Max. Next, we're going to—"

"It doesn't mean we're worse athletes," Maxie went on. "Low population's the most important factor, with bad weather second. If we traded places with Arkansas, then—"

At that point Harmony turned to Maxie and made a slashing motion across her throat. I didn't know what that meant, but Maxie went silent immediately.

"Thank goodness for Harmony," said Mrs. Salming.

And soon after that, the kids were spread out on the field, warming up. They did some stretching, lined up in rows, tossed baseballs back and forth, whipped sidearm grounders to each other, flung a few flies up high. Baseballs started getting loose, lots of them.

"You're staying right here, my friend," said Mrs. Salming. "How about we do a little catching up? What's new at the beautiful Blackberry Hill Inn?"

Hmm. A tough question. I had no idea. Neither could I think of anything old at the inn. I waited for something I could handle.

"Making a go of it, I hope? Times are tough."

Were they? I'd completely missed that. I turned my head for a better view of Mrs. Salming. Was she feeling all right? Sick people give off certain smells that are easy to detect, and I was picking up none of them.

"That's a funny face," she said, rumpling the fur on the back of my head in a nice way that felt good, if a bit on the rough side. "Some might say you're a tad ugly, but I don't think so. To me you're the handsomest boy in town."

Wow! Mrs. Salming thought I was handsome? Took her

a lot of words to say so, but I'd missed most of them, so no harm done.

"Speaking of beauty," Mrs. Salming went on, "how is Yvette?" She frowned. "And how in heck could anyone prefer the likes of Lilah Fairbanks to . . ." Mrs. Salming was quiet for a bit, her hand resting motionless on my head. There was a lot to like about Mrs. Salming. The bone, for one thing, plus a promising biscuit smell that rose from her purse.

"Any gentlemen callers sniffing around?" Mrs. Salming said.

What was this? If there was any sniffing to be done at the inn, that sniffing would be handled by me and only me. I awaited more info.

"Word is that Deputy Carstairs's divorce finally came through, and he's already expressed interest in—"

Mrs. Salming paused, shielded her eyes, peered up the street that led to the ball field. "And who would that be?"

A boy had just come over the hill at the top of the street and was running our way, running full speed. He raced onto the field and approached Mr. Salming, a boy who was pretty sweaty despite the rawness of the day, and whose face was a little messed up. It was Jimmy.

"Uh, hi, Coach," he said. "Sorry I'm late."

Mr. Salming gazed down at him. "Jimmy?" he said. "Jimmy Doone? Haven't seen you in some time."

100

"Uh, no," said Jimmy.

Mr. Salming eyed Jimmy's face. "You okay?"

Jimmy looked down. "Fell off a ladder."

Bro and Harmony exchanged a look. It was almost like they had a quick talk, although no talking happened— an unusual thing among humans, but not from the two of them.

"Well, glad you're here," Mr. Salming said. "Don't tell me you ran all the way from your place."

Jimmy nodded.

Mr. Salming smiled. "So conditioning ain't gonna be an issue," he said.

Mrs. Salming laughed, a very soft laugh, barely heard even by me. You would have missed it completely, but no worries.

Out on the field, Mr. Salming said, "Bring your glove?"

"Don't have one," Jimmy said. "But I'll be all right."

"I've got some extras. You a righty or a lefty?"

Jimmy shrugged. "Doesn't matter."

"I just meant do you throw from the right or the left?"

"Both, I guess."

Mr. Salming leaned back a bit, stared down at Jimmy.

"You wouldn't be having a little fun with me now, would you, Jimmy?"

"For god's sake, Bertram," Mrs. Salming muttered.

Jimmy shook his head.

"Left, right—makes no difference?" said Mr. Salming.

Now some of the kids were watching. "Not for throwing," Jimmy said. "For writing my left's a little better."

Mr. Salming nodded. He reached into the ball bag and tossed Jimmy a baseball. Jimmy reached up and caught it with both hands, in that same noiseless way Harmony and Bro made barehanded catches, their hands somehow soft and strong at the same time.

"Any catchers here today?" said Mr. Salming.

Maxie's hand shot up.

"You're not a catcher, Maxie. But Harmony is." He dug into the ball bag again, pulled out a catcher's mask, tossed it to Harmony. "Get behind the plate," he told her.

Harmony went behind the plate, got into her crouch, and lowered the mask over her face. Right! She was a catcher. I started remembering things from last season. Harmony was a catcher and Bro played shortstop, maybe because he liked to get dirty.

"Step on the mound, Jimmy," Mr. Salming said.

Jimmy stepped on the mound.

"Throw."

"Uh, with which hand?"

"You pick."

Jimmy stared down at Harmony. She tapped her fist in her mitt. And then Jimmy wound up—hey! kind of like on TV!—and threw.

Wow! The ball flew through the air, a real quick blur, and went SMACK right into Harmony's mitt.

"Ouch!" said Harmony.

"Oh, sorry, Harmony," Jimmy said. "I didn't mean—"

"Shut up," said Harmony. "I wasn't ready, that's all. My bad." She tapped her mitt again, hard this time. "Let's see what you got from the left."

Mr. Salming tossed Jimmy another ball. Jimmy turned sideways the other way, went into that TV-style windup again, and threw. Same as before: blur and SMACK. This time there was no ouch from Harmony. Instead, from behind the mask, came a quiet, "Yeah."

"Want to see righty again?" Jimmy said to Mr. Salming.

"Seen enough. But just to get my facts straight, the last time I saw you on the ball field was when you were on the eight-year-olds."

"Yes, sir."

"So where have you been playing baseball?"

"Nowhere."

"You haven't played since?"

"No."

"Then who taught you that windup? Was your dad a ball player?"

Jimmy looked down and shook his head.

"Then how, Jimmy?"

"Watching games."

"Where?"

"On TV."

"You watch baseball on TV?"

"In summer. After chores. Couple of innings, if I can."

Mr. Salming gazed at Jimmy. Mrs. Salming was leaning forward a bit, her hands clasped tight. After a silent moment or two, Mr. Salming picked up some bats and turned to the kids. "Looking forward to the season, everybody?"

"YEAH!"

"Then let's take some BP."

BP was when Mr. Salming pitched and the kids took turns hitting. What a great idea! Baseballs flew all over the place in BP, better believe it. One came bouncing right to me! I snapped it up, easy peasy.

"Now, Arthur," said Mrs. Salming. "Those balls cost money." She reached out, as though to possibly put her hand on the ball. I'm talking about my ball, which just happened to be in my mouth. What could she have been thinking?

Mrs. Salming reached into her purse and took out the biscuit. A nice big round one, I believe from a company called Waggies with which I was familiar. "How about we do a little trade?" she said.

Trade? What was that again? Some way of both eating the biscuit and chewing on the ball at the same time? I tried to figure out how to do that and had no thoughts. Mrs. Salming laid the biscuit right in front of me on the ground. I kept my eyes on it but also kept chewing on the ball. That was the best I could do.

"You're incorrigible," said Mrs. Salming.

Incorrigible? A compliment, for sure. Hadn't Bro said the exact same thing?

Not long after that, BP ended and Mr. Salming waved everyone over. "Good job," he said. "I'll be calling about who made the As, who made the Bs. Calling, not texting. So pick up. All right, in here, team." He raised his hand. They all raised their hands, forming a kind of tent of arms with Mr. Salming's hand at the top. "Bobcats!" they all cried. "Yeah!"

Bobcats? Bobcats was the name of the team? Bobcats sounded like a kind of cat. Why would anyone name a team after a cat? Do cats ever team up to do anything? This was a disturbing development, so disturbing I lost control of my ball. Mrs. Salming snatched it up on the first bounce.

"Good boy," she said, wiping the ball in the grass, for some reason. "Now eat your biscuit."

I started in on the biscuit. It tasted great! If something

had been bothering me, I forgot what it was right away. Meanwhile Harmony and Bro came over.

"Thanks for watching Arthur, Mrs. Salming," Harmony said. "Was he good?"

"The best," said Mrs. Salming. She rose, walked over to the mound. For a moment I thought she might be about to do some pitching herself, but instead she stuck my ball in the ball bag.

Meanwhile Maxie Millipat was talking to Mr. Salming. "Coach? Want me to take one of these balls and put a chip in it? We could track spin rate, velocity, trajectory, just about anything. I could even write some code for making changes in real time."

"I don't understand a word you're saying," Mr. Salming said.

"Change a curveball into a fastball in mid-flight," said Maxie. "That's just off the top of my head."

Mr. Salming gazed down at Maxie. "What I want you to do with the ball, Maxie, is watch it."

"Not following you, Coach."

"Eye on the ball, Maxie. Rule one in the game of baseball."

"That's rule one? But what about—"

And Maxie started in on something very complicated. We headed for home, Harmony carrying her catcher's mitt,

Bro wearing his glove on his head, me dragging my leash, my tail held at its highest. I had a big big thought: We were a great team, me, Harmony, and Bro, in no need of any more members, especially a certain one I won't name. I always try not to think of her but things always pop up to remind me. Bobcats, for example. Wouldn't Dogs be a better team name? Two four six eight, who do we appreciate, dogs! dogs! dogs!

We walked across the outfield, headed for home. Up ahead, Jimmy was also walking, but very fast, cutting across our path.

"Hey, Jimmy," Bro called.

Jimmy turned his head but didn't even slow down. "Yeah?"

"Uh, good job."

"Uh, you too."

Jimmy kept walking, getting farther and farther away from us.

"Jimmy!" Harmony called after him.

Jimmy turned his head, still not slowing down.

"Yeah?"

"What are you doing?"

"Going home."

"Walking?"

"Uh-huh."

"It's miles and miles."

"I'll run part."

"Um, how about—" Bro began.

"Coming over to our place?" said Harmony. "Our mom will drive you home."

"Yeah?" said Jimmy, and came to a stop.

ELEVEN

QUEENIE

BASEBALL PRACTICE? BASEBALL tryouts? Baseball game? Baseball anything? I really didn't care. Humans have many ways of keeping busy, almost all of them pointless. They're at their best, in my opinion, when sleeping.

We had humans here in the kitchen at the inn—Bro, Harmony, and Jimmy—none of them sleeping. The only sleeper was someone I don't even have to name. I'm sure you've already guessed. He was sacked out beside the big stove, one of his favorite spots. Every once in a while one of his paws did a strange vibrating thing. What would be a good way of stopping that?

The humans were at the table over in the little alcove where the family ate most of its meals, a cozy spot with a bay window and a view of the side yard bird feeder. There's also a bird feeder out back, which the birds seem to prefer. I myself am a big fan of bird feeders in general and wish we had more. Birds are not easy to catch, far from it, but it can be done, and one of the best times is when they're at a bird feeder and not in their usual hyperalert frame of mind. To get a claw into one of them, to feel that tiny heart beating so— Well, perhaps enough of that, or even too much.

Back to the kids at the kitchen table. They were eating popcorn and washing it down with soda. I could hear the fizzing from across the room, where I was curled up in a graceful way on the tall stool Bertha sometimes sat on while slicing and dicing, to give her feet a rest. Human feet: a big, unhappy, and often smelly subject we might get to later.

"What's the best way to go, Jimmy?" Harmony said. "Pitching one game righty and the next one lefty? Or switching it up during the game?"

"I don't know," Jimmy said. "Never thought about it."

"Frmmuch glopbrg," said Bro, or something like that, impossible to understand with his mouth full of popcorn. He washed it down with soda, maybe too much, which led to a coughing fit, followed by some gagging and spewing. Harmony reached out and smacked him on the back.

"Phew," said Bro. "Thanks."

Jimmy looked at one, then the other. "I thought brothers and sisters weren't supposed to get along."

"We don't," Harmony said.

"We hate each other," said Bro.

"Despise."

"Yeah, despise. What's that other word, Harm?"

"Loathe."

"We loathe each other, Jimmy," Bro said.

"Hate, despise, and loathe," said Harmony.

Jimmy did that thing of looking from one to the other again, and a smile began spreading across his face, still somewhat messed up. He started laughing, a low, happy laugh. It spread to Harmony and Bro. They all laughed together for a while. After that came a silence, a very silent silence following the noise of all that laughter. Bro turned to Jimmy and said, "I told Harmony."

For a moment, Jimmy looked angry. Then his face changed, smoothing out, and he said, "That's okay."

"Yeah?" said Bro.

"I kinda thought you would," Jimmy said.

Harmony leaned forward. "Walter can't get away with this," she said. "We should do something about it, Jimmy."

"It's not your problem," Jimmy said. "And there's no answer."

"That's why we should talk to my mom," Harmony said. "She's good at finding answers when nobody else—"

Jimmy jumped up and shouted, "No way! Don't you dare tell your mom!"

That was when Mom came in, carrying a bag of groceries. "Hi, everybody," she said. "Paying us a visit, Jimmy? That's nice." She gave his face a second look, but real quick. And you had to be real quick to spot it. "What is it I'm not supposed to hear?" She opened a cupboard and began putting the groceries away.

The kids looked at one another, maybe waiting for one of them to step forward, but no one did.

"The thing is," Mom said, rearranging boxes on the cereal shelf, "if I hadn't heard that I'm not supposed to hear, we'd be live and let live right now." She turned to the kids. "But I did hear."

Bro and Harmony were both watching Jimmy. He nodded. "I guess it doesn't matter now anyway. He's gone."

"Who are we talking about?" Mom said.

"Walter," said Jimmy.

"Whoa," said Bro. "He's gone?"

"Left last night," Jimmy said. "He told my dad it was either him or me."

"But that's crazy," Bro said. "He's just the hired hand and you're the son."

"I guess . . ." Jimmy began, his voice thickening. He tried again. "I guess that's why my dad said he was . . . was stuck with me."

"Oh, no," said Harmony.

"Kids?" Mom said, softly closing the cupboard. "Can we back up a bit?"

They backed up, one of those tedious human things where they're trying to all get on the same page. Among me and my kind, we don't care the slightest about that. Finally they came to the end, Mom in the know about everything—just like me, I suppose. Hmm. Interesting thought. Perhaps I'd circle back to it sometime. But right now, Mom was saying, "What about your mom, Jimmy?"

Jimmy shrugged. "I was two when they got divorced, and I haven't seen her much."

"Sorry," Mom said. "Didn't mean to pry."

Jimmy smiled. "Too late to stop now."

Then they were all smiling, kind of unexpected, even puzzling, from my point of view, but actually rather nice.

"Can we give Jimmy a ride home?" Bro said.

"Be my pleasure," said Mom.

A moment later they were all on their way to the front door, excepting Arthur, of course, still in some doggy dreamland, no doubt all about food. Notice I didn't say excepting Arthur and me. For some reason, I followed them to the door. Why? I'd already had a too-long outing today, and I don't particularly like car travel. There are depths in me that even I haven't yet explored. Let's leave it at that.

"Hey," Harmony said. "Check out Queenie."

And then everybody had their eyes on me. Quite nice, of course, but also I envied them. Why couldn't I, too, have been feasting my eyes on me at that moment? Or just I alone?

"She wants to come with us?" Mom said.

"Looks like it," said Harmony.

"Odd," Mom said.

We rode in Mom's car, me in the back between Harmony and Bro, and Jimmy up front with Mom. The sun wasn't shining anymore, and we had one of those light drizzles going on. The air got very humid. I don't like that. I also don't like not humid enough. I like just right. My mood deteriorated a bit. Nobody's fault. Maybe my fellow riders were also feeling the humidity. No one was saying anything. The only sound was the occasional swish of the windshield wipers, not one of my favorites.

After a while, Mom glanced at Jimmy and said, "Maybe Sweet Lady Em will be back by now."

"Yeah," said Jimmy, gazing straight ahead.

"Someone's bound to see her," said Mom. "Cows aren't good at hiding."

I'd never heard that before, but it made sense. That was Mom, every time.

We turned off the road—I believe the road that leads

out of town, but most of my travel takes place on my own in the dark of night, so I'm no expert on the road system—and onto a narrow track, paved only for stretches here and there.

"Keep your eyes peeled, kids," Mom said.

"For what?" said Bro.

"Why, Sweet Lady Em, of course," Mom said. "Maybe she decided the wandering life's not for her, and she's coming back on her own."

"Um," Bro said.

"Go on," said Mom.

"Well," he said, "that's if she wandered off in the first place."

"I don't understand," said Mom.

"Which, uh, she couldn't do with the barn door locked," Bro said.

"Ah," Mom said.

There was a long silence. A barn came into view, with a small house beyond it, both buildings in need of a paint job, in my opinion. Mom drove up to the house and stopped the car. Jimmy opened the door.

"Jimmy?" Mom said.

He paused, looked back at her.

"Drop by our place anytime you like," she said. "You're always welcome."

Jimmy nodded and got out.

"See you," said Bro.

"Yeah," said Jimmy.

He closed the car door and headed toward the house.

"The door's open," Harmony said.

"Huh?" said Bro. "He closed it."

"I'm talking about the door to the house," Harmony said.

And yes, the door to the house was open. Jimmy appeared to notice that, and seemed to slow down.

"Do you think he left that door open, too?" Harmony said.

"What do you mean—too?" said Bro.

"Well, we don't know for sure, do we?" Harmony said.

"I believe Jimmy," Bro said.

"So do I," said Harmony. "But we don't actually know."

Jimmy went into the house. The door closed. The car was running, but we didn't drive away. I began to get anxious.

"Mom?" Bro said.

"Just a minute," said Mom. "I want to be certain that—"

The door to Jimmy's house burst open. Jimmy came running outside, his mouth wide open like he was screaming, although I heard no sound.

Mom jumped out of the car. So did Harmony and Bro. And me.

"Jimmy! Jimmy! What is it?" Mom said.

Jimmy just put his hands to his head.

Mom turned to Harmony and Bro. "Wait here." Then she ran past Jimmy and into the house. I was right beside her, Harmony and Bro a step behind. Perhaps they'd missed Mom's instructions. We all came to a stop right away. There in the hall lay Mr. Doone, motionless, eyes closed, blood all over the floor.

"Oh my god," Mom said. She reached for the kids, drew them close. That was when Jimmy came back into the house, walking unsteadily, almost stumbling. He knelt and took Mr. Doone's head in his hands.

"Dad! Dad!"

Mr. Doone moaned a low moan.

Mom whipped out her phone. "We've got an emergency!"

Bro stepped forward and pulled Jimmy away from Mr. Doone, very gently. Mr. Doone moaned again. His eyelids fluttered slightly but stayed shut. Sirens started up in the distance.

I myself returned to the car, not fast, not slow. I just went. Mom's door was open. I slipped inside and eased myself under the driver's seat.

TWELVE
ARTHUR

I DREAMED I WAS HUNGRY. WHAT KIND of a dream was that? More like a nightmare. I opened my eyes and found that I was hungry for real. All at once I had a sure grip on . . . on, well, everything! What a great feeling! Here's one thing about me: When I'm feeling good, I like a little company. Feeling good is even better if there's company, in my opinion. I looked around, saw that I was in the kitchen, lying by the stove, one of my favorite spots, partly because it was nice and toasty and partly because the kitchen is a good place to be if you like company. But right now I seemed to have the kitchen to myself. I was all alone. All alone and hungry. Was I scared? Not one bit! Old Arthur is braver than you might think.

Still, where was everybody? No matter how brave you are, you . . . you need a little company. Hey! The company thing again, and so soon. That had to mean something. I got up, gave myself a quick shake, and trotted out of the kitchen.

No one in the front hall. No one in the back hall that led to the family quarters. No one in the small parlor, the Big Room, the breakfast room. Not even anyone on the grandfather clock. I did not like this, not one bit. What if I was all alone forever? No Mom. No Bro. No Harmony. No Bertha. No Elrod. No Big Fred. No Quee—

Maybe best to stop at no Big Fred.

I paced back and forth in the front hall. Through the windows I could see the sky darkening and darkening. No Mom. No Bro. No Harmony. Darkening and darkening! *Mom, Bro, Harmony! Mom, Bro, Harmony!* I paced and paced, ramping up to pretty much my fastest trot, tuckering myself out. But what good would I be all tuckered out? I eased off a bit, and in that moment heard a footstep upstairs. I went still, cocked my head to one side, which is how to listen your very best. And I heard silence, silence, silence, and then: another footstep, not loud but sort of firm. Mom's footstep? Bro's? Harmony's? No, none of them. Did we have any guests? Maybe not. It was mud season, meaning lack of guests was a big problem. Meanwhile in the middle of all this thinking, I found I was already halfway up the broad staircase that leads to the guest rooms.

The smell began to change. There was always less human scent on the guest floor, and more floral scent, since Mom kept a vase or two of fresh flowers in the upstairs hall, even in winter when we had to buy them. On his last visit, Mr. Pruitt, the accountant, had turned a page in Mom's big book and said, "Another invoice from the florist, Yvette? How about cutting back a little?"

And Mom had said, "An inn without flowers is not an inn, Mr. Pruitt."

That had stuck with me. Now whenever I'm in any sort of place and I don't smell flowers I know right away: Not an inn, Arthur, my friend.

I walked along the upstairs hall, past a vase of yellow flowers on a stand, and past several doors, the rooms on the other side all silent. The guest rooms are named after flowers and have tiny paintings of flowers on their doors. Passing by the one with the red flowers, I heard a faint thump, like something light had landed on something soft.

I paused.

Silence. It went on and on. I began to get restless. And anxious. And worried. A bark rose up inside me, not a loud one, but there was no keeping it in. I let it out, low and rumbly, actually one of my favorite barks. It says, "Dude!"

The door flew open. And there was Ms. Pryor. Right, we had a guest. I'd almost forgotten. She had a red leather belt in one hand, the leather very soft and smelling lovely. What would gnawing on such a fine leather belt be like?

120

Good, of course, but there was only one way to find out how good.

She looked my way, possibly not happy to see me. At first, maybe because I'd been wanting company, I was happy to see her. I knew from how my tail was wagging. But as I looked at her, the wagging slowed down and finally came to a stop, the end of my tail drooping to the floor.

Ms. Pryor frowned. "What was your name again? Did I ever hear it? No doubt something cutesy."

What was this? Something about my name? Arthur is my name. Is that cutesy? If so, cutesy must mean very very good. I love my name. My name and me are like this! It's Arthur, by the way. Please don't forget.

"Are they back?" she said, speaking in that voice humans use when they're talking to themselves. I've heard it a lot from many kinds of humans, and I've actually come up with a thought on the subject. That voice you hear when they're talking to themselves is their real voice! Ms. Pryor's real voice scared me a bit.

She stepped past me, walked down the hall to the top of the stairs, and listened, cocking her head somewhat like I do. Uh-oh? Were we alike? That was a disturbing idea, but before I could deal with it, Ms. Pryor returned, stepping around me again and entering the room. Her backpack lay on the bed, looking pretty stuffed, pockets and

121

openings zipped and snapped closed except for one. Ms. Pryor rolled the red leather belt up tight, stuck it in the open pocket, and was starting to pull the zipper when her phone buzzed. She took it from her pocket, peered at the screen, frowned, and put the phone to her ear.

"What's wrong with you?" she said. "I told you never to call this number."

A man spoke on the other end. I couldn't hear what he was saying, but I recognized the voice. Where from? I came close to remembering, so close I felt a bit proud of myself. But despite trying oh so hard, I got no further than the smell of wet mops.

"Did I hear correctly?" Ms. Pryor's face went red. The combination of the redness of her face and the silvery blondness of her hair made me want to be somewhere else, hard to explain why. But . . . but no one else was home. Didn't that mean I was in charge? And being in charge meant staying right here. It was so clear to me that I didn't need to know why, a good thing since trying to know the why of things can be confusing.

Ms. Pryor's voice got lower and sharper at the same time, a combo I'd never heard before. I backed up the tiniest bit. You wouldn't even have noticed.

"How could you let it get so far out of hand?" she said.

The man started to explain, but she cut him off.

"Don't want to hear it. There were two of you and one of him."

The man spoke again, and again she cut him off.

"What I want you to do now? Get lost until you hear from me. That's what I want you to do." Ms. Pryor clicked off. Her eyes got an inward look. I could feel her thinking, real fast.

"So many moving parts," she said. "But how can I leave now?" She turned in my direction and blinked, like maybe she was surprised to see me. How come? This was my territory. "Why are there so many stupid people?" she said.

There were many stupid people? I didn't recall meeting a single one.

"What's the ratio—nine stupids to one smart? Or is it even worse than that?" She shook her head. "I can solve this," she said. "I can solve anything. But it would be a lot easier without all these unnecessary people."

I had no idea what Ms. Pryor was talking about. All of a sudden I was very thirsty. My water bowl was down in the kitchen, but I knew I had to be here. Meanwhile Ms. Pryor had returned to the bed and was starting to unpack. Was trotting past her into the bathroom and taking a few quick sips from the toilet a good idea? I was going back and forth on that when I heard a car pulling into the driveway, and not just any car but ours, which

I knew from this high-pitched whee-whee-whee it was making these days, a noise that troubled me, although no one else seemed to hear it.

Ms. Pryor went still. After a moment she walked to the window and looked out. Then she turned to a wall mirror, did a little something to her hair, and headed out of the room and into the hall, locking the door. She stepped around me one more time and started toward the stairs.

I followed. She must have heard me because she glanced back.

"What's your problem?" she said.

I had no problem. Except for thirst. And the smell of wet mops. And being left alone in the house for so long. Plus I was getting hungry. And there were other problems, tumbling one after another into my mind. But none of that kept me from following Ms. Pryor, although now from quite a bit farther back.

We went downstairs, Ms. Pryor in the lead and me last until we were almost at the bottom, when I darted ahead— hardly losing my balance at all!—and reached the bottom first. Which was actually how I landed—bottom first— but I scrambled up so quickly you wouldn't have noticed. And there, kind of wet, were Mom, Harmony, and Bro!

Plus Jimmy, carrying a gym bag, and also that other member of our family, riding for the moment in Harmony's special backpack. Why was there no special backpack for me?

But no time for that now, because right away I knew that they were all upset, maybe even Queenie, too. There were all kinds of signs, but mostly I just knew. They all looked my way. That got my tail going, of course. We were so happy to see them, me and my tail. But then their gazes went to Ms. Pryor.

"Well, hi there," she said. "I've just been spending some quality time with this adorable pooch of yours. He's so cutes—so cute! Why do you know—" Ms. Pryor broke off. Her eyebrows rose. "Oh, dear. Is something the matter?" She put her hand to her chest.

Mom nodded. "I'm afraid so," she said. "Kids, take Jimmy upstairs and get him settled."

The kids headed for the door that led to the back stairs. On the way, Harmony opened the pocket on the backpack. Queenie slipped out, and before the door had closed behind the kids, she was somehow up in her spot on the grandfather clock. I'm not jealous. Don't think that for a second. I have no desire whatsoever to sit on the grandfather clock, and even if there was a way I could actually get there, I'd never—

I left that one in mid-thought, wishing I'd abandoned it right from the get-go. Most thoughts were like that, in my experience.

Mom moved behind the desk, checked the computer screen. She looked pale. I went over and pressed against her leg. Mom was trembling a bit. Oh, that was bad. All I could do was press a little harder.

Ms. Pryor came halfway across the hall and stopped. "What . . . what's wrong?" she said. "Is there anything I can do?"

"No," Mom said. "That's very kind of you." Mom stood straighter. I felt her pulling herself together. "We've had a terrible thing happen. There's been . . . well, an assault."

"Assault? Oh, dear!"

"Yes. The . . . the victim is Jimmy's dad." Mom gestured toward the door to the back stairs. "Jimmy—a friend of my son's."

"Yes, yes," Ms. Pryor said. "I met Jimmy yesterday, when we had that incident at the falls."

"Of course," Mom said. "You'll have to forgive me if—"

"And, oh my god!" Ms. Pryor said, her voice rising over Mom's. "I met *him*, too. We . . . we shook hands!" Ms. Pryor rubbed her hands together, almost like she was washing them. "The father. Mr. . . . Doone, isn't it? He had that rifle or shotgun or whatever it was—I don't

126

know guns. But . . . but what happened? Did he get into a gunfight?"

Before Mom could answer, the front door opened and Deputy Carstairs came in, rain dripping off the bill of his blue hat.

THIRTEEN

QUEENIE

"EVENING, YVETTE," DEPUTY CARSTAIRS said. "And you too, Ms., uh, Pryor, was it?"

"Correct," said Ms. Pryor.

What was this? More activity? I'd had plenty of activity for one day, enough activity to last for days and days. All I wanted was to lounge on top of my clock and do absolutely nothing. Why must there be all this drama? It was very inconsiderate. I gazed down at Deputy Carstairs, father of Harmony's friend Emma. I have no problem with Emma—she's actually not terrible at stroking my back and seems to enjoy it, although who wouldn't? But I have no time for Deputy Carstairs. He reminded me of Dad in some ways, and I was not a big fan of Dad, either, back in the days when Dad was here. In fact, I have a terrible memory of an event that took place right here, in this very front hall. This was back in . . . what to call it? The Lilah Fairbanks period? Close enough. Lilah, in case I haven't mentioned it yet, was the interior decorator Mom hired to spruce the place up. That was the expression she used, rather strange, since I expected the inn to soon have Christmas trees in every room, which didn't happen. What did happen was a feeling that disturbed the air—a little like just before thunder and lightning—whenever Lilah Fairbanks and Dad happened to be alone together. Then came that terrible moment: me here in the front hall, Dad and Lilah alone together, Dad hanging a painting Lilah had bought, a painting Mom didn't even like—I saw what she did to it afterward—and Lilah directing him. And leaning forward to straighten the painting, Lilah had placed her hand on Dad's back and kept it there. Then slowly he'd turned and . . . and need I go on? The point—the reason I brought this up—is that the look on Dad's face when Lilah was around reminded me of the look on Deputy Carstairs's face when Mom was around. Dad's a handsome man, I suppose, and Deputy Carstairs is not, although his eyes aren't so bad. But did we need him, or Dad, or anybody else around here? We were perfect just the way we were, with one obvious exception.

Meanwhile Deputy Carstairs was talking to Mom. "Is your son home?" he said.

"Of course," said Mom. "Why?"

"I'd like to talk to him."

"Talk to Bro?" Mom said. "What about?"

"We've got a serious case on our hands," Deputy Carstairs said. "Well, not you—I mean the department. Although in a small town like this, it really is everybody." He paused, glanced at Ms. Pryor—who was watching him in this way she had of seeming to look right into people— and then at Mom, who was also watching him, but in her own way, not like Ms. Pryor's.

"Go on," Mom said.

"Mr. Doone's in a coma—the EMTs took him straight to Regional Hospital," the deputy said. "The state sent down a forensics expert. She says Mr. Doone was hit on the side of the head with a blunt object, most likely made of wood, possibly a two-by-four. My job's to find whoever did the hitting."

"I don't—" Mom began, but Ms. Pryor interrupted.

"Is he going to live?" she said.

"The docs can't say for sure," Carstairs said. "But the odds aren't good."

"Did they quantify those odds?" said Ms. Pryor.

"Excuse me?" Carstairs said.

"Usually odds are expressed in numbers."

"They didn't give me any numbers."

"Then we'll just have to hope for the best, won't we?" said Ms. Pryor. "Good luck with your case." She crossed the hall and headed up the stairs toward the guest rooms.

Mom turned to Carstairs. "I don't see what this has to do with Bro."

"Just procedure," said the deputy.

"What does that mean?" Mom said.

"Procedure? It's, like, how we do things."

"I know what procedure means, Al," Mom said. "But what does your procedure have to do with my son?"

Deputy Carstairs blinked. "Well, he's a friend of the Doones—"

"He's a friend of Jimmy's," Mom said.

"Right, right, a friend of Jimmy's. And also someone who spent time in the company of the victim yesterday. Therefore he may have some potentially useful observations regarding state of mind."

"Whose state of mind?" Mom said.

"Mr. Doone's," said the deputy. "And—" He cut himself off.

"And what?" said Mom.

"Nothing. I was getting ahead of myself. Just Mr. Doone's state of mind."

"Bro is eleven years old," Mom said.

"I know that," said the deputy. "Emma's the same age."

Mom thought for a moment or two, her eyes deep, dark pools. From the direction of the kitchen I heard the sound of water being noisily slurped from a bowl. Life, which should be so easy, hardly ever is.

"Yvette?" said Carstairs.

Mom blinked. "All right," she said. "On one condition—I'm in the room the whole time."

"Goes without saying."

"And I can stop this . . . procedure whenever I want for any reason or none."

"That sounds like another condition," the deputy said. "Maybe two or even three."

Mom folded her arms across her chest.

"Didn't mean that, Yvette. Meant to be a light remark."

Mom raised one eyebrow. I'd hardly ever seen her do that and didn't know what it meant.

Our little discussion took place behind closed doors, in the breakfast room. Arthur's slurping had come to an end and now he was quiet, probably sleeping but possibly just dozing. Sometimes he watches dog programs on TV, every once in a while squeezing into the space behind the TV to see where the dogs are. It's embarrassing, but at the moment I heard no TV sounds.

Bro sat in his usual place at the table, with his back to the bow window. Mom's usual spot was across from Bro, but now she was at the head of the table. Deputy Carstairs sat at the other end in Harmony's chair. I didn't like that at all. As for me, there's a comfortable window seat that follows the whole curve of the bow window. From one end I could keep an eye on everyone, while listening to the rain on the window and enjoying the feel of the seat cushion, especially soft.

"Well, Bro," said Deputy Carstairs, "good to see you."

"Um," said Bro.

"Word is you had a heck of a hockey season."

"Uh, thanks."

"Won the regionals, I hear?"

"Lost in the final," Bro said. "Three one."

"Just getting there's an accomplishment. And if I were a betting man, I'd bet that lone goal came off your stick."

"Harmony's," said Bro.

"All in the family—an athletic family, no doubt about it. And now baseball's started?"

"Yeah."

"Mr. Salming's the coach?"

"Uh-huh."

"What do you think of him?"

"Me?" said Bro.

"Why not you?"

"I'm just . . . you know . . ."

"A kid?" the deputy said.

"Yeah."

"Kids have a right to their opinions, too," the deputy

said. His eyes were on Bro. Mom's eyes were on the deputy, and they were narrowed, very slightly.

Bro ran his hand through his hair, messy to begin with and now more so. "He's a good coach."

"Glad to hear it," said the deputy. "I understand Jimmy was at the tryouts."

"Uh-huh," Bro said.

"He made quite an impression on Mr. Salming. What was that about?"

"Jimmy can throw from both sides, left and right. And he throws hard."

"He's a strong kid, huh?" said the deputy.

Mom's mouth opened a bit, like she was going to say something, but she did not.

Bro shrugged. Then he happened to look at Mom. Their gazes met, just for a second. Bro turned to Deputy Carstairs.

"You talked to Mr. Salming?"

"I've known him for many years. He was quite an athlete himself, in his day."

"But . . . but you talked to him about the tryouts?"

A quick expression crossed Deputy Carstairs's face, an impatient kind of expression. Human impatience is a huge, unhappy subject. I have no plans to go into it, now or ever.

"I've already talked to many people with knowledge of Mr. Doone and his family. That's normal in an investigation like this."

Again Mom's mouth opened like she was about to speak. Again it closed without a word being uttered.

"So, uh, that's why you want to talk to me?" Bro said. "I know Jimmy, but not Mr. Doone. I mean I know him—I knew him to say hi, but . . ."

"No problem," said the deputy. "Tell me about Jimmy."

"What, um, do you want to know?"

"What's he like? Friendly? Easy to get along with?"

"Sure."

"Interesting," said the deputy. "Normally the friendly type has lots of friends. So far—and it's still early—I haven't turned up anyone who says they're friends with Jimmy."

"I'm friends with Jimmy," Bro said. "I like Jimmy. He has lots of chores. That's why."

"That's why what?"

"Why he maybe doesn't have as many friends as some other kids."

"Fine," said the deputy. "Fine and good. What do you two talk about?"

Bro thought for a moment. His face changes when he thinks, seems a little older. "Just stuff," he said. "Baseball. Things like that."

Deputy Carstairs nodded. "Did Jimmy happen to mention a certain dairy cow, named—" He took a notebook from his chest pocket, wet his thumb on his tongue, leafed through.

Maybe I should stop right here and mention that Mom, who tolerates a whole lot in life, has a few things she can't abide. One is that exact kind of thumb wetting that Deputy Carstairs just did. Once when she paid Mr. Sparks, the electrician, in cash—Mr. Sparks always preferring cash—he'd wet his thumb and started peeling off her change and she said, "Just keep it."

All that explains the expression that crossed her face as the deputy paged damply through his notebook. "—cow name of Sweet Lady Em, I believe." He put the notebook away. "Any mention of that?"

Bro nodded.

"What sort of mention?"

Bro thought again.

"Is Sweet Lady Em a prize cow of some sort?" Deputy Carstairs said.

"Yeah."

"Has something happened to her?"

Bro nodded. "She's missing."

Oh, didn't I know it! Sweet Lady Em was missing, all right. Here's a fact that will chill you to the bone. Not long

136

before the deputy's arrival, Bertha tried pouring me some store-bought cream! Out of a cardboard container! Need I even mention that I turned up my nose and walked away in the most dignified manner imaginable? As for my nose, it's the cutest nose in the world, as numerous humans—always of the smart type—have pointed out in my presence.

"Any idea why she's missing?" the deputy said.

Bro shook his head.

"What does Jimmy say?"

"About what?"

When humans are trying to be patient but they're real impatient inside, their faces tell the story. For example, Deputy Carstairs's mouth was set in a smiling position, but his eyes were not along for the ride.

"About Sweet Lady Em being missing," he said.

"He doesn't know how it happened."

"What are the possibilities?"

"I don't know," Bro said. "But Jimmy says he locked the barn door and I believe him. He's very . . . organized."

"Oh?"

"He has routines for everything."

"Good for him," said Deputy Carstairs. "His father must have appreciated that."

Bro said nothing.

"Or maybe he didn't?" the deputy said.

Bro kept on saying nothing. I saw a look on Mom's face that I'd never seen before on her, or anybody: part puzzled, part scared, part angry. Perhaps this was a good time for Deputy Carstairs to leave. I began making plans.

He sure didn't seem to be leaving on his own. Instead he leaned forward and said, "What happened to Jimmy's face?"

Bro looked over at Mom. It was one of those *what-do-I-do-now* looks you sometimes see on human faces, perhaps not often enough.

"Al?" Mom said. "Where are you going with this?"

Deputy Carstairs took out his notebook again, wet-thumbed to another page. "Don't know if you're aware, Yvette, but Mr. Doone had a hired hand out there at the farm for the past year or so, a high-school dropout name of Walter Feniak. Walter's the son of an old buddy of Mr. Doone's from up in Maine. Ran into a bit of trouble and his dad sent him down to work on Mr. Doone's farm, get him away from bad influences, if nothing else. Turns out Walter's gone back home to Maine, apparently just yesterday. Naturally when I found that out, I had to establish the exact time he left. Colleagues of mine in the Maine State Police questioned Walter within the last half hour. They've got positive proof he was back at his dad's by midnight last night, ruling him out as a suspect in the attack on Mr. Doone." Carstairs closed the notebook, looked at Mom. "I got to speak to Walter myself, not five minutes ago. He told me an interesting story—a story I'd like to run past Jimmy."

"What story?" said Mom.

"The background, according to Walter, is that Jimmy cottoned on to a notion that Mr. Doone actually preferred Walter to his own son. Don't know whether that was truly the state of affairs and we may never know, but that's the background. It all seems to have come to a head over the issue of this cow, Jimmy claiming he'd locked the barn door, Walter claiming he hadn't, and Mr. Doone taking Walter's side. This led, again according to Walter, to a confrontation in the barn, where Jimmy took a swing at Walter with a baseball bat. Walter, afraid for his life, ducked and threw a punch. The punch caught Jimmy in the eye and ended the fight. Walter decided there and then to go back home." Carstairs tucked the notebook in his pocket.

"That's not what happened!" Bro said.

"No?" said Carstairs. "Were you there?"

Bro turned red, didn't answer.

"And neither was I," said Carstairs. "So the only fair thing"—he turned to Mom—"is to hear Jimmy's side. I need his help."

"But I heard Jimmy's side!" Bro said. "There was no bat!"

Carstairs's gaze stayed on Mom. "I think your mom understands I have to hear that from Jimmy."

Mom gazed right back at Carstairs. Her eyes were beautiful, but I wouldn't have wanted that look aimed my way. And of course it never could be, Mom loving me the way she did. And who could blame her?

"I'll go talk to Jimmy," she said.

FOURTEEN
ARTHUR

HERE'S SOMETHING I FIGURED OUT all on my own: Harmony's room is right above the kitchen! Isn't that amazing? Maybe not her room being above the kitchen. After all, it has to be some-where. Wow! Is my brain working or what? The feeling is actually a bit unpleasant, so I hope it doesn't become a habit.

Where were we? Harmony's room? Right! It was all about my hearing. For a long time I wondered why I heard things that humans seem to miss. Then it hit me: My hearing is better than theirs! And one thing I sometimes hear while lying in the kitchen next to my kibble bowl, waiting for someone to fill it, is Harmony moving around on the floor above. No two humans make the exact same walking sounds. Harmony's walk is quick, quiet, and firm. Bro's is a bit slower, way more noisy, and just as firm. Bertha's is heavy and has a little hitch to it. Elrod's is sort of like a tipsy elephant. Mom's—well, you get the idea. The point is that awakening on the kitchen floor and finding no one around, I cocked my head for sounds, and heard Harmony's footsteps from above. Here's a secret shared by Harmony and me: She keeps a box of treats in her desk drawer, small bone-shaped biscuits in a small box. Small biscuits, yes, but very tasty.

The next thing I knew I was flying up the back stairs—and if not quite flying, then at least advancing steadily—and making my way down the hall that led to the bedrooms. I realized, possibly on the late side, that I might have heard a bit of conversation while passing the breakfast room, but it's hard to be on top of everything when your mind's on biscuits.

I strolled into Harmony's room, a neat and tidy room with two big windows and Harmony's autumn leaf collection framed on the wall. She was gazing out the window, her back to me, but she turned when I came in.

"Oh, good," she said. "Maybe you can help."

Sure thing! I was totally ready. Were we going to do treat first and help second? Or the other way around? My very favorite way was treat, help, and then another treat. I moved over to the desk, my head very close to the biscuit drawer—what a lovely smell!—just to give Harmony a hint.

"Come on, Arthur."

She left the room. Help first, treat second. Well, all

right. I followed her down the hall to Bro's room at the very end. The door was closed. Harmony knocked. That's a rule here at the inn: You come to a closed door and you knock. "We don't barge," Mom says. And Bro always used to say, "How come?" And Mom would say, "Because of the golden rule." And Bro would say, "Huh?" But now he doesn't anymore. He just knocks.

A voice came from inside the room. "Yeah?" Hey! Not Bro. It was Jimmy. I'd forgotten that Jimmy was here. Now it all came back to me. Bad things were going on, their exact nature a bit of a mystery.

"It's me," Harmony said.

"Come in."

Harmony opened the door and we went in. Bro's room has two windows, just like Harmony's, and is the same size and shape. Other than that, nothing is the same, especially when it comes to the neat and tidy part. For example, Bro's hockey stuff was still not put away even though hockey was done for the year and Mom had told him a thousand times, which sounds like a lot. His hockey stuff and his baseball stuff had sort of merged together in the middle of the floor. I shouldn't leave out his set of drums, which he'd wanted very badly and gotten for his last birthday, and maybe would play for the first time any day.

But not now. Bro wasn't even in his room. Instead there

was Jimmy, lying on Bro's bed, his gaze on the ceiling. He had a tear streak on each cheek, but he wasn't crying. Humans have something like weather going on inside them. I have a nose for it. The weather inside Jimmy was bad right now.

"Hungry?" Harmony said.

"No."

"Thirsty?"

"No."

"Arthur wanted to see you."

I did? News to me. But now that Harmony mentioned it, why, yes. I wanted to see Jimmy.

He sat up. "Yeah?"

That was when Harmony touched the back of my head, sort of a tiny push. We've got all kinds of signals, me and Harmony. This one meant *Hop up!*

I hopped up on the bed and then gave Jimmy's face a quick lick. Entirely my own idea. I wanted to get rid of those tear tracks, but my tongue turned out not to be quite accurate enough for that. Jimmy opened his arms, very slowly put them around me, and hugged. His heart was pounding away. I remembered one time—this was in hunting season—when a wounded deer came into our yard. We'd tried to rescue it, me and Bro, but it hadn't let us get close enough, although I'd been close enough to hear its heartbeat, a lot like Jimmy's at the moment.

144

"Do you have a dog, Jimmy?" Harmony said.

"No."

"A cat?"

"No."

"A farm without a dog or a cat?"

Their eyes met. A farm without a cat made sense to me. That was as far as I could get on my own.

"He," Jimmy began. He swallowed and tried again. "He said it was just more mouths to . . . to . . ." All at once a terrible sob rose up in Jimmy—I felt it on the way—and he started crying. I just stayed right there in his arms and let his tears wet my fur.

Harmony approached the bed, not quickly but with no hesitation. She didn't say anything, just put her hand on Jimmy's shoulder and kept it there while he sobbed and shook. I began to get scared, like I wanted to be out of there and fast. Then I happened to look into Harmony's eyes, those big brown eyes full of golden glints, a bit like Mom's eyes but even more so, if that makes sense. I calmed down, not down to total calm, but enough to stay where I was.

Well, not quite. I actually slipped off the bed and sat beside it. Harmony took over with the hugging. Jimmy cried in her arms. Harmony cried, too, but without making a sound. After some time, Jimmy settled down. They separated, Jimmy sitting on the edge of the bed, Harmony setting Bro's desk chair upright—it was lying on its side for some reason—and taking a seat.

Jimmy took a deep, quivering breath. "Sorry, Harmony."

"You've got nothing to be sorry for," she said.

"I just meant . . . dragging you into it."

"It's not about me," Harmony said.

Then they just sat there, Jimmy breathing slowly, his chest rising and falling, and Harmony with her hands in her lap. After a while, Jimmy blinked a long long blink. When his eyes opened he said, "The last time we were together was bad. If he . . . if he doesn't . . . Is that what I'll always remember?"

"Tell me a good memory," said Harmony.

"A good memory of me and my . . . my dad?"

"Yeah."

Jimmy thought for a bit. What was going on? Something about good memories? I myself had so many! For example, once I was down by the road out front of our place, marking my fire hydrant. Mine, although others seem to think they can mark it, too: dogs, foxes, coyotes—and a surprising number of humans, all male. But forget that part. There I was, marking my hydrant, when one of those big brown delivery trucks came up the street. As it went by, not even slowing down, the driver's window opened and out flew half a sandwich! I'm not making this up, wouldn't even know how. Salami and corned beef, an amazing combo. And that's just the very first happy memory that came to mind. I was waiting for the next one when Jimmy spoke.

"Once he taught me how to shuck oysters."

"What does that mean?" Harmony said.

"Open them up with a knife."

"Do you often eat oysters?"

"Just that one time—two Christmases ago. A guy who works at a restaurant that's a customer of ours dropped off a couple dozen. My dad could shuck them like nothing— zip zip zip."

"Yeah?"

"The trick is finding just the right spot to stick in the knife. It's like a hinge. You don't even need a lot of force. It turned out that he'd worked at an oyster bar up in Maine one summer in high school. I never knew." A tiny smile crossed Jimmy's face, there and gone. "Zip zip zip. 'Open sesame,' he'd say every time. It was funny." Jimmy looked down. "Hard to explain."

"No," said Harmony. "I get it. What do they taste like?"

"I can't put it into words," Jimmy said. "They sort of have the feel of soft-boiled eggs, but they're cold and taste like . . . like the sea."

"I want to try one," Harmony said.

Mom appeared in the open doorway.

"Try what?" she said.

"An oyster."

"Yeah?" said Mom, looking a little surprised. Her gaze went to Jimmy, to Harmony, back to Jimmy. "Want anything to eat or drink, Jimmy?"

He shook his head. "I should be going."

"Going?" said Mom.

"Back," Jimmy told her.

"I think it's best you stay here with us."

"But my chores," Jimmy said. "The animals need to be fed and watered, and what about the hens? The Leghorns lay eggs just about every day and—"

Mom held up her hand. "Don't worry about that for now. Someone from the Munsons' farm is going to take care of things for the time being."

"The Munsons' farm?" Jimmy said. "But Dad hates the . . ." He went silent.

Mom's voice got gentle. "Mrs. Munson called and volunteered."

Jimmy looked worried. "How much does she want?"

"Nothing," Mom said. "Meanwhile we're trying to contact your mother."

"What for?"

"Don't you think she'd want to know?"

"Her . . . her life's a mess already."

"That doesn't—" Mom stopped herself. After a bit of silence, she said, "What about your dad's brother—Carl, I think?"

Jimmy shook his head. "They're . . . I can't think of the word. Like strangers."

"Estranged?" Harmony said.

"Yeah. Plus he works on an oil rig in Dubai or some place."

"One thing's for sure," Mom said. "You're not estranged from us. And we eat supper every night. Tonight's spaghetti and meatballs."

"I'm not hungry."

"Then please just come and sit with us," Mom said.

A long pause. "Okay," Jimmy said at last.

"Also," Mom said, "Deputy Carstairs wants to talk to you."

"What about?"

"His investigation—he says he wants your help. But you don't have to talk to him, and if you do I'll be there."

"He wants my help?"

"That's what he said."

"You'll be there?"

"The whole time."

"All right," said Jimmy.

And soon after that, we were out the door, me in the

lead. Some conversations are very complicated. You just have to be patient and wait till something understandable goes by. Meatballs are understandable.

Meatballs and only meatballs were on my mind as we went down the back stairs. Sometimes you just have to hand it to humans, even if, like me, you don't actually have hands. Paws are better in many ways, if you don't mind me saying so, and maybe I'll get to that subject some other time. But just think! Who else but humans could dream of taking two of my favorite things, namely meat and balls, and making them one! Meatballs and nothing but meatballs were on my mind as we passed the side door. And then: the unexpected.

"When was the last time Arthur did his business?" Mom said.

"I don't know," said Harmony.

"Then we'd better let him out." Mom opened the side door. "Arthur—out."

Me? Out? I did not want to go out. I wanted meatballs. As for the last time I'd done my business, I had no idea, but I didn't need to do it now. Although on second thought, I sort of did. Oh, no. Second thoughts were a big problem. I hardly ever have them, but when I do they always lead to no good. *Go away, second thoughts*, I thought. Yikes! Was that a third thought? At that moment I realized that I seemed to be outside, the side door shut behind me.

For a while I stood right outside the door, my nose almost touching it, waiting for someone to open up. No one opened up. I waited some more. I sat down and waited. I lay down and waited. I got up and waited. My mind emptied right out. I felt nice and peaceful. And in my nice and peaceful state, I realized something: I needed to do my business.

On this side of the house was the shuffleboard court, where no guests ever played, and beyond it a big patch of forest. Dad had built a tree house in there, where Harmony and Bro played when they were little. I'd never been in the tree house myself, although I'd wanted to, very badly, especially when I happened to see a certain party up there one day. She wasn't with the kids, but by herself. That was when I first realized that Queenie did some roaming outdoors. How did she get out of the house? I never found that out, although I tried. My idea was to follow her around the house until she went outside, and then I'd know. A brilliant idea, one of my best ever. But Queenie didn't like being followed around—a possibility I hadn't considered—and she'd lost her temper, a very unpleasant development. The point of all this is that these woods are very good for doing your business. Well, maybe not you, but certainly me.

So there I was, doing my business in a pleasant little grove of trees, rain no longer falling and the sky almost fully dark, when I heard the nearby hum of a car engine. Car engines make a special kind of hum when the car isn't moving, a sort of frrm frrm frrm, frrm frrm frrm, sometimes with a little hiccup in between the frrms, meaning the car will soon be in the shop. That was what I heard now, the hiccupy kind of engine. I followed the sound through the woods to a narrow dirt road that ran in one direction down to a pond where we like to swim on hot summer days, the kids and me.

And there, parked by the side of the road, stood a van. Was this narrow dirt road part of our territory? Why wouldn't it be? One thing I knew for sure: I did not like strangers on our territory. I went closer, close enough to see that this van was the tall kind, muddy white, with a roof rack on top. Was there something familiar about it? I sniffed the air and smelled coffee, booze, and a tiny hint of cow scent. Cow scent? Was that important? I searched my mind and found only one thought: *This muddy white van is on our territory.*

Who was in charge of protecting the territory at the Blackberry Hill Inn? Me, Arthur. And when you're in charge, you take charge! I stepped right up to the van and started barking my head off, my loudest, harshest, most savage bark. It even scared me a little bit, and when I'm scared I bark even harder. The front doors of the van flew open and out jumped two shaven-head bushy-bearded dudes, one huge and one not. They smelled like wet mops and seemed familiar. And then it all came back to me, that tire-changing episode and lots of back-and-forth about a cow. I even remembered the small one's name—Roscoe— and came very very close to remembering the name of the cow as well. My mind was humming! But what else would you expect from the head of security?

I barked and barked, gave them a barking they wouldn't forget anytime soon. The huge one held a baseball bat. Was I afraid? Not in the least. I did that thing where I go forward and backward at the same time, and scared the pants off them, although somehow their pants stayed on, at least for now.

"Put that away, Curly," Roscoe said. "It's just that pooch from before."

"Why do I have to take orders from you?" said the huge one, who had to be Curly, if I was following this right, even though he didn't have a hair on his head. That made me even madder, hard to say why.

Roscoe turned to Curly. "How's your judgment been recently?"

Curly's face got uglier, and it was plenty ugly to begin

with. "We go down, we go down together." He flipped the bat into the woods and started to get back in the van.

"What are you doing?" said Roscoe.

"We're supposed to get rid of it, remember?"

"Not here, you moron."

Curly stepped down off the running board. "Who you calling a moron?"

Roscoe didn't answer. He took a flashlight from his pocket, switched it on, and walked off in the direction the bat had flown. I followed, barking at his heels. Then, just as the bat appeared in the cone of light, I heard a voice inside me: *Arthur! Grab that bat!* I raced forward just as Roscoe was bending to pick it up, and we ended up grabbing it at the same time. Roscoe tried to pull it away. Oh, yeah? I jerked my head back and forth, growling and growling, digging my teeth into the wood of the bat. It started to slip from Roscoe's hands. I tugged even harder and—and all at once, I was off the ground and in the air. I twisted around and saw that Curly had me by the collar. I jabbed my head forward and bit him on the wrist, not much of a bite because of the bat in my mouth, although it wasn't in my mouth for long. But that meant this next bite would be the real thing. I opened wide and—

And Curly threw me into the trees. For what seemed like a long time, I flew through the air. That was the painless part. Then I landed. I wouldn't call that part painful, exactly, more like I just couldn't breathe. I lay on wet leaves, trying and trying to breathe, and finally I drew a breath, a breath of lovely night air, cold and damp.

I rose. Curly, Roscoe, the muddy white van, and the baseball bat: all gone. Meaning off my territory? Hey! Was I the winner? I started feeling pretty good about myself.

FIFTEEN

QUEENIE

ALONE IN THE BREAKFAST ROOM with Deputy Sheriff Carstairs. How do I end up in situations like this? I have no problem with being really alone, all by myself. That's probably best, but I'm always happy to be in the company of a very few—namely Mom, Harmony, and Bro—and sometimes happy to be in the company of a few others—like Bertha, say; as for Deputy Sheriff Carstairs: nope.

Yet here we were, me on the window seat, Carstairs at one end of the table in the chair where Harmony always sat. What made him think that was okay? I gave him a look that asked that very question in no uncertain terms, a hot, golden look that could not be ignored. He did not appear to even see it. Some humans don't notice me. In fact, many creatures don't notice me. Birds, for example. Or mice. Until it's too late. There are upsides and downsides to so many things in life. Perhaps Carstairs was the unnoticing type when it came to me and my kind. I filed that thought away. I had no intention of hunting the deputy sheriff. Not now.

He took out his notebook, leafed through, stopped at a page. His eyes went back and forth, back and forth. Then he spoke. Some humans talk to themselves. I've picked up a lot of information because of that, much of it boring. Mostly they talk about their worries. Sometimes they talk about what to do next. That seemed to be where Carstairs was headed.

"What I need is a theory of the case," he said. "That's almost always about why. But. But. But." He sighed. "You can't let the theory run too far in front of the facts, especially when so many of them are missing." He gazed at the ceiling. "That was Hunzinger's downfall." Carstairs looked down, and all of a sudden he was noticing me, actually meeting my gaze. "The town wants this case solved. I solve it and I win the next election. Sheriff Al Carstairs. Why not me?" He wrinkled up his nose, trying to charm me, perhaps? Like that was going to work? His daughter, Emma, does that same wrinkle-nose thing, but on her it looks cute. Unlike him, she has pigtails, so she's off to a head start when it comes to cuteness. Was she leaving town with her mom? Something about a divorce? So many humans have untidy lives. I just can't relate.

Meanwhile the deputy's nose had unwrinkled at last. "Why not me?" he said again.

Grow some pigtails and get back to me. That was my answer, an answer I was still enjoying when the door opened and in came Mom and Jimmy.

"Jimmy's agreed to talk to you," Mom said. "In my presence."

Carstairs rose, his head almost hitting the little crystal chandelier Mom got at a lawn sale. "Wouldn't have it any other way," he said. "First off, Jimmy, I'm very sorry about your dad and am hoping real hard that he'll pull through."

Jimmy just stood there. Sometimes humans don't know what to say. This was one of those times.

"That'll be up to fate, and all the good people at Regional Hospital," Carstairs went on. "All I can do is find whoever did this and get him locked up for a very long time. You might not care about that now, but one day you will."

"I care—" Jimmy's voice broke. He tried again. "I care right now," he said.

Mom touched Jimmy's arm. At the same time she gave Carstairs a look that . . . that reminded me of me.

"Um," he said. "Appreciate it, Yvette. That is, you allowing me to—"

"Let's get started," Mom said.

They sat at the table.

Carstairs rubbed his hands together, the way humans sometimes do when they're about to begin. "Is there a baseball bat at your place, Jimmy?" he said.

"A baseball bat? Yeah, my dad's old one from high school."

"Wood or metal?"

"Wood."

"Where is it kept?"

"In the barn."

"What's it used for?"

"Nothing. There's stuff like that in the barn. Old stuff."

"Picked it up lately?"

"The bat? What for? Like to practice my swing?"

"Or for any reason whatsoever."

Jimmy shook his head.

Carstairs gazed at him. Jimmy looked down. A lock of his hair fell over his messed-up eye. The sight had a strange effect on me. "How about we leave the subject of the bat?" Carstairs said.

"Okay."

"You'd like that, Jimmy?"

Jimmy shrugged.

"Let's move on to enemies."

"Enemies?"

"Do you have any enemies?"

"Me? No."

"What about your dad? Any folks he didn't get along with? Maybe who didn't like him very much?"

Jimmy looked at Mom. "He fights with just about everybody, doesn't he, Mrs. Reddy?"

Mom smiled a very small smile. Her voice was gentle. "I don't know about that."

"What do you mean by 'fights'?" said Carstairs.

"You know," Jimmy said, turning to him. "Gets into arguments."

"Physical arguments?"

"No."

"Was there anybody he got into particularly nasty fights with?"

Jimmy nodded. "The environment lady from the town."

"Mrs. Gibbons?"

"She came out and stopped us when we were filling in the little pond at the back. She said we need a permit. They were screaming at each other."

"Whew," Carstairs said. "That sounds bad. But a lot of force must have gone into the attack on your dad, meaning the attacker was strong. Mrs. Gibbons is seventy years old and weighs maybe ninety pounds."

Jimmy spread his hands, a human gesture that meant he

had nothing to offer. So perhaps we could now bring this little confab to a close and send Carstairs on his way? I wanted things to get back to normal. That's all I ever want really. What's so hard to understand?

Carstairs stayed where he was. I can't say I was disappointed because I'd never held out much hope for him in the first place, although I'd always preferred him to the old sheriff, Hunzinger. Hunzinger had a strange smell, a repellent combo of garlic and chewing tobacco. Carstairs's smell wasn't particularly offensive, if a little heavy on the aftershave. He leaned forward.

"Where's the baseball bat now, Jimmy?" he said.

"The bat?"

"Yes, we're back to the bat. Where is it?"

"It's not in the barn?"

"Nope. Not in the barn, your house, any of the sheds. We've searched. It's gone."

"I don't understand," Jimmy said.

Carstairs sighed. "Oh, Jimmy. I feel for you. I really do. That was a lousy thing for a father to do—favoring an outsider, a hired hand, over his own son."

Jimmy went pale.

"But," Carstairs went on, "you're a big, strong kid. You shouldn't have swung that bat at Walter. You could have really hurt him."

Jimmy stood up, a wobbly sort of rising. For a moment I thought he would fall. Across the table, Mom rose, too.

"I . . . didn't do that," Jimmy said. "I'd never do that."

"I know, son," Carstairs said. "You'd never do that if you were in your right mind. But you weren't in your right mind. It was all so unfair—and that's the honest truth. Then it got even more unfair, when your father blamed you for the loss of the cow. He didn't even care what happened to your eye, did he, Jimmy? And all of a sudden you couldn't take it anymore and you just snapped."

"What . . . what are you saying?" Jimmy said.

I hadn't been picking up anything interesting from Jimmy in the smell department—just normal boy stuff like chewing gum and stinky sneakers. But now I caught a hint of something sharp and sour. That was human fear.

Mom spoke, her voice icy cold. "Yes, Al, what are you saying?"

Carstairs didn't look at Mom, just made an impatient backhand gesture in her direction, meaning *not now*, or *be quiet*, or something like that. Mom's face turned white. Mom's not the angry type. I'd hardly ever seen her angry at all. Now she was furious, even starting to shake from how strong it was inside her. I was up on my feet right away.

Carstairs, his eyes on Jimmy, their expression kind of gentle, said, "Did you hit him with the bat, Jimmy?

Lash out against all the bad treatment? Lash out against your dad?"

"That's outrageous!" Mom said. "I had no idea you were—"

But whatever Mom was about to say stayed unsaid. Jimmy backed away, almost a lurch, a lurch that knocked over his chair. It tumbled across the floor, crash crash crash, and Jimmy raced out of the room. Carstairs—surprisingly fast for such a tall guy—sprang up and ran after him.

"Stop, Jimmy!" Carstairs yelled. "You're making it worse."

Jimmy didn't stop. He charged across the front hall, threw open the front door, and sprinted outside, where night was already falling. Carstairs hurried after him, through the hall and into the open doorway. But not quite outside. Just as his lead foot hit the threshold, his trailing foot struck something. Not hard, which was a good thing, since that something happened to be me. Very strange—I had no memory of even leaving the breakfast room, yet here I was, beyond doubt. As for Deputy Carstairs, he cried out—perhaps uttering the kind of words I wouldn't repeat—and fell facedown on the lawn. I heard Jimmy's running footsteps, the sound diminishing fast.

Swift and silent—in my own special, me-ish way—I joined the shadows.

SIXTEEN

ARTHUR

MORE SLEEP? MORE DREAMS? I seemed to be so sleepy and dreamy these days. And nights. Funny how you can be sleeping and dreaming and know you were sleeping and dreaming and even where—in this case, in the kitchen beside my water bowl—and then all at once you forget the whole thing and get totally lost in the dream.

And what a dream! So busy, so noisy, so scary. First came running footsteps, not far away. Then there was some shouting. I recognized that voice. The shouter was Deputy Sheriff Carstairs. Why did he have to be in my dream? Why couldn't I be dreaming about our family visit to the Green Mountain County Fair, specifically the barbecue tent near the entrance? That's the most exciting place I've ever been in my life, and every night I try to dream about it, and every night it doesn't happen. It only happens when I don't try! How do you like that? When I finally realized the barbecue dream would only happen if I didn't try, I tried not to try. That got very confusing so I just gave up and whatever—

What was this? A loud crash? A scream? A thud? Deputy Carstairs making more noise, this time like he was in pain? Then more running footsteps, footsteps I recognized, namely Mom's? Mom's footsteps. Phew. She was often in my dreams. I saw her lovely face. It faded and then there was only sound. Sometimes I have sound dreams, no picture. They're just as real for me, maybe more.

"Al? Al? Are you all right? Don't tell me you and Jimmy got into a fight."

"For god's sake, no." Carstairs grunted, the kind of grunt humans make when they're getting up from lying down. "It was that nasty cat of yours."

"Excuse me?"

"Sorry, Yvette. I didn't mean *nasty*. It was an accident. I tripped over her and—"

"Where is she? Is she all right?"

"I'm sure she's all right. It's me that—"

"Queeeeniieee! Queeeeniieee!" Mom cried. "Al? What are you doing?"

"Calling in. We're going to raise a search party, find that boy."

"Al!"

"What?"

"You don't seriously think he attacked his father."

"Awful things go on, Yvette, things we see in law enforcement. There's no question of incarceration or anything like that."

"He's eleven years old!"

"That's why. But I've got to bring him in."

A car door opened and closed. The car drove away. A siren started up, fading and fading. I began to see things, dreamy things like Harmony and Bro floating down the back stairs, circling over Mom, grabbing her hands, hoisting her off the lawn. They drifted into the night. I rose off the floor and drifted after them. But where were they? Anxiety grew inside me, and just as I was starting to get scared, a big tent appeared in the night. I came down from the sky and entered the tent. The smells were out of this world! I was in the barbecue tent! All my anxieties vanished. I couldn't even remember having them. Mr. Doone set a plate of ribs at my feet. Mr. Doone? That was a little strange. But those ribs! Out of this world! And so was I!

I opened my eyes. Daylight streamed in through the kitchen windows. Morning already! Up and at 'em, Arthur old boy. The early bird gets the worm, as humans say. But who else but a bird would want one? Certainly not me. Once I actually saw a bird tugging a worm out of the ground. The worm seemed to be resisting, but the bird was stronger and pulled it free. And at that very moment, just when the bird was about to gobble up the worm—something I'd never seen and was sort of looking forward to—there was a snow-white blur and Queenie . . . but no need to go on. Enough to say that I still haven't seen a bird downing a worm.

But . . . but Queenie? Some memory about her stirred in my mind. Had I dreamed about her? I searched my mind and came up with nothing. No worries. What was the point of worrying about nothing?

I got up and had a good stretch, butt way up and head way down. Ah! I felt not bad at all; in fact, pretty darn good. Is there anything that sets you up for the day like a good sleep? Well, yes. A proper breakfast. I glanced around—and there was Bertha placing bacon strips in a pan. This day was off to a great start.

Bertha glanced over at me. "What are you so cheerful about?"

Wow! An easy question. That hardly ever happens, at least to me. I was cheerful because of a great night's sleep and bacon in my immediate future. But we had one little problem. When I'm cheerful I like everyone around me to be cheerful, too. Bertha was not cheerful. She had a dark, worried look in her eyes, and heavy things were going on inside her. I could feel them.

Meanwhile lovely sizzling sounds were coming from the pan. The air itself seemed to sizzle with bacon smells. Right away I was hungrier than I'd ever been. Perhaps I crowded in quite close to Bertha. She looked down and said, "Is bacon all you care about? How can you even be thinking about bacon at a time like this?"

How could I be thinking about bacon when it was sizzling practically under my nose? Was that the question? This one seemed too easy even to be asked. Uh-oh. All at once, maybe for the first time in my life, I suspected a trap. What were you supposed to do if you suspected a trap? I had no idea and was waiting for one to come when Mom walked in.

Oh, poor Mom! So tired and anxious! Normally when she comes down in the morning, she's dressed in fresh clothes and looks very fresh herself. But here she was wearing muddy rain gear and muddy boots. There was even a muddy smear on one side of her face. Plus she had dark patches under her eyes, like she hadn't slept a wink.

Bertha turned to her. "Any luck?"

Mom shook her head. "Al Carstairs still has a couple of teams out there, but nothing so far. The kids and I tried all sorts of places where we thought he might go—the ball field, the woods behind the school, that abandoned warehouse by the tracks. No sign of him."

"The kids were with you all night?"

"I sent them home at three thirty. It took some doing."
Bertha handed Mom a mug of coffee. "How are they?"

"I've never seen them so angry."

"Harmony, too?"

"Oh, yes. Not that they're saying much, but they're boiling inside." Mom glanced around. "Any sign of Queenie?"

"I assumed she was in one of her spots."

Mom left the room. Bertha and I followed. We checked the grandfather clock, the top bookshelf in the Big Room, the ottoman by the fireplace, the window seat in the breakfast room. No Queenie.

"She's been gone all night," Mom said.

"But she's pretty resourceful," said Bertha.

"So are foxes and coyotes," Mom said. Then she put her hand on Bertha's shoulder. "Sorry, Bertha. Didn't mean to be snarky."

Bertha didn't say anything, just put one big, strong arm around Mom and gave her a hug. As for what was going on or why Mom had been up all night, you tell me. There was really only one clear fact: Queenie was gone. Queenie was gone? Queenie was gone!

"Why is Arthur rolling around like that?" Mom said.

I went still, found that I was lying on my back, paws raised in the air. When had that happened?

"I'm frying up some bacon," Bertha said.

"Ah," said Mom, gazing down at me.

I popped right up, and we went back into the kitchen. Mom set two places at the counter. Bertha flipped the bacon strips—sizzle, sizzle—and said, "What's with Carstairs? I always thought he was reasonable."

"He thinks he's being reasonable."

"It's reasonable to think an eleven-year-old boy took a baseball bat to his father?" Bertha said.

"I don't know," Mom said. "Emotional abuse might have made Jimmy—"

Bertha interrupted. "Whoa! So you think he's guilty?"

"In my heart? No. But my head's not completely sure. The situation with Walter—just think of the humiliation. A person can only stand so much."

"Maybe," Bertha said. "But Mr. Doone rubbed a lot of people the wrong way. Aren't there any other suspects?"

Before Mom could answer, Ms. Pryor walked in. "Oh, sorry," she said. "Didn't mean to interrupt."

Mom turned to her. "You're not interrupting. What can we do for you?"

And Bertha added, "Breakfast will be up in a jiff."

"Thanks," Ms. Pryor said. "But I'm checking out. The usual story—vacation cut short by unexpected work."

"I'll get your bill," Mom said.

They went into the front hall. I followed. Not that I'd forgotten my bacon, nothing crazy like that. I just felt like being close to Mom.

They stood by the desk, Mom printing out a sheet of paper, Ms. Pryor handing over a credit card, all the usual checkout things I'd seen many times but actually didn't understand at all.

"I've enjoyed my stay," Ms. Pryor said, "despite all these . . . events. Is it true that very nice boy attacked his father? I saw it on the news before I came downstairs."

"Is that what they're saying?" Mom said.

"Maybe not in so many words," said Ms. Pryor. "So strange that I met both of them. The father seemed like the violent one, if you ask me."

Mom's eyes got an inward look. That meant she was having a thought. Mom had lots of thoughts, more than enough for just one mind, which made me feel pretty good about perhaps not having many myself. Not so easy to explain why.

"I wonder if that's relevant to the case," Mom said.

"What do you mean?" said Ms. Pryor.

"That scene out at the falls. Could it have anything to do with the attack on Mr. Doone?"

Ms. Pryor looked surprised. In fact, very surprised. "How would that be?"

"I don't know," said Mom. "I wonder if Deputy Carstairs has considered it." She glanced at the paperwork. "Is this the best address to reach you? In Menlo Park?"

"Yes," said Ms. Pryor.

"Could I have a phone number as well?"

"May I ask why?"

"It's just a hunch," Mom said, "but maybe there have been other incidents at the falls between Mr. Doone and people he thought were trespassing. And maybe one of those didn't end with a handshake the way yours did. Maybe he got into a feud with someone and . . . and I don't really know, but just in case Deputy Carstairs has any interest in this—"

"Or you can get him interested," Ms. Pryor interrupted, a friendly smile on her face.

"There's that," said Mom.

Ms. Pryor gave her an admiring look. "You're trying to help the boy."

Mom nodded.

"Here's my number." Ms. Pryor leaned over the desk and wrote on Mom's sheet of paper. Then she hoisted on her backpack. "Best of luck," she said.

"Same to you," said Mom.

Ms. Pryor walked out of the inn and closed the door softly behind her. I looked up at Mom. She looked down at me. "Menlo Park," she said.

Menlo Park? Was that supposed to mean something? I searched my mind and was still searching it when Harmony and Bro came in through the door to the family quarters. They both looked sleepy, their hair messed up and faces kind of rumply, but they were all dressed for the outdoors, or close to it: Bro still had on pajama pants, blue with a hockey stick pattern.

"Any news?" Harmony said.

Mom shook her head.

Bro opened the front door.

"Where do you think you're going?"

"To look for Jimmy, of course," Harmony said.

"Not without breakfast," said Mom.

"C'mon, Mom!" said Bro.

Mom didn't say anything, just pointed to the kitchen. The kitchen! Where my bacon was probably getting cold. Not that I cared. Bacon, hot, cold, or in between! I was first through the kitchen door, and by plenty. You may hear that Arthur's not particularly swift. That may be true about my normal top speed, but my bacon top speed? Clear the decks!

SEVENTEEN

ARTHUR

WHAT'S MENLO PARK?" MOM SAID.

"A town," Bro said.

"Where a bunch of the big tech companies come from," said Harmony. "Why?"

"That's where Ms. Pryor lives," Mom said. "She's gone home."

"She's smart, huh?" Bro said.

"What makes you say that?" said Mom.

Bro shrugged.

"There must be something," Mom said.

"You know," said Bro. "In general."

"She's got this real fast brain ticking away inside her," Harmony said. "You can practically hear it."

"Yeah," said Bro. "That's it."

Mom gazed at the two of them and quietly said, "What have I done?"

That made Bertha laugh, but I didn't get it at all. Also I'd never heard of Menlo Park and didn't care. All I cared about was bacon, specifically just one more measly scrap.

"You've had more than enough, buster," Bertha said. She was sitting at one end of the kitchen counter, Mom at the other end, the kids in between. I myself was at Bertha's feet, close as close could be. There was no one else around, so who was this Buster character? Was Bertha getting me confused with someone else? Did that explain why she wasn't tearing off a little morsel from that last strip of bacon on her plate and dropping it down to li'l ol' me?

"Is he barking for food?" Mom said.

"I'm afraid so," said Bertha.

"None of that, Arthur," Mom said. "Or you'll be standing in the corner."

Oh, no! Standing in the corner? That was my punishment. I hated my punishment, even hated just the word *punishment*, of all the human words that went constantly flowing by, the very worst. I didn't want to be punished. But I wanted that bacon!

"Okay," Mom said, pointing to the corner. "That's it. Go."

"Check out his tail," Bro said, his mouth full of cereal. "You're upsetting him."

Something about my tail? I can usually see it just by turning my head the slightest bit. Which I did, but it wasn't in sight. That meant it was drooping. I knew tails belonged up nice and high, but—but my bacon! Your tail would be drooping, too.

"He's never going to change," Harmony said.

Mom sighed. "Bertha?"

"You're too softhearted," Bertha said. And down came a bacon scrap, perfect in every way.

"Someone's gotta be," said Mom.

Then came a slight pause when everyone was looking at Mom, almost like she was some new person who'd just walked in. I looked at her, too, but in my usual way. She was the same old Mom to me.

Outside it was gray and drizzly. We went for a long walk, me, Bro, and Harmony, making a big circle into town, past Willard's General Store all the way to the village green, then down to the rail trail, woods on both sides, and a cold drizzle falling the whole time. Actually quite refreshing, if you've got a coat like mine.

"Arthur?" Harmony said. "Remember what you're doing?"

What a question! Of course I remembered. I was doing my job, which meant marking every fire hydrant we passed as well as the occasional parked car, plus chasing any squirrel we ran across up a tree. So far I was batting a thousand, whatever that happened to mean.

"I don't think he does," said Bro.

Harmony turned to me. "Sit."

I sat.

"What are we doing?" she said.

Going for a walk? That was my answer, not a bad one and super quick on the draw! I was so pleased with myself I gave Harmony's hand a nice lick. Almost always a bit of a disappointment on my end, by the way, Harmony's hand usually tasting of soap. I've had much better luck with Bro's hand.

"He forgot," Bro said.

"Arthur!" said Harmony. "Listen up! We're looking for Jimmy and Queenie. Use your nose! Got that?"

Whoa! We weren't just out for a stroll? That changed everything. I raced into the woods, sniff-sniff-sniffing with all I had in me, searching for a whiff of Jimmy. And was there someone else I was supposed to be sniffing for? Not that I remembered. I hadn't been with Jimmy often, but his smell was in this part of my mind—a very big part—where I keep all the smells. Yours, too, if we ever meet. As for Jimmy's, it was somewhat like Bro's with a slight add-on that reminded me of maple syrup. I have no interest in maple syrup itself, my one encounter with a pancake smothered in the goopy stuff ending with a very sticky-roof-of-the-mouth situation.

Meanwhile I was picking up no trace of Jimmy's smell. A fox had been this way not long ago, and a little before that, some of those wild turkeys have gone by. I was no fan of foxes or wild turkeys. The scent of the fox seemed to be following the scent of the turkeys. Here's something pretty unusual about me: My nose can predict the future! That's why I've been following my nose around since day one.

The fox and turkey scents were unlosable. I took off at a fast pace. Harmony and Bro hurried along behind me, somehow keeping up without actually running.

"You smell one of them, Arthur?" Harmony said. "Is it Jimmy? Queenie?"

Jimmy? Oh, right. Jimmy was perhaps the point of all this. No, I picked up no trace of his scent. As for Queenie, what did she have to do with anything? Although, oddly enough, there were traces of her here and there, laid down before the turkeys had passed by. Queenie, then turkeys, finally fox. Kind of like a parade! Had I come very close to cracking a joke? Wow! If I kept going like this, there was no telling how I'd end up.

"Look at his tail," Bro said. "He's onto something."

"At least in his own mind," said Harmony.

The scent of my little parade led us out of the woods, onto the rail trail, then back into the woods on the other side.

"That reminds me of Mom," Bro said.

"What does?"

"When you said 'at least in his own mind.' Mom says stuff like that."

"Does anything I say remind you of Dad?" Harmony said.

"That right there," said Bro.

"You think you're funny." Harmony punched Bro on the arm, not hard.

Bro fell down, rolled around like he was in agony.

"But you're not," said Harmony. "Not funny at all."

Bro popped up. We kept going, came to a worn, old fence, lots of rails missing or broken. Hey! I knew this fence. On the other side was the whole wild part of our property that led back to the shuffleboard court, still a long way away, but the point was that my little scent parade passed right through a gap in the fence, meaning those turkeys, that fox, and Queenie had dared to set foot on my land. How infuriating! Although perhaps not in Queenie's case, since she lived at the inn. Did that make it her land, too? I didn't want to think about that, so I kept going, rounding a fallen tree and—

And there on the other side lay a pile of turkey feathers. I sniffed at them. Ah, blood. Not visible blood, but the smell was there, as well as the smell of fox and turkey. The future, exactly as my nose had predicted. I turned to Harmony and Bro, my tail wagging in that very powerful manner that gets my whole back end going with it. I,

Arthur, solved the case! If the case was about turkeys and foxes, and why wouldn't it be? Foxes and turkeys are one of those happening combos, as you must see by now.

"What's this?" said Bro.

"Remains of a dead turkey, I think," Harmony said.

"Could Queenie have . . . ?"

Harmony thought. "She does have a thing about birds. But she's so small compared to one of those wild turkeys."

They gazed down at the feathers, both of them looking worried. Worried about Queenie? Queenie had nothing to do with this turkey. There wasn't a trace of her scent around, just fox and turkey, meaning the fox was the perp. I gazed at Harmony and Bro. How come they didn't get that?

"He's staring at us kind of funny," Harmony said.

"What's on his mind?" Bro said.

"If anything."

"That's more Dad talk."

Harmony gave Bro's arm another soft punch. He started to fall down. "Give it a rest," said Harmony, and somehow Bro stayed on his feet.

I sniffed around in a little circle, one of my best techniques. Ah, this was interesting. The turkey scent disappeared completely, like the rest of the turkeys had just vanished into the blue after their buddy's bit of bad luck. But the fox had kept going, headed deeper across my land. And what was this? More Queenie scent, coming in from one side? The fox scent changed direction, overlaying Queenie's scent.

I followed. The two-part scent trail led up a muddy slope and into a small clearing. I'd been here before, more than once. On the other side was a big, spreading tree, and up in that tree were the remains of the tree house Dad built. It was kind of slanted and topsy-turvy with a side wall missing, but the roof looked okay. The tree house had a small door, hanging open. And in that doorway lay Queenie, curled up in her usual way. She gazed down with her golden eyes. Was she happy to see us? Not happy? I had no idea.

"There she is!" Harmony said.

"Hey! Arthur! You rule!" said Bro.

I was just about to start feeling very good about myself when I heard movement from inside the tree house.

EIGHTEEN
QUEENIE

H UMANS ARE TOO RESTLESS, IN MY opinion. They're forever working on projects, most of them useless in the end. There's a lot to be said for simply being still. But once in a while, humans hit on a primo idea. Tree houses, for example. I've been in houses and I've been in trees, but never once thought of combining them. Was something lacking in me? Hard to imagine.

Our tree house here at the Blackberry Hill Inn did not look as primo as it did when Dad first built it. It's the best thing he did while he was part of our lives, probably the only good thing. There's a nice room inside with a couple of chairs and even a sort of blow-up couch, now deflated, and wooden footholds that used to be brightly colored, nailed into the trunk so humans can climb up. Footholds unneeded by me, of course.

Suppose you were lying in front of a tree house door and a group of cats was coming your way. First of all, that could never happen. We don't "group." We don't "hang out." We don't "party." But if a group of cats were coming, you wouldn't hear them. Not so with humans, especially if they're on an outing with dogs, or even just one dog. So it was no surprise to me when Harmony, Bro, and Arthur stepped out of the woods and into the clearing. I'd been expecting them for some time.

"There she is!" said Harmony.

"Hey!" said Bro. "Arthur! You rule!"

Excuse me? What was Bro talking about? There were times when he didn't make sense. That never happened with Harmony. Still, I loved them both. Life has its mysteries. As for the other party, he was wagging his tail in that ridiculous way of his, the whole back half of him on the wobbly move. For some reason, he was very pleased with himself. He adores being pleased with himself and is easily pleased, a very fortunate combo for him.

"Queenie, we were so worried about you," Harmony said. "Come down."

Come down? Why would I want to do that? I was perfectly content. Plus I felt—and how strange for me!—certain responsibilities. I could sense the object of my responsibility close by, getting restless and anxious.

"Maybe she's afraid to come down on her own," Bro said. "I'll go get her."

I gave him a golden-eyed look that said, *Bro! Make sense. I'm begging you*. Well, not begging. Unlike a certain party, I don't beg. He wasn't begging now, maybe because he'd finished overeating for the moment, maybe because he was doing some prancing, still feeling proud of himself for god knows what.

Bro did not get the message. He walked to the tree, stepped on the first foothold. That was when Jimmy came out of the tree house and stood beside me on the warped plywood threshold. Yes, Jimmy, the object of my responsibility. But why? Why did I care? What was Jimmy to me or me to Jimmy? Well, maybe not that last part, Jimmy probably being an admirer of beauty. But basically I had no answer.

"Jimmy!" Bro said. "Are you okay?"

"Yeah," said Jimmy.

"Were you here all night?" Harmony said.

"It wasn't too bad."

"But everyone's looking for you," said Harmony.

"They'll give up eventually," Jimmy said.

"Huh?" said Bro. "What does that mean?"

"It means he's not thinking straight," Harmony said. "Jimmy, come on down."

Jimmy shook his head. "I'm not going to jail."

"Who said anything about jail?" said Bro.

"That's where they put criminals," Jimmy said.

"But you're not a criminal," Bro said.

"Carstairs thinks I am."

"He can't possibly believe it, not deep down," Harmony said.

"But he does, Harmony! He said so."

"That's not the way my mom heard it," said Harmony. "She told us—"

"I'm not talking about at the inn," Jimmy interrupted. "This was later."

"I don't get it," said Bro.

"It was right here," said Jimmy. "Last night. A search party came into the clearing."

"And they didn't find you?" Harmony said. "Why wouldn't they check the tree house?"

"Because of Queenie," said Jimmy.

And then all eyes were on me. I sat motionless, my own eyes gazing at nothing and everything, just one of my many interesting expressions. I don't blame anyone for taking long looks at me. I do the same whenever a mirror's handy. A shame Dad hadn't installed one in the tree house. Was there a way to get him to come back just to handle that one thing and then leave immediately?

". . . they didn't even see the tree house," Jimmy was saying. "I heard them coming and lay down flat, looking through the doorway. They started pointing lights around the clearing, but before any got aimed up here, Queenie kind of flew down to the ground and ran right past them. Carstairs said, 'There's that stupid cat. Maybe she'll lead us to the kid.' Queenie headed into the woods, and they took off after her. A long time later, Queenie came back by herself. I'd fallen asleep by then, but she made these purring sounds and I woke up."

Then they were all looking at me again, perhaps even more closely than before. A nice enough feeling, but of course I showed nothing.

"She hardly ever purrs," Harmony said.

"So what does it mean?" Jimmy said.

"What does any of it mean?" said Bro. "Are you saying she led the search party away from you? Like, on purpose?"

"Sure looked that way," Jimmy said.

"But she's a cat," Bro said.

"So?" said Harmony.

Jimmy reached over and stroked my back. He wasn't great at it, nowhere near Harmony's class, but I didn't put a stop to the stroking, refrained from taking any action, such as clawing him, for example. Oh, dear. How could I even have such a thought? For a moment I came close to . . . how would you put it? Having a doubt about myself?

But in the nick of time, I realized that having such very slightly dark thoughts was simply one more good thing about me. Queenie the mysterious, even to herself at times!

"But what I'm trying to tell you," Jimmy said, "was this conversation when they came into the clearing. One of the other guys said, 'What happens to the kid?' And Carstairs said, 'He'll be in juvie until he's eighteen. After that, who knows?'"

"Juvie's real?" Bro said.

"Huh?" said Harmony.

"It thought it was just to scare kids," Bro said, "like the bogeyman."

Jimmy laughed, a strange and sad laugh that sounded almost like a sob. "It's real, all right. That's where everything went wrong."

"What do you mean?" Harmony said.

"That's what my dad told me, this one time he'd had a few drinks. I don't mean there was only one time he had a few drinks. Just that one of those times he said he'd been locked up in juvie as a kid and when he came out he wasn't the same person."

There was a long silence. The drizzle was very light now, but I could hear it in the air, like bits of paper getting softly torn.

"What did he do?" Bro said.

"Stole a car and took it joyriding," said Jimmy.

"They sent him to juvie for that?" Harmony said.

"He got into a wreck," Jimmy said. "A woman died."

More silence. It went on and on, the kids all looking at one another and then not looking at one another. Finally Bro raised his foot onto the foothold and climbed up to the tree house. Harmony followed close behind. Harmony and Jimmy sat down on the wooden chairs, Bro on the deflated couch. Down below I heard Arthur clawing at the tree trunk. Why couldn't he climb trees? There really isn't much to it. Poor fellow. I took a short, silent leap onto Harmony's lap, and, at least for the moment, stopped thinking of others.

"So what do we do now?" Bro said.

"*I'm* staying here," said Jimmy.

"But . . . but for how long?"

"Till they stop looking."

"And then?" said Harmony.

"Go somewhere far away."

"Like where?" Bro said.

Jimmy shrugged.

"That doesn't sound like a good plan," Harmony said. "I think you should come back to our place."

"And then?" Jimmy said.

"We'll talk it over with my mom," said Harmony. "She'll come up with something."

"There's nothing to come up with," Jimmy said. "I'm not going to juvie."

"We'll figure out how to make that not happen," Harmony said.

Jimmy shook his head. "Once adults get involved it'll happen. They have all these systems. The systems take over and that's that."

Harmony went still. I could feel it. Had all this talk of adults and systems—of no interest to me—affected her in some way? I scratched her leg, very lightly, just letting her know it was time to get back to normal.

"C'mon, Jimmy," Bro said, "let's go back to our place. We'll figure something out."

Jimmy rose, a real sudden movement. His voice rose, too, loud and high. "What's wrong with you?" he screamed at Bro. "Are you an idiot? I'm not going to juvie. They lock you up and turn you into someone bad. So shut your dumb mouth."

Bro jumped up, stepped right in front of Jimmy. "You're the idiot." Bro's voice rose, too. "Only an idiot would act guilty if he didn't do it, and you're acting guilty."

What was this? Was some sort of throwdown about to happen? What a disagreeable possibility! Yet there they were, Jimmy the taller of the two and pretty strong-looking, but Bro had real big muscles for a kid.

"Stop this right—" Harmony began, but that was as far as she got when Jimmy suddenly took a swing at Bro. His fist caught Bro thump on the shoulder and spun him around, but in that spin, Bro caught the front of Jimmy's sweatshirt in one hand, yanked him close, balled his other hand into a fist, and punched Jimmy in his already bruised face real hard.

But no, not quite. At the very last instant, his fist already on the way, Bro somehow put on the brakes and pulled that punch back. He let go of Jimmy and stepped away. Bro's face was as white as bone, and so was Jimmy's. They both stood there, breathing heavily, like they'd just run a long way. Harmony rose—me sliding down to the floor— and stepped between them.

"You're both idiots," she said. "Sit down."

They sat down. Color came back to their faces, actually a bit too much. Harmony stayed on her feet.

"When you're accused of a crime and you didn't do it," she said, "what do you need?"

The boys shrugged, the exact same kind of shrug at the exact same time, like they'd rehearsed it.

"An alibi," Harmony said.

"I don't have an alibi," Jimmy said. "I was at baseball and then at your place, but what if I . . . if I did it just before I left home?"

"Do something like that and then just go to baseball, like nothing happened?" Bro said.

"Good point," said Harmony.

"But it's not proof," Jimmy said. "Face it, I'm—" He slumped forward, covering his face with his hands. Tears leaked out from between his fingers. "Let me stay here," he said, his voice rough and cracking. "Don't rat me out. Please, please, please." He rocked back and forth.

Bro and Harmony looked at each other. Sometimes they talk without making a sound. I do the same, but no one understands me—except for Mom and Harmony, and only sometimes. Bro got up, touched Jimmy's shoulder.

"We won't rat you out," he said.

"But you have to promise to stay right here," said Harmony.

Jimmy nodded.

"Say it out loud," said Harmony.

Jimmy lowered his hands, took a deep breath. "I promise."

"We'll be back with food, a sleeping bag, and drinks," Harmony said.

"You don't need to do that," Jimmy said.

"Shut up," said Harmony.

Then she scooped me up and carried me out of the tree house, Bro climbing down after us. Arthur came waddling over, delighted to see us, like we'd been gone for ages. We crossed the clearing and soon came to the path that led through the woods to the shuffleboard court. Bro and Harmony were silent for a long time, thinking hard—I could feel how hard—the whole way except when they glanced back to check on Arthur, running out of gas the way he does and falling farther and farther behind.

At last Bro said, "What are we going to do?"

"Without an alibi there's only one thing to do," said Harmony.

"Find the real attacker?"

"Yup."

NINETEEN

ARTHUR

ONE DAY VERY SOON I'LL FIGURE out how to climb trees. I almost succeeded at the tree house. Watching Bro climb the tree trunk, I suddenly had a brain wave. That was exactly how it felt, like a huge wave rolled in and slapped me good and hard right upside the brain. And the message it pounded into my head was this: You just charge straight up the tree! Wow! Why hadn't I thought of that? No idea, but it didn't matter because now it had come to me on its own. Arthur, my man! Just charge directly on up that tree. Aren't Bro and Harmony—and Queenie, ha!—going to be surprised?

So I gathered my paws under me and CHARGED directly on up that tree. CHARGE, ARTHUR, CHARGE! ATTABOY! YOU CAN DO IT! LET'S HEAR IT FOR ARTHUR! WHATEVER YOU DO, DON'T PUSSYFOOT! And I came very very close to reaching that first foothold. In fact, I believe the tip of my nose actually grazed it. But at that huge moment, I thought: *Pussyfoot?* What a terrible time to think pussyfoot! Because pussyfooting was how Queenie climbed trees. She didn't charge at all. She simply pussy-footed. And then, BUMP, I landed on the ground at the base of the tree. I lay there on my back, paws in the air and tongue hanging out, which is how I do my best think-ing. And as I lay thinking—thoughts like, *How does one pussyfoot, exactly? And do you need pussy-type feet for pussyfooting or will doggy-type do the job?*—I happened to glance up and there was Queenie watching me from the doorway of the tree house. I did not like the look on her face, not one little bit. *Forget all about pussyfooting*, I told myself. *Never think of pussyfooting again.*

Strength, determination, raw power—they all flowed in, filling me to the brim, and I charged like no one has ever charged before. Unluckily for me, I turned out to be still a little winded from my previous try. Perfectly understand-able in such a situation that this time I didn't come quite as near to reaching that first foothold.

BUMP.

I lay on my back, thinking things over again. Up above, Queenie was no longer watching. I lay on my back thinking and thinking, and stayed that way until a bit later, when everybody except for Jimmy came down from the tree house and we headed for home, Harmony carrying Queenie on her shoulder the whole way. Why not me? Was there some reason I wasn't carryable? None that I could see. I nosed around Bro's legs, trying to get across to him the simple idea: *Pick up Arthur. Carry him on your shoulder.*

But Bro didn't even seem to notice me. Instead he turned to Harmony and said, "It's a good idea, Harm."

"Finding the real bad guy?"

"Yeah. But where do we start?"

No answer from Harmony. We kept going. After my little rest at the bottom of the tree, I'd gotten back all my energy, so it was no surprise that I was able to keep up, no problemo. At least at first. But I hadn't been prepared for the pace Bro and Harmony were setting. Was there some reason for walking so fast? Where was the fire? I sniffed the air and smelled no smoke. That was a little joke I shared with just me. Meanwhile I was falling behind a little. No shame in that. But the way Queenie watched me from up on Harmony's shoulder was very bothersome.

After a while, Harmony said, "What about starting with Sweet Lady Em?"

Queenie stopped watching me, turned toward Harmony. Her golden eyes seemed to be on fire. What was up with her? Was there some reason she couldn't stay at the tree house? She could make a very nice life there, pussyfooting up and down to her heart's content.

"Finding her, you mean?" Bro said.

"Or at least figuring out what happened," said Harmony. "Do you believe Jimmy?"

"About him locking the barn door? Yeah."

"So do I," said Harmony.

"And Sweet Lady Em didn't unlock the door herself," Bro said.

"Meaning someone unlocked the door and opened it. Would that someone just let her wander off?"

"Nope. Her cream is special."

"Making her valuable," Harmony said. "She got stolen."

"A cownapping," said Bro.

Harmony laughed. "Yeah, a cownapping. You'll be a stand-up comedian someday."

"You think?"

"No."

"Ha-ha," said Bro. "At least I'm funnier than you."

Harmony was quiet for a moment or two. Then she said, "You're right about that."

"Yeah?" said Bro.

Harmony nodded. "But the point is—stealing a cow is a crime. So that makes two crimes in a very short period at the very same place. Coincidence or—"

"Connected," Bro said.

"Meaning the thief and the attacker are the same person," said Harmony.

"Does it have to be one person?"

196

"No. Thinking of anybody in particular?"

"Kinda," said Bro. "Somewhere in my mind, but I can't get to it. Does that ever happen to you?"

"Sure."

"You're just saying that."

"Bro. Don't start this."

"But how come you're smarter?"

"I'm not."

"But you're a grade ahead of me."

"Are we really going to go through this again? Like now, when Jimmy's all alone back there?"

Bro didn't answer. We kept going, me maybe falling farther behind. I actually lost sight of them once or twice, as the trail wound through the woods. But soon I caught a glimpse of the shuffleboard court between two trees, and I sped right up, like I always do when home is in sight, actually trotting as I came alongside Harmony and Bro.

"Harm?" Bro said at last.

"Yeah?"

"Let's find that stupid cow."

They bumped fists.

But what was this? Cows, again? I'd actually picked up traces of cow scent in the woods, back at a crossing trail that led to . . . well, I wasn't sure where, and after so much exercise found myself a little too hungry and thirsty for deep mental work.

■ ■ ■

"Any luck?" said Mom from behind the desk as we entered the inn.

"Um," said Bro.

"We've got Queenie!" Harmony said, holding Queenie up like a shiny trophy. I wanted to be held up, too, and pressed against Harmony's leg, perhaps more vigorously than I'd intended, to give her the idea. Instead she said, "Arthur! What the heck!" And, "Oops!" And then she dropped Queenie, a good result, but Queenie landed oh so softly and ran over to Mom, right up her leg and into her arms, where Mom cradled her. So, a bad result. Queenie turned her golden eyes on me and gave me a bored sort of look, like she was about to yawn. A very very bad result.

Mom kissed Queenie on the top of the head. I, Arthur, have a head with a top that likes getting kissed. Just mentioning that in case you had doubts. But the top of my head did not get kissed. Instead Mom put Queenie down on the desk—where she curled up in a way that said, *This is my desk and there's nothing you can do about it*—and asked, "And what about Jimmy? Any sign of him at all?"

Bro looked at Harmony. Harmony took a deep breath and said, "Well, Mom—"

But before she could continue, the door opened and a small man in a dark raincoat came in. He had wispy white

198

hair and carried a worn leather briefcase. Worn leather is a particular interest of mine. Gnawing on leather is a nice way to pass the time, as you may have already discovered, and worn leather is the best.

"I'm looking for Ms. Yvette Reddy," the man said. He had a thin, scratchy voice and thin, colorless lips.

"That's me," said Mom.

"Pleased to meet you," he said. "My name's Edwin P. Hale, of the law firm Hale, Hale, and Hale, practicing in Wilmerville for the past century and more."

"Nice to meet you, Mr. Hale," Mom said. "These are my children, Harmony and Bro."

"Nice to meet you," said Harmony.

"Hey," said Bro.

"And hey to you, young man," said Mr. Hale. "But don't expect a high five. High-fiving at the age of eighty-two looks ridiculous. Keeping up with cool is impossible. Remember that."

Harmony and Bro both raised their eyebrows in the exact same way, like something important had just been said. If so, I'd missed it myself.

Mom smiled. "Sounds like good advice," she said. "What can we do for you, Mr. Hale?"

Mr. Hale glanced around. "Is there somewhere we can talk?"

"How about the office?" Mom said.

"Perfect," said Mr. Hale.

"May I take your coat?" Mom said, going over to him. She helped him with his coat, hung it on the rack. Underneath the coat, Mr. Hale wore a dark suit, white shirt, and bow tie. None of that was important. The important thing is the smell that came wafting over from the pocket of his suit jacket: the smell of a biscuit, I believed the kind that came in the big yellow box, which just happens to be my favorite.

Mom led Mr. Hale around the reception desk and through the doorway into her little office. Around then was when Mr. Hale appeared to notice me for the first time, possibly because I'd bumped up against him on the biscuit side. He glanced down and said, "Well, well, what a fine-looking pooch!"

Fine-looking pooch? Fine-looking pooch! You hear that all the time, although perhaps not about me until right now. Had Mr. Hale come to book a room? Maybe for a nice long stay?

"His name's Arthur," Mom said as they took their places at her desk, a much smaller desk than the one at reception.

"Excellent name," said Mr. Hale. "And is there a Guinevere in the house?" he added, losing me completely.

"Not exactly," Mom said.

"A mixed blessing in any case, the Guineveres of the world," Mr. Hale said, moving me beyond complete non-understanding into whole new blankness. But then he quickly switched to another track, back in a direction I knew as well as anybody. How did he do that? By reaching into his jacket pocket, taking out the biscuit—the yellow box kind, for sure—and saying, "Can I give him this?"

"Now you can't not," Mom said.

Mr. Hale laughed. A moment later the biscuit was mine. Would Mr. Hale be living here permanently? The Violet Room was our nicest. Yes, the most expensive, but we'd be happy to give him a deal.

Mr. Hale laid his briefcase on the desk, opened it, and took out some papers. "Most of my work these days concerns wills and estates," he said, "meaning I help folks make sure that their property and belongings are distributed the way they want after they're gone. In this case, I represent my longtime client, Mr. Gorman Doone, presently lying in a coma at Regional Hospital, his prospects dim, according to the doctors. As you may know, Mr. Doone has one child—a son, Jimmy, missing very temporarily, I hope—a half brother, Carl, now living in Dubai, from whom he's been long estranged—and an ex-wife, Rhonda, Jimmy's mother, address unknown at present, from whom Mr. Doone is also estranged. Any questions so far?"

"No," said Mom.

I had one: Did Mr. Hale have any more biscuits on hand, outside in his car, for example? I gazed up at him with my question in mind, but he wasn't looking my way.

Mr. Hale picked up some papers, stuck glasses on the end of his nose. "It was Mr. Doone's very strong wish that in the event of his death, all his earthly goods, including the farm, all equipment and livestock, and all cash and investments—of which I'm afraid there is very little—be passed on to, quote, 'my son, Jimmy, who deserved better.'"

Mr. Hale took off his glasses. "Any idea what he meant by that last part, about deserving better?"

Mom gave Mr. Hale a long look. "No," she said at last.

Mr. Hale nodded. "I never go into things like that with a client unless they open the door to those sort of questions, and Mr. Doone is not the door-opening kind. The main point is that Jimmy becomes the sole heir. That's in the event of death. In the present circumstances—meaning if Mr. Doone becomes incapacitated—he has directed that the same transfer take place, reversible if Mr. Doone somehow recovers. That presents an obvious problem, since the boy is eleven years old and won't reach the age of majority in this state for another seven years. Therefore the law requires that the estate be held in possession of the trustee chosen by Mr. Doone in the interim. Usually an adult family member or an attorney is chosen for the role, but neither choice appealed to Mr. Doone."

Mr. Hale turned a page, put his glasses back on, read for a moment or two, took off his glasses, looked at Mom, and said, "He picked you."

Mom, who always sits up straight, sat straighter. "Me?"

Mr. Hale handed her the page. "I'll leave you a copy, of course."

Mom read what was on the paper. "But I hardly know him."

"Nevertheless," said Mr. Hale.

Mom shook her head. "I'm sorry, Mr. Hale. For something like this, I'll need more than 'nevertheless.'"

They had what looked pretty much to me like a staredown. Mr. Hale was the one who looked away.

"Well, Ms. Reddy, I did ask him about that. His answer was, quote, 'because of her cards.' Evidently you're in the habit of sending him cards?"

"Why, just Happy New Year cards, Mr. Hale. I send them to all my clients, suppliers, and former guests."

"Cards with a handwritten message?" said Mr. Hale.

"Handwritten, yes, but it's the same message on every one."

"Nevertheless," said Mr. Hale. Nevertheless again?

Hadn't Mom just finished blowing that one up? The word seemed to stay in the air, and then Mr. Hale said it again. "Nevertheless, it means something to Mr. Doone. What is your Happy New Year message, Ms. Reddy?"

"It's actually pretty much a cliché, and not even nicely phrased," Mom said. "I've never been clever enough to improve it."

"But what is it?"

Mom took a deep breath. "'I plan to look for the beauty in life this year, and hope you will, too.'"

A long silence. Then Mr. Hale said, "There's your answer."

TWENTY

QUEENIE

IN ONE CORNER OF THE BIG ROOM stands the foosball game. It's played on a sort of table with knobs and rods and tiny metal players, some red and some blue. Guests play on it from time to time, occasionally challenging Harmony or Bro if either of them is around. That's always a mistake since Harmony and Bro never lose except to each other. Once a businessman with a loud voice asked Bro if he cared to bet a dollar on a game. Bro borrowed four quarters from Harmony and won. This businessman was the type of human who can't stand to lose and makes you keep playing until he wins, which did not happen in this case. Instead the bets kept getting doubled until Bro had won two hundred smackers, and it might have been more, but they called it quits when the businessman's girlfriend started yelling at him. That brought Mom in from the front desk. She made Bro give back all that green.

"But why, Mom?" Bro said later. "I won it fair and square."

"We don't hustle the guests," Mom told him.

The point of all this was that while Mom and Mr. Hale were in the office, Harmony and Bro were playing foosball, me curled up on a nearby footstool. Foosball is much too noisy and, well, idiotic for me, and Harmony vs. Bro foosball is the worst. They scream and yell, accuse each other of cheating, and even get into physical fights. Not they themselves, of course, but the tiny metal players, although it's hard to understand how that could be since they're on tracks. But somehow they get to whacking each other, and once a tiny player even flew off the table and whizzed by me. A horrible game, and I was glad when Mom came in the room. The kids stopped playing at once.

"What did that old guy want?" Bro said.

"He's a lawyer," said Harmony. "I bet he wants to defend Jimmy."

"That didn't come up—but not a bad idea," Mom said. "What brought Mr. Hale here is something I'd never have thought of. In case he ended up . . . well, the way he has ended up, all Mr. Doone's possessions go to Jimmy. Since Jimmy is underage, there has to be a temporary trustee. That turns out to be me."

"Huh?" said Bro.

Mom went into a long explanation. This sort of thing— where humans get very complicated and do a lot of brow-wrinkling and head scratching—is of no interest to me and I tuned out completely.

This time when Mom finished, Bro said, "Does this mean Jimmy's going to live with us?"

"How would you two feel about that?" Mom said.

"Cool," said Bro.

Harmony was silent. Mom turned to her, raised her eyebrows the slightest bit.

"It's a big decision, isn't it?" Harmony said.

"True," Mom said. "And we're getting ahead of ourselves. For one thing, maybe Mr. Doone will come out of the coma. Also we should try to get in touch with his mother, and maybe the uncle, too. Meanwhile Mr. Doone's instructions are to not sell the farm if at all possible but instead hire someone to work it and pay that person from the earnings. I wouldn't want to start any of this without Jimmy's permission. So first we need Jimmy. The poor kid." She went over to the window, gazed out. A helicopter hovered in the sky, not far away. "Where could he be?" Mom said.

Bro and Harmony looked at each other. The answer to Mom's question was: Jimmy's in the tree house. But neither of the kids said that. In fact, they said nothing. Why not? This was disturbing. I didn't want to be disturbed. I slipped off the footstool, made my way to the back stairs and down to the basement. When you're disturbed it's a good idea to get busy, focus your mind on other things. Such as mouse hunting, for example.

Mice have a surprisingly strong smell for such little critters, and there was plenty of it in the basement, although not particularly fresh. I entered the oldest cobwebby part, came to the furnace and the coal chute, dim light coming through the single high window and shining on the scythe, still lying on the dirt floor. The sight made me go still. I actually forgot about mice for the moment and thought only of Ms. Pryor. Some humans are very smart. Mom, for example. But also Ms. Pryor. Some of the smart ones are also tricky. Not Mom. But Ms. Pryor? Oh, yes.

I moved away from the scythe, sprang onto the coal chute, gazed out the window. We certainly needed guests at the inn, but I had no desire to ever see Ms. Pryor again. My desire now was all about finding a mousy little playmate and . . . and having a bit of fun. I'm the playful type, maybe something that's not fully appreciated in this establishment. But why feel sorry for yourself? Is it my loss or theirs? Never mine! I am me! End of story.

I am me! I am me! I am me! I let that thought happen to its heart's content. Is it possible that thinking good thoughts makes good things happen? Possibly not for most, but perhaps for me, because all at once, up there on the coal chute, I caught a whiff of extra-fresh mousy scent. Life is good, my friends. It is also for the living, although in this case maybe not for all concerned. I followed the scent to the end of the coal chute, where it led up to the little hole in the top pane. A little hole, but manageable for someone who combined my size with superb body control. That would be me.

The very next thing I knew I was on the side lawn, not far from the shuffleboard court. I had a crazy but exciting idea: How about playing a bit of shuffleboard with my mousy pal? And very conveniently the mousy scent led exactly in that direction. I turned toward the shuffleboard court and—

"Hey! There's Queenie!"

What was this? Harmony and Bro coming out the side door, both carrying plastic bags? An unexpected development, and even though I loved them both, not a particularly welcome one.

They came over to me, bent down.

"How did you get outside, you little devil?" Harmony said. I loved when she called me that. It meant I was . . . what's the best way to put this? How about: the cat's meow? Yes, that says it all. I am the cat's meow. What can top that? Don't even bother trying.

Meanwhile she'd scooped me up and given me a kiss on

the nose. I can't stand anyone touching my nose, but I made an exception for Harmony.

"We're marching you right back inside," she said.

Meanwhile Bro had wandered over to the broken window. "Here's where she got out."

Harmony carried me closer to the window. "That hole's too small," she said.

I waited for Bro to argue with her, to say something about repairing the window, maybe even repairing it himself with duct tape, which was how Bro repaired everything, but he just shrugged, maybe because Harmony was hardly ever wrong about anything. This was working out well for me. No repairs to that window, if you don't mind.

We started for the side door, meaning I was about to be deposited back in the house, mousing expedition finito. But at the last second, Bro's hand actually on the doorknob, he paused.

"Bertha thinks Queenie can tell Sweet Lady Em's cream from the store-bought kind," he said.

"So can I," said Harmony. "Can't you?"

"I don't like cream," Bro said. "The point is maybe we should bring her with us."

"Why?"

"To help look for Lady Em."

"Bro. Queenie's not a dog."

210

"I know it doesn't make sense. But . . ." He went silent. Their gazes met for a moment or two.

"Okay," Harmony said. "Why not?"

And very soon after that, I was in my special backpack and we were moving quickly through the woods beyond the shuffleboard court. I wasn't paying much attention. My mind was stuck on: *Queenie's not a dog.* True, of course. Could anyone be less doglike than I? But what if . . . oh, horrible simply to form the thought . . . but what if I had been a dog? Queenie, the dog. Here, Queenie. Shake a paw! Wanna play fetch? Uh-oh, none of that, Queenie. Or that or that or that. Be a good little Queenie doggy. Need to do your business? Here, Queenie. Shake a paw! Wanna—

In short, a nightmare.

"Trustee?" Jimmy said.

Oh, no. That again? And so soon? We were up in the tree house. Bro laid out what we'd brought: a sleeping bag, a blanket, water, tortilla chips, salsa, potato chips, a bunch of tiny jars of jam, M&M'S, some other kind of chips. Harmony explained the whole trustee thing. A cold wind blew in from the side with no wall.

". . . but Mom doesn't want to make any decisions you don't like," Harmony was saying.

There was a long silence. Jimmy rubbed his eye. It

looked better today, not very swollen, the skin around it more yellow than purple.

"What if I go to jail?" he said. "What happens then?"

"You're not going to jail," Bro said. He took the top off one of the tiny jam jars, ripped open a pack of chips, dipped a chip in the jam, and handed it to Jimmy.

"But what if? Then what happens to the farm?"

"Jimmy!" said Bro. "You're not listening."

"But it's a real question. If I . . . if I did what they said, then wouldn't it be wrong for me to have the farm?"

"I don't know," Harmony said. "There's what's wrong legally and then there's what's just plain wrong."

Jimmy gave her a long look. He seemed about to say something, but before he could, Bro said, "Who cares? You didn't do it."

Jimmy lowered his head.

"What?" said Bro. "What are you say—"

Harmony moved one of her fingers the slightest bit. Bro went silent. I smelled jam, strawberry to be specific. I'm a fan of strawberry jam. The tiny jar lay open on the floor.

Jimmy, still looking down, said, "I thought about it."

"You thought about . . . about doing something to your father?" Bro said.

Jimmy nodded. "And now he left everything to me. When I'd been thinking that about him. Why?"

"You're his kid," Harmony said.

Tears filled Jimmy's eyes and overflowed, although he didn't cry out loud. Then we just sat there. The wind rose higher, blew some dead leaves across the floor.

"In the meantime you've got us," Harmony said.

"You're taking a big risk," said Jimmy, wiping his face on his sleeve.

"True," Bro said. He pointed his chin at the jam-smeared chip, still in Jimmy's hand. "Try that. A good combo—I invented it myself."

Jimmy sniffled once or twice, then tried the chip. "Not bad," he said.

"Here's another." Bro took a chip from the bag, dipped it into the open jam jar, discovered the jar was empty. He picked it up, peered inside. Yes, empty for sure. He glanced around the tree house, his gaze passing right over me, lying in the far corner, my eyes closed to the tiniest possible slits.

"Want your cream?" Harmony said. We crossed our meadow and were now in the woods—not the little woods where the tree house stood, but the big woods that separated our place from the Doones' farm. Or possibly just Jimmy's farm now, or even . . . even ours? For the first time in my life, I wished I'd paid a little more attention to some of the human back-and-forth, usually so tedious. Was there some possible future where I ended up as the boss of Lady Em? Oh, how

lovely that would be! But didn't I deserve it? So here's my answer, Harmony: YES! I WANT MY CREAM.

"Then you're going to help us find her," said Harmony.

Fine, but how? No ideas came to me, not a single one. If Lady Em had been a mouse or a bird, then no problem. I hunted mice and birds. I did not hunt cows. For a second or two I was almost mad at Harmony.

We walked out of the woods, made our way down a long slope. A house came into view, with a barn nearby, both of them shabby, especially compared to the inn, always so sparkling thanks to Mom. This of course was the Doones' farm, and perhaps mine someday soon. I had no doubt that Mom could fix it up just fine.

It was very quiet at my new farm, if you don't mind me calling it that. No farm animals of any kind, no squirrels, no humans; only one lone bird, very big and very dark, circling high above. We followed a crushed-stone path that led past the house—there were strips of yellow tape criss-crossed over the door—and around to the barn. The front double doors were closed and padlocked. A plastic bag hung on the handle, with a folded-up note inside. Harmony opened the bag and read the note out loud:

"'To Deputy Carstairs, Mr. Hale, Mrs. Reddy, or anyone else this may concern: For the time being, I have moved the livestock and the chickens over to our place. Easier to care for them at home, and I will return them when things are settled. Sincerely, Trudy Munson.'"

Bro rattled the lock. It stayed locked.

"We could go ask Mrs. Munson for the key," Harmony said.

"And what if she wants to know why?" Bro turned and began walking around the barn.

We followed him. "You're a natural-born criminal, aren't you?" Harmony said.

Bro came to a small window, dirty and cracked. He got his hands on each side of the frame, pushed, grunted, pushed harder, grunted harder—and then, with a slight cracking sound, the window slid up.

"I'm going to be a jewel thief in Beverly Hills," Bro said.

Harmony laughed, a laugh she tried and failed to tamp down. Were we having fun? If so, in what way?

Moments later, we were all in the barn. It was empty and dark, shafts of dull light coming through windows here and there. I picked up distasteful smells—pig, for example. El Jefe, who lives in our new barn, not the falling-down old one, was the only pig I knew personally, a relationship I had no wish to pursue. I was remembering every smelly detail of our one encounter and not paying much attention as we passed the empty stalls.

"Wonder which one was Lady Em's?" Bro said.

And all at once I smelled cream. Just a tiny whiff, but cream for sure.

MEOW!

"Whoa!" Harmony said. "Did you hear that?"

"Hard to miss," said Bro. "She's trying to tell us something."

"Bro! She's a cat!"

MEOW!

Harmony gazed down at me like she was trying to see deep inside. Through the mesh of my pocket in the backpack, I gazed up at her in a way that lets no one in.

"This is the stall," Harmony said.

We went in, walked around. Not much to see: straw on the floor, a worn wooden stool, a squashed soda can.

"What are we looking for?" Bro said.

"I don't know," said Harmony. "Maybe—"

All at once, Bro bent down, fished through the straw, and pulled out the stub of a fat cigar. "Aha!" he said, and held it up for Harmony to see.

"I don't get it," Harmony said. "Does Mr. Doone smoke cigars? So what?"

"Maybe he did, maybe he didn't," Bro said. "But I know someone who does for sure. His name is Roscoe. He's got neck tattoos."

"Yuck," said Harmony.

TWENTY-ONE
ARTHUR

BERTHA?" SAID MOM. "CAN YOU HOLD the fort for a bit? I'm going for a walk."

"Putting on your thinking cap?" said Bertha.

"Exactly," said Mom, putting on her jacket but not a cap. That was a bit confusing. Maybe Bertha had said "thinking jacket" and I hadn't heard right. Lying on the mat by the umbrella stand, I wriggled around, got myself even more comfortable, settling in for a nice afternoon nap, or if it was still morning, that would be fine, too.

But then: "Rise and shine, Arthur. We're going for a walk."

Rise? Shine? Walk? Me? I didn't want to do any of that, and as for the shining part, didn't even know how.

"Ar-thur?"

Uh-oh. When Mom says my name like that—Ar-thur—it's game over. She doesn't yell at me or talk in a cold way. In fact, she sounds like she's enjoying herself—and maybe even enjoying me. So why should that be game over? I had no idea. It just was.

And the very next thing, there I was, outside with Mom. No leash, not ever with Mom. I always walk right beside her, like a champ from obedience school, although my actual stint at obedience school probably could have gone a bit better. Am I a growler? Certainly not. I'd never growled in my life before obedience school. So why had I growled at the nice obedience school lady every single time I laid eyes on her? For the longest time she was so good about it. And then she wasn't. Mom didn't even get her money back.

We headed down our long driveway toward the road. Mom is always alert but today seemed even more so, her eyes taking in everything there was to take in. How tiring that must be! I take in everything, too, but through my nose, and it requires no effort at all. I just have to breathe, and I've always been a good, steady breather.

"Where is he, Arthur?" Mom said. "Where could he be?"

Who were we talking about? I waited for Mom to give me a clue, but before she could, a car turned off the road and into our driveway. A long black car: I perked up at the sight. These long black cars are called limos, which I knew from the time a rock band had stayed with us for a few days. They told Mom they were hoping the peace and quiet would help them think up some new songs. I was never clear on whether new songs happened, probably not, because from the moment they came to the moment they left, there was no peace and quiet. We had the cops, the fire department, the EMTs, plus the rock band ate and drank everything in the house, including cases of champagne Mom ordered special. In short, they threw money around like crazy. Bro caught quite a lot of it. But the point is they were the best guests we ever had. And here came this new limo. I tried to see if a rock band was inside, just waiting to jump out, but the windows were tinted almost black.

The limo rolled up the driveway and stopped beside us. A window at the very back slid down. A man peered out. He seemed to be alone and did not look at all like any of the rock band dudes. For example, he didn't need a haircut. He had a full head of hair, dark with some silvering at the sides, but neatly trimmed, with no crumbs stuck in it here and there, rock band style. His skin was smooth; his teeth big, white, and even; his eyes watchful.

"Yvette Reddy?" he said.

"That's me," said Mom.

The man opened the door and got out. He turned out to be a very lean dude, possibly a bit of a hipster, although weren't hipsters supposed to be a little younger? But he was wearing skinny black jeans and bright red sneakers, which I knew to be hipster style on account of Harmony dressing as a hipster on Halloween. This hipster dude, if that was what he was, gave off very pleasant aromas of aftershave and deodorant, although I couldn't detect much in the way of actual human smells.

"I'm Sergei Bender," he said. "I'm interested in rural real estate, and I have a proposition for you."

"If this is about the inn," Mom said, "it's not for sale." She frowned. "Your client isn't Ms. Pryor, by any chance? Ottoline Pryor from Menlo Park?"

"Doesn't ring a bell," he said. At that moment, I caught the first human smell coming from him, the smell of a man on high alert. "And my firm is based in Brooklyn." He handed Mom a card.

Mom read it aloud. "'Mellontic Investments.'"

"At your service," said Sergei Bender. "Is there somewhere we can talk? I promise not to take much of your time."

Mom glanced around. "Arthur and I are going for a walk. You're welcome to join us, Mr. Bender."

"Perfect," said Mr. Bender. "And, hey, it's Sergei, please." He looked around. "And when will Arthur be joining us?"

"This," said Mom, "is Arthur."

Sergei gave me a quick glance. "Ah," he said. "The dog."

Yes. Exactly. The dog. Some humans don't seem to notice me, even when I'm right there, within easy biting distance. Uh-oh! Where did that thought come from? Very bad, I know. Still, I forgave myself, and right away, my go-to move in situations like this.

We took the old road that came out behind Willard's General Store, and turned onto a path that led to Willard's Pond. This was one of my favorite walks, not too long, and flat almost all the way. Up above the sun was trying to poke through but couldn't quite manage it. That happened a lot in mud season. What was the sun all about, anyway? Whoa! What a strange thought. I gave myself a quick shake to get rid of it.

"You'll be relieved to know," Sergei said, "that we don't want to buy your inn. What we're interested in," he went on as we came to the pond, mostly open water except for a few dirty ice chunks floating here and there, "is the farm belonging to the, uh, unfortunate Mr. Doone. I believe you're the trustee."

Mom turned quickly to him. "But how do you know that? I just found out."

We stepped onto the boat dock, made of thick boards held up by sturdy posts, but a little unsteady compared to solid earth. I wasn't a big fan of the boat dock.

"Quite the dock for such a small pond," Sergei said.

"It feeds into a nearby creek that's navigable for miles downstream," Mom said.

"Oh? What's the name of the creek?"

"Blackberry," said Mom. Sergei's eyes shifted, and he seemed about to say something, but before he could Mom went on, "But you haven't answered my question—how do you know about me being the trustee?"

"Information is our currency now, Yvette, not money," Sergei said. "I deal in information. And information travels at the speed of light. I mean that literally."

"Well, I don't operate at the speed of light," Mom said. "And I don't want to. Now please answer my question."

"It's a matter of public record," said Sergei.

"But right away? I thought that took months."

"Then let's just say the relevant document will be a matter of public record, and the information came to me a little early. But that's a side issue. I'm here to make you a very generous offer for the Doones' farm."

"If you've seen the document . . ." Here Mom paused and gave Sergei a very close look. His face showed nothing that I could see, but the high-alert smell got stronger. ". . . then you know," Mom went on, "that Mr. Doone doesn't want the farm to be sold. And if it is to be sold, he wants his son, Jimmy, to make that decision after he turns eighteen. So my job as trustee is to make sure that's exactly what happens."

"Very conscientious," Sergei said. "I admire that. But as

a trustee, isn't it your real duty to take care of Jimmy's interests? What if that means selling now instead of later?"

"Why would it mean that?"

"Because," Sergei said, "my kind of offer almost surely will never come again. In which case you'd end up doing Jimmy less good than you could have."

Mom gazed out over the pond. I gazed out, too, for no particular reason. And what was this? Some sort of little red ball was floating out there and drifting slowly toward the sandy beach just beyond the end of the dock. A memory stirred in my mind but refused to come closer, which was how my mind worked. No problem. I've come to understand that my mind knows what it's doing! What a thought, especially since my mind must have made it! That meant . . . I actually had no idea what it meant and in fact had gone as far as I could, or even further.

Mom turned to him. "I assume you know Jimmy's gone missing."

Sergei nodded. "I hear he's the main suspect. A sad story."

"It is a sad story," Mom said. "But I don't believe he's guilty."

"Why not?" said Sergei. "Deputy Carstairs seems to think it's an open and shut case."

"You've spoken to him?"

"Briefly."

Mom shot him a glance. "Well," she said. "You warned me."

"Oh?" Sergei looked surprised.

"That you're traveling at the speed of light."

Sergei laughed. "Of course at the neuron level we're nowhere near the speed of light, but with AI brain implants it's bound to happen one day."

Mom shuddered. Had something frightened her? I couldn't think what, but I edged over toward her just the same. Whatever it was had me to deal with, and I'm a pretty tough customer, as I'm sure you know by now.

"I just don't believe Jimmy has that kind of violence in him, no matter what the provocation," Mom said. "Call it an informed guess or just a feeling. But when we get him back I promise to tell him about this conversation."

Sergei raised his hands, very long and skinny type hands. "Whoa! You don't want to even hear the offer?"

"Not now," Mom said.

Sergei stared down at her. He was much taller than Mom, something I hadn't realized until now. "I can't believe you're not taking this more seriously, Yvette."

"I think I am, Mr. Bender."

"Do you realize that any deal will benefit you, too?" he said.

"How so?"

"You'd be a facilitator. We always pay a fee to facilitators. It's safe to say yours would be in the mid–six figures, and that's the floor."

Mom stared back up at Sergei. They were standing quite close together, but there was space to squeeze in between, which I did.

"Whatever happens, there'll be no fee, Mr. Bender."

There was a silence. Then Sergei backed up a step and smiled a big smile that actually looked warm and happy. "Why did it take me so long to see this? You're a world-class, natural-born negotiator!"

Mom's jaw dropped. She looked stunned. I'd never seen her like this before. Then she gave her head a little shake—reminding me of me!—and said, "I've got to get back to work."

"I'll stay here for a bit, enjoy the rustic beauty." Sergei held out his hand. They shook. "To the future," he said. Mom withdrew her hand.

Mom and I walked off the dock. I noticed the red ball, now lying on the beach. Why not scoop it up? You don't come across such an interesting red ball every day. So I made a quick detour, scooped up the red ball—a strange ball, somehow hard and soft at the same time—and trotted back to Mom. She stood at the start of the path to

Willard's General Store, looking back at Sergei. He was talking on his phone.

And here was a funny thing: My red ball was making a tiny beeping noise. Beep beep beep. Mom didn't seem to hear it.

TWENTY-TWO

QUEENIE

"T HEY HAD THIS BIG WHITE VAN," Bro said.

"Who are you talking about?" said Harmony.

"The two guys with the neck tattoos. Roscoe was the small one. They were changing a tire. The big guy did all the work. Roscoe just watched."

"They both had neck tattoos?" said Harmony.

"And bushy beards."

This conversation—about van, beards, and neck tattoos— was of no interest to me. I was in a bad mood. Here we were in Sweet Lady Em's stall, Sweet Lady Em being the source of my cream, but Sweet Lady Em was absent. The thoughtful thing on her part would have been to leave behind a bottle or two of cream, nice and fresh, but no. Instead we had this stinky cigar stub, which Bro seemed to find very interesting, and I most certainly did not.

"I'm not sure where you're going with this," Harmony said. She was speaking for both of us, and not for the first time.

"It was the morning all this started," Bro said. "Mom sent me over to see about the cream, and Jimmy and I went looking for Lady Em." Bro got a look in his eyes like he was gazing at something far away, but there was nothing to see except the rough wooden wall of the barn.

"And?" said Harmony.

"Well, they were changing the tire on the van."

"You mentioned that."

"We asked if they'd seen a cow. They said no. Then they finished changing the tire and drove off. But first Roscoe tossed his cigar stub into the bushes."

"He was smoking a cigar?"

"Like this one." Bro held up the cigar stub he'd found in the straw. "Didn't I say that?"

"Not exactly," said Harmony. Her eyes got very bright. "You're thinking DNA?"

"Yeah," Bro said. "Even if I don't know what it is."

"Genetic material," Harmony said. "Everyone's is different. It's in your sweat, your nail clippings, your—"

"Spit?"

"Uh-huh. So let's—"

"Go find that other cigar stub."

There's the human world and there's my world. Right now the human world seemed to be about cigar stubs. My world was about cream. Could we go home now? I'd had more than enough.

We didn't seem to be going home. Instead we were walking down a dirt road I didn't know, me not walking but in the backpack, the air cold and drizzly. I stuck a claw through the mesh of my little pocket—surprisingly strong mesh, as I already knew—while I sketched out a plan or two.

We rounded a bend. "Maybe here," Bro said, stopping by the remains of an old stone wall. Behind the wall stood a tall and skinny tree, its bare branches rattling in the wind. The sound irritated me, this middle-of-nowhere place irritated me, just about everything was irritating me right now. Except for me, of course, and Harmony and Bro, I suppose.

"There's bushes on both sides of the road," Harmony said.

"Yeah," said Bro.

"So which side?"

Bro's gaze went to the bushes on one side, and then the other. "Hmm," he said.

"The wall side?" said Harmony.

Bro squeezed his eyes shut.

"Yes? No?" said Harmony.

Bro opened his eyes. "I don't know," he said. "But he also tossed his coffee cup over the wall. So—"

"His DNA will be on it, too," Harmony said. "Mr. Carstairs can charge them with littering."

Bro gave her a long look. Then he started laughing. He laughed and laughed. "Maybe you're funny after all." He laughed some more.

"Give it a rest," said Harmony, moving around the wall, meaning I went, too, although I had no desire to see what was on the other side. But there was no missing the crumpled-up coffee cup, lying at the base of the tall, skinny tree. "Got it!" Harmony took a glove from her pocket, put it on, and picked up the coffee cup.

Bro came to look. He sniffed at the cup. Humans weren't good at sniffing scents, in my experience. Was Bro somehow an exception? I shifted around so I could see Harmony's face, and on it I caught a very quick look of enjoyment, like she was enjoying him sniffing at the coffee cup. And not just enjoyment: There was love, too. Harmony loved Bro? I'd never thought about that before. Did he love her? Quite possibly. This was all somewhat interesting, although not interesting enough to pursue. At least not now, when all I wanted was to go home.

But that didn't happen. Instead we began searching through the bushes, first on the wall side of the road and then on the other. And back to the wall side! Was this a kind of torture, dreamed up just for me? What was going on?

Bro turned to Harmony. "How about bringing Arthur here? He's good at things like this."

"He's good at finding food," Harmony said. "But yeah, why not?"

What was this? Arthur good at something? I made myself concentrate on this tedious matter of . . . what was it about again? Cigar butt in the bushes? Good grief. Who cared? But adding Arthur to the mix—just imagine how he'd prance around if he happened by total luck to actually stumble on this supposed cigar butt!—was an intolerable idea. I put my nose—my button nose, cute as cute can be, in case you need reminding—into a gap in the mesh and breathed in a bit of air. Not anything you'd call a sniff—that's not my style. I simply took in a gentle breath, and in that tiny stream of air passing through my nose there was a trace—faint but foul—of stale cigar. I followed the scent with my eyes, and sure enough there was the cigar butt, lying pretty much in plain sight on a soggy leaf. An old brown leaf left over from the fall and close to the color of the cigar butt, I suppose, but . . . but really. Can't we do better?

MEOW!

"Whoa!" said Bro. "What's with her?"

MEOW!

"Maybe she has to pee," Bro said.

Harmony shook her head. "She can hold on forever."

MEOW! MEOW! MEOW!

"But you could be right," Harmony added. And she pulled the Velcro strap on my pocket and in one quick and I'm sure very graceful movement I was out of there and on solid ground, free as a bird. Hmm. Interesting expression. Birds probably do think they're free, roaming around the big blue sky. Perhaps that's why they're always so surprised when I . . . introduce myself to them; let's put it that way.

Meanwhile although it's true I can hold on forever—as opposed to a certain party who hasn't quite made it to the door on many occasions, doing his business in my line of sight from up on the grandfather clock, our gazes often meeting, his guilty, hapless, and dumb, mine, well, aristocratic. But the point was I didn't need to pee at all right now. What I needed to do was put a stop to this cigar affair. An obvious way would have been to glide over to the cigar, pluck it off the leaf, and hold it up for all to see. Which would have meant allowing the odious thing to come in contact with my mouth. Out of the question.

Instead I walked in a casual circle, pausing here and there with one paw delicately raised—

"Is she deciding where to pee?" Bro said.

"I don't think so," said Harmony. "And she'd never let you see her pee."

"Why not me?"

"Anybody, Bro. Good grief! She won't let anybody see her pee."

—and finally sat down not far from the cigar butt. I love Harmony and Bro, but they weren't at their best right now. Why couldn't they wrap up this moronic back-and-forth and—

"Hey!" said Bro.

Finally.

Then came big excitement: the gathering up of the cigar stub, comparing it to the first one, blah blah blah about DNA, and who knows what else. I myself didn't actually catch the what-else part, but instead slipped silently away. Have I mentioned I wanted to go home?

I was some distance removed, sheltered in a thick grove of Christmas-type trees beside the road, when I heard faint voices crying, "Queenie! Queenie!"

Too late, my friends. I headed for home.

My plan was to head directly home, or as directly as possible. I'd never been on this dismal dirt road before, so the path from here to home was a bit of a mystery. No problem. All I had to do was follow my own scent trail all the way, a delightful prospect, since my scent happens to be . . . well, I won't describe it to you. Don't be offended, but you haven't got the nose to appreciate a scent like mine. I'm sure you're a very nice person otherwise, or at least somewhat nice.

Back to me, happily following my scent and looking forward to a lovely rest on my grandfather clock, or perhaps among the soft paperbacks on the Big Room bookshelf, when I suddenly picked up a mousy whiff. This mousy whiff was gamier than the mousy whiff down in the cellar, meaning we were dealing with a field mouse. What fun! Field mice were a little quicker than house mice in my experience, making our occasional playtime more sporting. Being a good sport was important. That's one of our family beliefs at the Blackberry Hill Inn.

I followed the scent of my field mouse buddy up a long rise, beyond the Christmas-type trees and into thick underbrush. The little scamp had spent a lot of time in this underbrush, darting here and darting there, god knows why, but at last he'd popped out and entered some woods, the trees mostly the kind that were bare in winter. His scent grew stronger and stronger and then there he was! Sitting at the edge of a small clearing, his paws up to his mouth, chewing away on some tiny treat. Just adorable! I got down low, low as a shadow, and slinked my way closer and closer, until I was right behind him in easy pouncing distance. Did I pounce right away? Would that be sporting? Instead I waited until he'd finished with his snack, then gathered myself into a powerful ball and—

Whoosh!

Whoosh? From directly at my back? At moments like this my body takes over. I sprang—not at the mouse, but sideways, as high and as far as I could. A red blur flew by just underneath me, the fur of that blur brushing my own fur. Fox! Oh, no. I'm not afraid of foxes, but if I were afraid of foxes I'd be very afraid. Big, quick, fast, smart, and sneaky. I know from experience. They can do everything I can do just as fast and just as quick, except for climbing trees, although the silver kind actually can climb trees, something I'd learned to my shock, and yes, horror, on a long-ago outing to the maple sugar forest beyond Willard's Pond, where I've never been again.

But this was the red kind of fox. I shot up the nearest tree. The fox's jaws snapped shut just short of my tail. That could have been very bad. My tail ends in a lovely golden tuft. I'd hate to lose that tuft. In fact, the moment I was settled on a thick, high branch, I twisted around to check it, and there it was, my golden tuft unharmed.

Down below, the fox was staring up at me, her eyes full of bad desires. And what was this? My mousy pal was still hanging around? Was that wise? Had it been me—

But too late for that thought. The fox, without seeming

even to have been aware of this third party, suddenly was way beyond mere awareness. I caught a brief glimpse of the mouse struggling between foxy jaws, and then: no more mouse. The fox trotted back and stood under my branch. She locked her eyes on me. The message couldn't have been more clear. Time passed. I wanted to be at home. Now and again, up there in the tree, I thought of making a quick break for it. Then I remembered the little mouse I'd never quite gotten to know, and stayed put.

It rained. It stopped raining. It rained again. The fox and I kept doing what we were doing. Was I hungry? Not a bit. Thirsty? Never! Well, actually yes and yes, but it was important to get the answer right, and the answer was no and no.

The rain turned to drizzle. The fox didn't move. Neither did I. And then, after the longest time, her ears twitched. She turned her head, and at that moment I heard human voices. I turned my head, too, to follow the sound. When I turned back, the fox was gone.

Three humans entered the clearing. Two were men, men I didn't know. But had I heard of them? Hadn't Bro been going on and on about two bushy-bearded men, one big, one small? Perhaps I should have paid more attention, but it really didn't seem very interesting at the time. Cigars, wasn't it? Cigars cigars cigars, ad nauseam, although I hadn't actually puked. No cigars in evidence now, but there was a hint of cigar in the air, rising from the beard of the small guy.

The third human was a woman I knew. It was Ms. Pryor.

TWENTY-THREE
QUEENIE

D O I STRIKE YOU AS THE SELFISH type? Of course not! And I'm sure you don't mind me answering for you. It will save time. I, Queenie, am not the selfish type. Instead I'm the type who . . . who does whatever unselfish types do. Such as . . . such as thinking of others! There we go. I knew something would come to me. I, Queenie, think of others. For example, here's a thought about others: What others would blame me—such a wonderful and superior creature, beauty on four legs—if I didn't bother to think about them? To think of myself for just one lousy darn minute, if you don't mind. Do I ask for much? Oh, far from it, and when I do I ask only for the simple things in life. Like being home. All I wanted was to go home! But was that happening? Oh, no, far from it. Instead I was still stuck in this stupid tree, while down below three unpleasant people were talking about unpleasant things in unpleasant voices.

Here's something I've learned about humans: The biggest

ones don't necessarily dominate. That's also true about what you humans like to call the animal world. As if you're not one of us. How amusing!

In this little scene we had one huge guy; one much shorter guy, although he was thickly built with lots of muscle; and Ms. Pryor. Ms. Pryor was taller than the short guy, but not nearly as tall as the huge guy, and much thinner than either of them. But she dominated completely. I could feel it.

"Summing up," she said, "the trustee turns out to be difficult."

"You want us to talk to her?" said the huge guy. Oh, dear. He had some sort of neck tattoo, curling up from under his jacket collar, a snake with enormous fangs. I've had several adventures with snakes, although none with enormous fangs, adventures that ended with my little snakeys lying very still. But who would want enormous fangs on their neck?

"Think for a moment, Curly," said Ms. Pryor. "How did your talk with Mr. Doone work out?"

"Hey! That wasn't on me. If Roscoe hadda just stuck with the program—"

"Oh, sure," said the smaller guy, Roscoe no doubt. "Put it all on me. Who was the one that got him all riled up? I had to grab that bat just to defend myself."

Curly laughed a nasty laugh. "Defend yourself? That's a good one."

Roscoe's face got purple. He took a step toward Curly. "Watch it, Curly, or I'll—"

"Neither of you will do a single thing without my say-so," said Ms. Pryor. "Now shut your ignorant mouths."

Both their mouths happened to be hanging open when Ms. Pryor spoke. They got them closed, closed nice and tight and in a hurry. Ms. Pryor glared at them.

"Do you understand the potential jeopardy you're in?" she said.

Curly and Roscoe gazed at her, Curly's face going from purple to ash-colored. Roscoe's eyes shifted, and he was shifty-eyed to begin with. "If we're in jeopardy, so are you."

"That's your problem, right there," Ms. Pryor said. "Do you know why Curly gets paid more than you?"

"He does?" Roscoe gave Curly an angry look. "Then you lied to me, you—" And he called Curly a name that won't be repeated here.

"It's not my fault, Roscoe," Curly said. "She told me—"

"Zip it," Ms. Pryor said.

Curly zipped it.

"The reason Curly gets a fatter paycheck," Ms. Pryor said, "is simple. He's stupid and knows he's stupid. You're stupid but think you're smart. That's the only kind of person who can imagine that I'd somehow be in jeopardy, too."

"But—but—but we were just following your orders!" Roscoe said.

"Which were quote to negotiate discreetly with Mr. Doone, end quote," said Ms. Pryor. "I have it on tape."

"Whoa!" said Curly. "Negotiate discreetly's what you always say. But you wink your eye at the same time."

"Is that so?" said Ms. Pryor. "There's no wink on the recording."

Now Roscoe's face went ashy, too, just like Curly's.

"But let's not fight, boys," Ms. Pryor said. "Everything's going to work out just fine. Our problem is this kid, Jimmy. The trustee isn't going to make any moves until she talks to him. Right now he's in the wind. Our yokel deputy has expanded the search to neighboring counties, but I'm just not feeling it. I'm thinking that he's hiding out somewhere nearby, maybe getting help from a buddy. Actually two buddies. We could . . . involve the buddies, but I'd prefer we find the kid ourselves. So you two are going to comb these woods, from the state road, past the inn, and up to the farm. Got it?"

The men nodded.

"Any questions?" Ms. Pryor said. "Go on, Roscoe, I know you've got at least one. I won't bite."

Roscoe hesitated. Maybe he was thinking that in fact Ms. Pryor would bite. I know I was. At last, he said, "But what if we find him and he doesn't want to sell?"

"That's a smart question," Ms. Pryor said. "The kind of question that can fatten a paycheck one day." She gazed into the woods. "I've been thinking about that poor kid." Curly and Roscoe looked a little puzzled at that, but Ms. Pryor didn't notice. "My take is that he was a little disturbed to begin with, due to his family situation. And he's at a vulnerable age. Check out the statistics on child runaways. Not pleasant reading." She turned to the men. "Still, I'd be shocked if you found that something terrible had happened to him."

The men were silent.

Ms. Pryor winked.

Not long after that, Ms. Pryor was gone, but Curly and Roscoe were still standing under my tree.

"What're we gonna do?" Curly said.

"Is there a choice?" said Roscoe.

They turned and started walking deeper into the woods. I had no desire to go deeper into the woods. I wanted to leave these woods, maybe forever, and simply GO HOME! But I climbed off my branch, down the trunk, leaping the last bit, and followed Curly and Roscoe. Why? I actually didn't know. Let's just say that my paws—probably the most beautifully shaped paws in creation—wanted to go that way, and I went with them.

Curly and Roscoe were not the silent-moving types. Maybe they didn't know how. They wore big boots that thump-thump-thumped on the damp ground, they bumped into everything possible, and they hardly ever shut their mouths. I followed in silence, behind bushes, over rocks, along the occasional branch, never on the path. I take pride in things. These two did not.

"What could we have done different?" Roscoe said.

"You not taking that bat to him might have been a start," said Curly.

"He came right at me! Maybe if you hadn't of told him he'd get that cow back if he cooperated, he wouldn't have gone off like he did."

"Huh? That was the assignment, you moron! He says yes to the offer, he gets his freakin' cow back. Turns it down and there's worse to come. That's all we did. Our job."

Roscoe poked Curly in the chest. "Who's calling who a moron?"

And they went back and forth on who was a moron and who wasn't. I tuned out. My mind was on the cow. Sometimes in this life all becomes clear, and all at once.

This was one of those times. These two . . . what would you call them? Bad men? Yes, these two bad men had stolen my cow. Not only that, but they knew where she was! No, they hadn't exactly said that last part. I'd made a mental leap. I'm a first-class leaper, physically and mentally.

Curly and Roscoe ended up deciding that neither of them was a moron—proving the opposite, in my opinion— and moved on. I moved with them.

"What about the kid?" Curly said.

"Huh? Weren't you listening? We gotta find him."

"Not that kid. The other one."

"Walter?" Roscoe said. "He's gone to Maine or wherever he came from."

"But what if he comes back?"

"Why would he do that? It'd be asking for trouble. We paid him good money—and all he had to do was unlock that door."

"I don't like loose ends," Curly said.

"Your whole life is loose ends," Roscoe said.

And they grumbled on and on. After a while, the woods started to seem familiar. Were we near the tree house? I thought so. Was that a good thing? No.

"Course he's—what's the word?" Curly said as they started up a long rise, huffing and puffing a bit, I myself not huffing and puffing in the slightest. I've never huffed and puffed in my whole life, don't really understand what either of them—the huffing or the puffing—actually is.

"What are you talking about?" Roscoe said, huff huff, puff puff.

"Walter," said Curly, huff huff, puff puff. "He's . . . he's, you know, tied up in this just like us."

Through the gap in the trees I saw a clearing opening up, a clearing I knew. On the other side was the tree house.

"Implicated," Roscoe said.

"Yeah, that's the word."

"Curly? Try not to think."

They entered the clearing. I circled right around, stopping beside a mossy rock very near the tree house. Jimmy was inside: I could smell him.

"What are we looking for?" Curly said.

"Anyplace the kid could be hiding," said Roscoe. "A cave, a woodpile, an old shack."

"And when we find him? Fake a suicide? How does that work?"

"It'll work, but I've got something better. And easier. That creek's not far from here, half a mile or less."

"He drowns?"

"A sad accident. On the run in the dark. Slips and falls in. Finito. Now we just gotta find him."

They glanced around the clearing, their bushy beards matted with rain, a very unpleasant sight. Any second now they were going to look up, and when they did they'd spot the tree house. Still, I might not have done what I did if it hadn't been for those ugly, wet beards. I live for beauty.

Which is why I sprang off my rock, flew across the clearing, and bit Roscoe on the back of his leg, just above the top of his boot. The calf, I believe? Very suitable for biting. My teeth—no, not huge, but as sharp as sharp gets, my friends—sank in nice and deep.

"Arrghh!" screamed Roscoe. And "Aiieee!"

Curly saw what had happened and aimed a powerful kick in my direction. Powerful, yes, but oh, so slow. I could have twisted around, leaped up behind him, and bit his calf, too, and way more than once. Which I didn't do, not the way-more-than-once part, restricting myself to one bite only. But a perfect bite, deep and, well, savage. A bite to remember!

"Arrghh! Aiieee!"

And then Roscoe grabbed a stick and Curly drew a tire iron from inside his jacket and they charged after me. I ran out of the clearing and into the woods. But nowhere near my fastest. I didn't want them to lose hope, not until we were far far away.

■ ■ ■

I came back much later, and alone. Jimmy was climbing down from the tree house slowly and with a lot of nervous looking around. Then he spotted me.

"Queenie? Queenie!"

He hopped down to the ground, crouched in front of me, his eyes wide open and worried. "What happened? Did they hurt you?"

Ha. That was a good one.

"Oh, I wish you could talk, Queenie."

He did? How strange! I had no desire to talk. Even if I could, I wouldn't.

He stroked my back. "What are you doing out here alone?"

I welcomed the question. The answer was: I'M TRYING TO GET HOME.

Jimmy peered into the woods. "They'll be coming back for sure. We can't stay here. But where should we go?"

HOME.

I scrambled up on Jimmy's shoulder. "You're funny," he said. An odd thought, but if Jimmy wanted to think it, I had no objection. I liked Jimmy.

He rose and left the clearing, me on his shoulder, nice and comfy, and we headed off in the opposite direction from where I'd had my fun little chase with Curly and Roscoe. The drizzle died away and things got very quiet.

Then, in the distance, I heard voices, two voices to be exact, voices I knew very well.

"Queenie! Queenie! Queenie!"

The very woods were ringing with the sound of my name. How thoughtful!

TWENTY-FOUR
ARTHUR

SOMETIMES—MAYBE MOST OF THE time—it's best to just kick back and not exert yourself too much. One way of not exerting myself that never gets old is to sit by the window at the back of the Big Room and gaze out. When that grows too tiring, all you have to do is close your eyes and lie down. Anyone can do it!

So there I was, all by myself at the window in the Big Room, eyeing the scenery, meaning the bird feeder, the flower beds, the apple trees, and beyond them our meadow and finally the woods. No birds at the feeder, no flowers in their beds, no apples on the trees, no action in the meadow, the woods misty and still. In short, not a very demanding view, which happened to suit me just fine at the moment. I wriggled around a bit and was getting even more comfortable when suddenly we had some action after all. From out of the woods came three people. Even though they were too far away for me to see their faces, I knew who they were just from how they moved. Hey! Where had I learned to do that? I couldn't remember. In fact, I couldn't remember how I'd ever learned anything.

Back to the three people: Bro and Harmony, with Jimmy in the middle. My tail started up right away, swishing back and forth across the floor. Sometimes my tail has a lot more energy than I do. Lucky tail. But I don't feel jealous of my tail, not one little bit. I'm happy for it. Go, tail!

Maybe I got distracted by my tail. When I went back to taking in the view, Harmony, Bro, and Jimmy were already in the apple orchard. That was when I noticed one other party in the mix. Why wasn't there a backpack with a mesh pocket for me? I was trying to figure out how to make someone think, *Hey, how about a nice backpack with a mesh pocket for old Arthur*, when they came out of the orchard, moving quickly now, and headed for the bulkhead doors.

The bulkhead doors stick out from the foundation of the house, not far from the back door. They lead to a flight of worn stone stairs that take you down to the basement, and maybe had something to do with deliveries in the old days, whenever those might have been. You can get to those worn stone stairs from inside the house, too. All you have to do is run to the back hall like so, or walk quickly, like I was actually doing, then take the stairs into the new part of the

250

basement, go past the small wood-paneled room that Dad and Lilah Fairbanks had been making into a wine cellar, even though—as I overheard Mom telling Dad—we had no wine collection and served breakfast only, and then there you were, at the bottom of the stairs to the bulkhead doors.

"Hey, here's Arthur," Bro said as he led the others into the basement.

"Shh," said Harmony.

Was I being noisy? Oh, no. I'd never want to displease Harmony. I lay flat down.

"What's with him?" Bro whispered.

"No clue," whispered Harmony. She motioned for Jimmy. Everyone went into the wine cellar. I got up and followed them, my every movement slow and cautious. When we were all inside, Bro closed the wine cellar door.

Then all eyes—excepting Queenie's, which were almost completely shut, just one of her many bothersome looks—were on me.

"Is he sick?" Bro said.

"He's acting drugged or something," said Harmony.

"Arthur," Bro said. "Lie on your back."

I lay on my back. Bro reached down and scratched my belly. All my paws started twitching like crazy.

"He's fine," Bro said.

He and Harmony turned to Jimmy. Jimmy was gazing

around the room, an empty room except for partly built shelves on one wall.

"What is this place?" he said.

"Nothing," Bro said.

"But it was going to be a wine cellar," Harmony said.

"It's nothing," Bro said.

They exchanged a look unlike any I remembered between them. Not unfriendly or angry, also not particularly friendly. I had no desire ever to see it again.

Harmony went closer to Jimmy. "The point is you'll be safe. No one comes here. There's just the laundry room, and it's the other way. The bathroom's down to the right. We'll bring you what you need."

"What about your mom?" Jimmy said. "Are you going to tell her?"

"I don't know," Harmony said.

"No," said Bro.

"Which is it?" Jimmy said.

"She knows you're innocent," said Harmony.

Jimmy shook his head. He had big circles under his eyes, maybe had lost some weight, was trembling the tiniest bit. I could feel that last part more than I could see it. All at once, I wished I'd learned the shake-a-paw trick. I'd tried and tried, first with Bro and then with Harmony, but I'd never gotten the hang of it.

"She'll tell Carstairs," Jimmy said.

"She won't," said Harmony.

"She won't want to, but she will," Jimmy said. "There'll be all these reasons."

"Like what?" Bro said.

Jimmy shrugged. "I don't know. Adult reasons. It's okay if you tell her. You have"—he shivered, a tiny shiver of the kind that usually went with a sob, but there was no sobbing—"a good relationship with your mom." He took a deep breath. "But I need to know if you're going to tell her."

"Because then you'll leave?" Harmony said.

Jimmy nodded.

"Leave?" said Bro. "And go where?"

"I'll be all right," Jimmy said. "I can take care of myself."

Harmony's voice didn't rise, but now she sounded angry. Had that ever happened before? "Jimmy! You're not answering the question."

"If I knew where I'd go, why would I tell anyone?" Jimmy said.

Then came a silence. Queenie stuck a claw through a hole in her mesh pocket.

"We won't tell my mom," Harmony said.

Bro nodded.

Jimmy held out his hand. Bro clasped Jimmy's hand and Harmony laid her hand on both of theirs. At that moment

Queenie did one of her meows, a sound that gives me a bad feeling up and down my back.

"Maybe she wants to stay with me," Jimmy said.

"Yeah?" said Harmony and Bro together.

Harmony unsnapped the Velcro tab on the mesh pocket. Queenie slid out, sort of hovered down to the floor—does she move like that just to annoy me?—and went to the far corner, where she sat down and closed her eyes to tiny slits. Why is it so hard to relax around her? Relaxing is . . . is the foundation of my life!

"Okay, then," said Harmony.

I followed Bro and Harmony out of the wine cellar and down the hall to the back stairs. Bro put his foot on the first step and paused.

"This feels bad," he said.

"I know," said Harmony.

"Mom's smart."

"I know."

"We should tell her."

"I know."

"But we'd have to tell Jimmy."

"I know."

"Stop saying you know."

"What do you want me to say?"

"Something that helps."

The looks on their faces said Harmony and Bro didn't like each other. I hated that. Was it all because this conversation was so confusing? That was my take. I hoped they'd move on to something else. Bacon was a good subject, for example.

"All right," Harmony said, "how about this? Telling Mom means we're putting the burden on her. Is that fair?"

"She is the mom," Bro said.

"Meaning she has to carry the load forever?"

"Well, not forever."

"Till when?" Harmony said. "We're not babies, Bro."

"Speak for yourself," said Bro.

And even though serious, maybe even dangerous, things seemed to be going on, Harmony laughed.

From the top of the stairs, Mom called, "What's the joke?"

The looks on the faces of Bro and Harmony at that moment! Scared out of their minds. Of Mom? I didn't get it.

Mom came down the stairs, a basket of laundry in her arms. "Tell me," she said. "I could use a laugh or two."

"Uh," said Bro. "Um."

"It was just Bro being funny," said Harmony.

"What's the punch line?" Mom said. "'Uh' or 'um'?"

"Ha-ha-ha," went the kids.

"Am I missing something?" Mom said.

"You know Bro," Harmony said.

"I *think* I do." Mom gave Bro a narrow-eyed look, then turned it on Harmony and kept it there longer. "Okay," she said, "what I need is one of you to help with the laundry." Then, even though I hadn't moved a muscle or done anything in the slightest to attract her attention, her eyes were on me. "And the other one takes Arthur on a nice long walk. He needs the exercise."

"Laundry," Bro said.

"Arthur," said Harmony.

Mom looked surprised. "Really?"

"Don't let him near the bleach," Harmony said.

I'd already had plenty of exercise these past few days, way more than enough! More than enough exercise had to be bad for you, stands to reason, too much of anything is bad for you. Except for treats, of course.

"Arthur?" Harmony said as we went past the village green. "If you don't stop dogging it, I'm putting you on the leash."

But . . . but dogging was the only way I knew how! This was maybe the most confusing moment of my life, and then, the very next moment, more bad news. Harmony looked down at me and said, "What we're doing now, Arthur, is a kind of end run."

256

We were going to run? Walking was bad enough, but running? I thought right away of the time Bertha decided to enter the Halloween 5K race, and Mom suggested she take me along on her training runs. A nightmare. And now Harmony. I got ready for torment.

But no torment happened. We kept walking, and after a while Harmony said, "To tell Mom or not to tell Mom. That's the problem. An end run is maybe how we make the problem disappear. See what I mean?"

I did not. The only part I understood was Mom. I loved Mom.

"We won't even have to make the choice," Harmony said as we walked up to a brick building with a blue light over the door. "If this works, the problem goes away." She opened the door and we went inside.

We were in a small lobby with a counter at one end. Behind the counter sat a uniformed woman. She gazed down at us, not with the friendly-type gaze I like to see.

"Something I can help you with?"

"I'd like to see Mr. Carstairs," Harmony said.

The woman gave Harmony a closer look. "Are you Emma's friend? From the inn?"

"Yes, ma'am," Harmony said.

The woman didn't actually smile, but her face relaxed a bit. "Can I tell him what it's about?"

"Business," Harmony said.

"What kind of business?"

"Police business."

The unfriendly look came back. The woman rose, went to a door behind her, poked her head inside, and said something I didn't catch. Then came the voice of Deputy Carstairs.

"Send her in."

A moment later we were in his office. The deputy was studying a big wall map. He turned and said, "This is a nice surprise. You two out for a walk? If I knew you were coming, I'd have let Emma know."

"I'm here about Jimmy," Harmony said.

Carstairs went still, just for a second. "Oh?" he said. "I'm all ears. Take a seat."

He sat behind his desk. Harmony sat in the visitor's chair. I sat beside her on the floor, a linoleum floor, not that comfortable, but from there I had a good view of the deputy's ears. They were on the small side, even for a human. He wasn't close to being all ears. I realized something very important about Deputy Carstairs: He couldn't be trusted.

For a moment, Harmony just sat there, with me beside her, of course. She sat very straight like always—maybe even straighter—but I could smell she was getting a bit nervous. I wasn't used to nervousness from Harmony.

Finally she put on one of her gloves, reached into her jacket pocket, and took out two cigar butts. Cigar butts? Had I come upon a cigar butt recently? Harmony had my attention!

She laid the cigar butts on Deputy Carstairs's desk.

"What have we here?" He wrinkled his nose, not a good look on him.

The golden glints in Harmony's dark eyes brightened. "Evidence," she said.

"Yeah?" said Carstairs, and he gave Harmony a smile, the kind of smile you see on adult faces when kids are being cute. "Can I ask of what?"

Harmony gave him a direct look. "A terrible crime," she said.

The smile stayed on Carstairs's face. "And what crime would that be?"

"The attack on Mr. Doone," said Harmony. She leaned forward. "There are actually two crimes, Mr. Carstairs. The first one was the stealing of Sweet Lady Em."

"Excuse me?" said Carstairs.

And Harmony started in on a long explanation, all about the cow that I'd been looking for, two dudes with neck tattoos who I knew, and lots of stuff I didn't get at all: how two crimes at the same place on the same day had to be connected, how the cow thieves had to be the attackers, and DNA. There was more, but it went by too fast.

"So," said Carstairs, leaning back in his chair, still smiling, "what you want me to do is send these"—he nodded at the cigar butts—"down to the lab, see if we get a match to some bad guy in the system?"

"Yes," Harmony said. "And also send out an announcement, like on TV and the internet, that Jimmy is innocent and you're looking for two guys with bushy beards and neck tattoos."

Carstairs's smile faded away. "Given any thought to what you want to be when you grow up, Harmony?"

"Maybe a hockey player," Harmony said.

"Uh-huh," said Carstairs. "But if that falls through, consider law enforcement. You've got the mind for it."

"Thanks."

Carstairs stroked his chin. "So let's put that mind to work on another part of this problem. If you had to guess, where do you think Jimmy might be?"

All at once I could hear Harmony's heart pitter-pattering in her chest. "I . . . I don't know."

"Let's think it through with that fine mind of yours. Does it make sense that he's out there all alone? What's he doing for food? And shelter? It's still below freezing most nights."

Harmony didn't answer. Suddenly she was watching Carstairs very carefully.

"Or is it more likely," Carstairs went on, "that he found someone to help him? Maybe his mother, somewhere in California, when last heard of?"

Harmony shook her head.

"Or his uncle in Dubai?"

She shook her head again.

"Or would it be someone much closer to home? Did Jimmy turn to a well-meaning friend—or two, or even three—in his time of need?"

Harmony met his gaze. I could feel the effort in her, like she was standing up to a very strong wind. "But how does any of that matter now? Once you get the DNA results—"

The desk phone buzzed and the voice of the uniformed woman came over the speaker. "Mayor on line one."

Carstairs picked up the phone. He gave Harmony a cold look, then made a little finger gesture for us to leave.

We left. Carstairs's eyes were on us until the door closed. I could feel them. Part of me wanted to get out of there. Another part did not. I'd smelled a biscuit in his desk drawer from the get-go and hadn't given up hope. What was the point of even having biscuits in a drawer if they never came out? This visit hadn't gone well.

TWENTY-FIVE

QUEENIE

"M OM?" BRO SHOUTED FROM THE laundry room. "What does it mean when all the lights start flashing?"

The laundry room was far away from Mom, probably working at her desk, so she didn't hear, but I, sitting beside Jimmy in the wine cellar, heard loud and clear. Jimmy was lying on the floor beside me, eyes open and staring as though at something distant. I rose and went to the door. I hadn't thought of laundry in some time, but it's a particular interest of mine, relaxing in a pile of laundry being one of life's small pleasures. I went to the door. Some humans have big problems when it comes to taking care of my needs, but not Jimmy. He rose right away and let me out.

I headed toward the laundry room, but before I got there, the back door opened and Harmony and a certain party came in from outside, the certain party huffing and puffing, his strangely enormous tongue hanging way out. I followed them into the laundry room.

"Bro?" Harmony said. "What's with all the foam?"

"It's soap. There's supposed to be foam."

"Not all over the floor," Harmony said. "Arthur! Stop that!"

Why would Arthur be slurping up mouthfuls of foam? Couldn't he tell from the smell that it was going to disagree with him? Arthur's inner workings—if any—were a mystery to me, although not one I cared about.

". . . didn't seem interested in the cigars," Harmony was saying.

"Why not?" said Bro.

"I don't know." Harmony grabbed a mop, started mopping very hard, like she was mad at all the foam. "Well, I guess I do know." She set the mop aside. "He still thinks Jimmy did it. Plus he knows we're helping him."

"He does?"

"Not really," Harmony said. "More like he senses it. It's kind of creepy."

"So what are we going to do?"

"There's only one thing to do," Harmony said. And then they spoke as one person with two voices:

"Solve the case!"

For some reason, that got Arthur's attention. He lost interest in the foam and started prancing around the laundry room, poking his nose into this and that, and suddenly snatching up a red ball from a pile of soggy towels. A strange red ball. It was making a very faint beep beep, right on the edge of what I can hear.

"What's that ball?" Bro said.

Harmony shrugged. "Some ball. He loves balls."

"But it's beeping," Bro said.

"It is?"

"You don't hear it?"

"Arthur," Harmony said. "Give me the ball."

Oh, the tedium! Arthur, give me the ball—like that was going to work. Had Harmony forgotten that one of Arthur's favorite games was don't give them the ball, but shake your head and circle around and clamp it tightly between your jaws and look like an idiot? I'll spare you the description of what went on in the laundry room. Harmony ended up with the ball.

She wiped it off—it badly needed wiping—and held it to her ear. "I don't hear anything."

"Huh?" said Bro. "It's going beep beep beep. I can hear it from here."

Just then Mom looked in. She took in the foamy situation but all she said was, "Everything under control?"

"Yup," said Bro. "But what's this ball?"

"Arthur loves that ball. He found it down at Willard's Pond."

"It beeps," Bro said.

"It does?" said Mom. "Let's see." Mom held the red ball to her ear. "I don't hear it."

This was interesting. Bro and I heard the ball. Mom and Harmony did not. Arthur doesn't have much going on inside his head, but the outside parts—ears and nose, for example—work very well. Therefore it was likely that Arthur, too, heard the beep, putting me in a group with Bro and Arthur. What did that mean?

"What's the deal with Willard's Pond?" Harmony said.

"I suppose it belonged to the Willards at one time, but now it's town land," Mom said.

"I didn't mean that," said Harmony. "Is it connected to Blackberry Creek?"

"It didn't used to be," Mom said. "But they dredged a channel during the Depression. It was part of the recovery program." She held the ball to her ear again and shook her head. "Are you sure, Bro?"

She tossed him the ball. He held it to his ear. "It stopped."

"Hmm," said Mom.

A little later we were in the kitchen, me and the kids, Arthur having fallen asleep in some random spot the way he does. Bro was eating a sandwich—peanut butter and cucumber slices, one of those odd Bro creations, and Harmony was gazing at the red ball, which sat on the counter.

"You don't believe I heard a beep?" Bro said. Or something like that—hard to tell with the inside of his mouth all clogged with peanut butter.

"I do," Harmony said. "That's the point."

"The point of what?"

"The disappearance of Sweet Lady Em, the attack on Mr. Doone, and now this."

"Huh?" said Bro.

"They're all puzzles. Puzzles coming all at once, in the same place and time."

"So?"

"So we should investigate this ball."

"Want me to saw it in half?"

"I was thinking of something more . . ."

"Subtle?"

Harmony smiled. "Exactly."

Bro took a bite of his sandwich and said something that sounded like "We could grbbrr fromersh."

Harmony didn't say anything, just watched Bro eating. When he'd swallowed his mouthful he tried again.

"We could show it to Maxie."

Harmony nodded.

Harmony rang the bell of a little white house that faced the village green. The door opened and a woman looked out.

She had a small paintbrush in her hand, a smear of blue paint on the tip of her nose, and a surprised look on her face.

"Is Maxie home?" Harmony said.

"Why, yes," said the woman. "You must be the Reddy twins. Harmony and . . . ?"

"Bro," said Bro.

The woman blinked a few times, very fast. "Right, and Bro. I'm Max's mom."

"Nice to meet you, Mrs. Millipat," Harmony said.

"You can call me Bettina," said Mrs. Millipat. "Max often mentions you. He says you're going to be big league ballplayers."

"I don't know about that," Harmony said.

"Did you want him to come out and play some ball? That would be nice. We're not what you'd call an athletic family. Why, I didn't even know what balls and strikes were until Max explained it the other day, and to tell you the truth"—she lowered her voice like a secret was coming—"I still don't understand."

"Um," Bro said. "Maybe later, Mrs. Millipat. Baseball and all that. Right now we'd just like to see him."

"Of course, of course, come on—"

That was when Mrs. Millipat first noticed me, waiting patiently in my mesh pocket.

"Is that a cat?"

"Her name's Queenie," Harmony said.

"Oh, dear," Mrs. Millipat said. "Captain Eddie gets nervous when cats are around."

"Captain Eddie?" said Harmony.

"I'm actually painting him as we speak." Mrs. Millipat gestured with the paintbrush. She peered at me. The surprised look was still on her face. I wondered if it was a permanent feature. "Can he get out of there?"

He? Good grief.

"Queenie's a she," Harmony said. "And she likes it in the pocket."

"I suppose it will be all right, then."

We went inside. First there was a little hall, and then the living room. An easel stood by the window and beside the easel, on a wooden perch, was a very large bird, mostly blue except for some yellow tufts spreading from its head.

"Captain Eddie," Mrs. Millipat said. "Isn't he the most gorgeous thing you've ever seen?"

Far far from it. Captain Eddie was aware of me immediately. His wings fluttered and he did look nervous, as promised. As well he might! A bird indoors! My goodness. Did I like my chances? Bet the ranch, people. I'd never even heard of Maxie until today. What a shame! But that could be fixed in the future. I'm the type who looks on the bright side.

"Max!" Mrs. Millipat called. "Some friends to see you."

From somewhere in the back of the house came a voice. "Friends?"

"He's in his lab," Mrs. Millipat said. She pointed down a corridor. "Last door on the left."

"Hey!" said Maxie, a bony sort of kid with a bunch of pens in his shirt pocket. "Hi! Hey!" He made his skinny little hand into a fist like maybe fist bumping was a good idea, then reconsidered and put his hand behind his back. "What're you guys doing here?"

"Visiting," Bro said.

"You've got your own lab, Maxie?" said Harmony.

I'd never been in a lab before. This one had a workbench with drones and pieces of drones, and parts of things I didn't recognize, plus lots of wires, cables, and a whole row of monitors.

"No chemistry experiments underway at the moment," Maxie said. "That came to an unfortunate . . . well, sort of end, at least for now. These days I'm working on drone coordination—getting a whole flight of drones to conduct maneuvers on their own, like a squadron of F-18s—but my long-term goal is time travel."

"Take me with you," Harmony said.

For a moment, Maxie looked surprised, just like his mom. But in his case, the expression didn't stay there. He laughed, turned red, laughed some more. "Cool," he said, like he was learning a new word. "That's cool. You guys are cool."

"Let's not get crazy," Bro said. "What do you make of this?"

He tossed Maxie the red ball. Some humans are good at catching things and make it look easy. Others can catch but not make it look easy. Some can't catch. That was Maxie's group. He dropped the red ball. It didn't bounce, just landed on the floor with a soft thud. Maxie picked it up. He turned it in his hand, studied it, poked at it, sniffed at it, held it to his ear.

"Hear it beeping?" Bro said.

"Nope."

"It beeps sometimes."

"I'm not surprised," said Maxie. "This is a very interesting ball."

"In what way?" Harmony said.

"That remains to be seen. But for example." He turned the ball this way and that, then pressed his finger into one side, just the very tip, a quick little poke. A tiny white flag popped up on the surface of the ball. SPRONGGG. It quivered for a moment and went still.

"Whoa!" Bro said. "What's going on?"

"Plenty." Maxie's eyes glittered. "Where did you get this?"

"Arthur found it," Bro told him.

"Who's Arthur?"

"Our dog."

That was when Maxie looked my way for the first time. "I always wanted a dog." At that moment I knew I had no use for Maxie. "I wanted a dog, but we got Captain Eddie."

"We've met," Bro said.

"He can say 'Do you wanna dance,'" Maxie said. "It was funny at first." He turned back to the ball, poked it again. This time nothing happened.

"Arthur found it in Willard's Pond," Harmony said. "Willard's Pond is connected to Blackberry Creek."

"Why are you telling me that?" Maxie said.

"I don't really know. It's on my mind."

Maxie glanced at her. "Connected above or below the falls?" he said.

"Below," said Harmony.

Maxie opened a drawer, rooted around inside, produced a small gizmo, black and silver.

"What's that?" Bro said.

"My own invention," said Maxie. "I call it the bloodsucker."

He held the bloodsucker very close to the red ball. Nothing happened. Then came some very faint sounds, a click, a whir, another click, and a tiny square panel on the surface of the red ball, previously invisible, swung open. A voice spoke. This was the kind of voice you heard in some houses, although not ours, a voice that sounded from speakers you might not even see, a voice with a name like Siri or Alexa.

The voice inside the red ball said, "Catastrophe Falls." The kids looked at each other, Harmony and Bro amazed, Maxie sort of . . . cool.

There was a long pause, and then the voice said, "Mellontic data collection." More clicks and whirs followed that, and then the ball went silent.

"Mellontic?" said Harmony.

"We can look it up," Maxie said. He turned to a monitor, tapped on a keyboard. "Here we go. *Mellontikos* means 'future' in Greek."

"So this is some kind of data collection in the future?" said Bro.

"I don't know," said Maxie. "Let's see if we can check out the data collection part." He searched through another drawer, found another little gizmo, this one a sort of gold prong. He stuck the end of the prong in the open panel of the red ball.

The voice spoke. "Welcome, Ottoline. Here are your test results, covering power, distance, volume, flow, height, velocity, and kilowatt hour projection, with allowances for seasonal variation and climate change." And then line after line of incomprehensible squiggles began scrolling down the screen.

"Well well," said Maxie.

"Well well what?" Harmony said. Sometimes, like now, she gets an impatient look on her face, all the features sharpening. It makes her even more beautiful, in my opinion. Nothing wrong with a little bit of temper—but only in the right sort of person, of course.

Maxie tapped the monitor. "Any guesses what this is about?"

"Maxie?" Harmony said. There was something you might call threatening in her tone. Just when you think Harmony can't get any better, she does.

"Uh, let me tell you," Maxie said quickly. "All that code, all those numbers—they're all about measuring the potential power of Catastrophe Falls."

"Power for what?" said Bro.

Maxie's eyebrows, maybe the thickest I'd seen on a kid, rose. "To make electricity, what else?" he said. "Like Niagara Falls, but way smaller. Falling water spins turbine blades, just like on a wind farm, except the wind only blows sometimes and a waterfall never stops."

The squiggly action on the screen certainly wasn't

stopping. Line after line kept going by real fast, a bit nauseating, actually. I looked away.

"Someone wants to sell electricity?" Bro said.

"Maybe," said Maxie. "Or use it themselves."

"For what?" said Bro.

"I know what I'd use it for," Maxie said, "if I had a big-time operation."

"What kind of operation?" Bro said.

"Tech," said Maxie. "For something really big you need a lot of servers. I'm talking thousands, tens of thousands, even more. And they all run on electricity. Supply your own electricity, you save big big bucks."

"But why?" Bro said. "Why all of this?"

"Not following you, Broster," said Maxie. Bro shot Maxie a look. "I mean Bro," Maxie said. "Not following you, Bro."

"Bro's point," said Harmony, "is that Catastrophe Falls is on land belonging to the Doones."

Bro nodded. "Which kind of means Jimmy, for now."

Harmony nodded. "And Jimmy's not a tech company."

"Hmm," said Maxie. He gazed at the screen. Around then the squiggles came to a stop. The voice inside the red ball spoke again.

"That concludes the report. Have a nice day, Ottoline."

"Is that a name?" Bro said.

"Auto like car?" said Maxie.

"O-T-T-O," Harmony said. "Ottoline's a woman's name, not common. But if there is some tech company involved, then she probably works for it."

"Hey!" Maxie said. "I've got an idea."

He turned to the red ball, held his finger to the white flag. "Hi," he said. "It's me, Ottoline. I need to make sure you've got our full company name right. Can you repeat it? Thanks, and have a nice day yourself."

Maxie looked up, pretty pleased with himself. Harmony and Bro seemed pleased with him, too. They all gazed at the red ball.

For a few moments there was no action. Then there was plenty. First the white flag turned red. Then it furled up and withdrew, back down into the ball and out of sight. After that a horrible alarm went off in the ball, like sirens in my skull, the most awful sound I'd ever heard. It only ended when the ball burst into flames.

Maxie ran to the corner, grabbed a fire extinguisher, and ran back. By that time there was no more red ball, just a little pile of ashes, snow white.

From outside the door came the voice of Mrs. Millipat.

"Max? I hope you're not doing any chemistry in there. You promised."

"Everything's all right, Mom," Maxie said. "It's just physics."

TWENTY-SIX
ARTHUR

WE WERE IN THE KITCHEN, MOM and me. There's a very small TV that Bertha sometimes watches while she's working. The rest of the time it lives in one of the cupboards, but now Mom was watching it. She hardly ever watches TV, and never in the kitchen.

". . . still no sign of the young man, James Doone, officially called a person of interest in the assault on his father, Gorman Doone, still in a coma at Regional Hospital. Our reporter caught up with Deputy Sheriff Al Carstairs." I glanced at the screen. There was Deputy Carstairs talking to a woman with a microphone. "Are you searching for anyone else?" the reporter said.

"Not at this time, no," said Carstairs. "But if Jimmy sees this, I want to say to him, Jimmy, you're not safe out there, wherever you are. Please, for your own good, come forward and identify yourself to the nearest law enforcement officer."

"But if you're not looking for anyone else," the reporter said, "isn't it fair to say that Jimmy is a suspect?"

Carstairs frowned at her. "He is not a suspect at this time. He's a person of—"

Mom snapped off the TV, put it back in the cupboard, closed the door. Closed it firmly. You could almost say slamming it, but Mom wasn't a door slammer. Meanwhile it was getting dark outside. That meant one thing and one thing only. I ambled over toward my bowls in the corner in an ungreedy-like way. Water bowl full, food bowl empty. These were metal bowls that made noise when rattled around a bit. I rattled the food bowl, sneaking a look at Mom. She was staring out the window in an unseeing sort of way. I rattled the bowl some more.

Mom turned to me at last. "Arthur! Do you ever think of anything besides your stomach?"

Why, yes, of course! I could have even come up with some examples, if given time. But Mom, although brilliant, had forgotten a key point. While I thought of many things, my stomach had a mind of its own and thought only of itself. I rattled the bowl around some more.

"You're incorrigible," Mom said.

Incorrigible! I'd forgotten that one! Bro had said the same thing. And so had Mrs. Salming. It had to be true! Arthur the Incorrigible. I loved the sound of it, kind of . . . heroic. Yes, that was it. And when you're a hero, you have nothing more to prove. Heroes could just kick back and chow down to their heart's content. Rattle rattle rattle.

"Good grief." Mom went to the broom closet where the giant-sized kibble bag was kept and was about to open it when the kids came in, Queenie riding in Harmony's special backpack. Did I have a special backpack? No. But did heroes bother themselves with little upsets like that? No way! Or possibly sometimes, when they were ravenous, for example.

"Hi, Mom," said the kids.

"Hi, kids," said Mom. "I just had the TV on. No news about Jimmy. You two holding up all right?"

The kids nodded. Harmony let Queenie out of the backpack. She headed straight to the door that led to the basement and disappeared.

"Pizza's on the way," Mom said. "And Emma's here. I invited her to stay for supper."

"Emma's here?" said Harmony.

"She dropped by to see you. I sent her up to your room."

Harmony went out the door that led to the family quarters and headed upstairs. Bro sat down at the counter. Mom glanced over at him, then went to the fridge—leaving the broom closet door unopened!—took out an apple, sliced it up, set the slices in front of Bro, together with a jar of peanut butter. Bro dipped an apple slice into the jar and started snacking away. Was he a bit unusual for a human when it came to food choices? Just one more reason for loving Bro.

"Bro?" Mom said. "Something on your mind?"

"Kinda."

"Don't talk with your mouth full."

Bro chomped and chewed for a while, then said, "Mom?"

"Still here."

"Is Ottoline a real name?"

"Why, yes—a woman's name, not popular these days or maybe ever. What brings this up? Ms. Pryor, I assume?"

"Ms. Pryor?" said Bro.

"Her first name is Ottoline."

Bro's mouth fell open. There was still some appley peanut butter mush inside.

"You didn't know?" Mom said.

Before she finished saying that, Bro was up and running, out of the kitchen and through the doorway to the family quarters. And I was right behind him! Sometimes the excitement just takes over and there's nothing you can do.

"Bro?" Mom called after us. "Bro?"

We reached the upstairs hall with Bro in the lead, but not by much. Harmony was just coming out of her room.

"Guess what," Bro said.

"Is she downstairs?"

"Huh?"

"Emma. Is she downstairs?"

"No. Well, I don't know. But guess what."

Harmony didn't answer. Instead she went down the hall, peering through doorways into Bro's room, the bathroom, Mom's room.

"Where is she?" Harmony said.

"Emma?"

"Yes, Emma! I've got a bad bad feeling."

"About Emma?" said Bro.

"About Emma in this house."

Bro went still. "Uh-oh."

"Yeah," Harmony said.

Then we were on the move, back down to the first floor, in and out of every room, except the kitchen. Were we looking for Emma? No Emma. I knew Emma, of course, Deputy Carstairs's daughter. And with those pigtails she was easy to spot. Imagine having two tails! Wow! For a moment, I wished I had another one. Then I thought: *What if my two tails didn't get along?*

By this time, we were down in the basement. First we checked the old, scary part where I never go, with the dirt floor and big clunky rusted-out stuff I didn't even know the names of. Bro snapped on all the lights, but it was still scary.

Then we headed into the new part. We checked the laundry room, the—

And there was Emma, coming out of the sports equipment room. She didn't see us, but turned the other way, moving down the hall, moving in an extra-quiet way like she was on her tiptoes, even though she wasn't. She came to the wine cellar, reached for the doorknob, put her hand on it.

"Emma?" Harmony said.

Emma screamed and wheeled around so fast her pigtails rose up sideways like wings. "Oh my god. You scared the life out of me."

"Did we?" Harmony said.

Emma held her hand to her chest. "My heart is pounding."

"Yeah?" said Harmony, gazing right into Emma's eyes.

Emma looked away. "I . . . I came to see you and got . . . got a little bored, so I went looking for . . . for the foosball game."

"It's in the Big Room." Harmony said that very quietly, but somehow it sounded like . . . like a threat? From Harmony? What was going on?

"You've been in the Big Room, lots of times," Harmony said.

"And you hate foosball," said Bro.

There was a moment of stillness. Then Emma burst into tears. "I'm so so sorry," she said, actually more like a wail than just saying something. "He said you'd be in big big trouble, Harmony. You and Bro, both of you. If Jimmy's here, you'd get sent to juvie for harboring a criminal. If . . . if I was any kind of a friend I should come and find out the truth, no matter how . . . how bad. You'll thank me for it one day. He promised me!"

"That will never—" Harmony began, and then the door to the wine cellar opened.

Jimmy stood in the doorway. And what was this? Queenie was perched on his shoulder? I didn't understand things even more than I'd thought.

"I knew something like this would happen, Bro," he said. "It's not going to work."

"It can still work," Bro said.

"We just have to think," said Harmony.

"Oh, Jimmy," Emma said. "I'm really really sorry, I know you didn't do anything bad and—"

"Shut up," Jimmy said.

Emma covered her face with her hands. Jimmy turned and took a step toward the nearest door, the one leading to the shuffleboard court. Bro put his hand on Jimmy's arm. At that moment, Mom called down the stairs.

"Kids? You down there? Emma's dad's here to take her home. Come on up. There'll be enough pizza for everybody."

In a very soft voice, maybe to herself, Emma said, "He's here? He promised he wouldn't do that."

"Right," said Jimmy. A look crossed his face, angry and dangerous. He shook loose from Bro's grip, dropped Queenie to the floor, bolted down the hall and out the door. Queenie followed, so fast she was just a whitish blur.

"Kids? What's going on?"

Harmony and Bro looked at each other. Then they looked at Emma.

"I won't tell him," Emma said. "I'll make up something, like . . . like . . . But please. Don't—"

"Let's go," Bro said.

And he and Harmony followed Jimmy, running outside and into the night. I didn't think for a second but raced after them at top speed. I'm at my absolute best when I don't think.

TWENTY-SEVEN
ARTHUR

WE FLEW THROUGH THE NIGHT! I'D never run so fast, not even during the incident with the coyote pack. At first it was very dark, which doesn't bother me at all, what with my nose and my ears, plus I'm pretty sure my eyes work better than yours at night. Well, they couldn't be worse, could they? No offense. Then things began to get brighter. I looked up and saw a huge cloud, like a lid, moving slowly across the sky and uncovering the moon, one of those full, round moons, my personal favorite. Bro and Harmony, somewhat ahead of me despite how fast I was running, came to a halt.

"Where did he go?" Bro said.

"It's they," said Harmony. "Queenie's with him."

"Should we call her?" Bro said.

"Call a cat?" said Harmony.

"Can't hurt to try."

Harmony glanced around. We were in the woods, standing by a big round rock, a rock I'd marked many times and now decided to mark once more. I'm the type who tries to do his duty.

Maybe they were going to call Queenie—good luck with that—but before they could, a light shone from back at the inn, a very powerful white light that penetrated all the way through the trees, leaving us just beyond its reach in the shadows. Harmony put her finger across her lips, the signal for quiet.

Bro turned to me and whispered. "Arthur! Find Jimmy! Find Queenie!"

I was happy to, just as soon as I finished up my current task. Once you've started doing what I was doing, there's no stopping until you're done. I'm sure that's not news to you.

"Arthur!"

What a long marking session this was turning out to be! I felt pretty pleased with myself and would have done some tail wagging, but I actually can't wag my tail and mark at the same time. Why was that? Was some sort of trick involved? Playing dead was my only trick so far—and a very good one—but maybe I could learn another, given time. Meanwhile the kids were gazing down at me, their eyes silvery gleams in the moonlight, actually a little scary.

"Is something wrong with him?" Harmony said. "How come his tail's twitching like that?"

"Maybe he's having a seizure," said Bro.

Me, a seizure? I didn't even know what that was. I finished up with my marking duties, gave myself a good shake, and got ready for the next assignment, unfortunately now forgotten.

"Come on, Arthur," Bro said. "We need you tonight."

How nice to be needed! I felt so happy!

He squatted down in front of me. "Find Jimmy. Find Queenie."

That was it? Consider it done! Their scents were all over these woods. I gave Bro's face a quick lick and got right to work.

"Whoa!" said Bro.

"He's headed back home," said Harmony.

Why, of course! I was just following their scent trails, so thick and unlosable, and that's where they led, back toward home and that strange bright light, bobbing through the trees.

Bro ran up and grabbed my collar, but very gently. "That's where they came from, Arthur," he said, also very gently. "But where did they go?"

Ah!

I reversed course immediately. Do I need to be told twice? Or even once? I'm at your service, even if it meant going in the exact wrong direction from where—with any luck at all—my dinner was waiting. Don't forget I still hadn't had my dinner. I was out in the middle of nowhere, performing at a very high level, and on an empty stomach.

I trotted back to the big rock—and actually considered marking it again, deciding at the last second—

"Oh my god!"

—or maybe slightly later, that this was not the right time, and kept going, through a thicket full of burrs, up a rise, and into a grove of trees, the kind with spiky leaves that stay on the branches all year long. The scents of Jimmy and Queenie were very strong here, all closed in by the trees. For a moment I thought they might even be in this little grove. But no. I went round and round in a swirl of scents, and then sort of got pulled out of the grove in a way that's hard to describe, and I trotted down a long path—not a real path, but a scent path—that led to a meadow with an old, falling-down barn at the back end, silvery where the moonlight shone on it, black in the shadows. Hey! That was our barn, the old one. Wow! I was missing absolutely nothing tonight. And on an empty stomach, a stomach that was starting to growl, so we'd probably be having to cut this excursion short.

Have I already mentioned the old barn? I don't mean the new barn, down a little lane past the tomato patch, where we keep the snowblower, the lawn mower, some chickens, and El Jefe, the pig, who is no fan of mine, by the way. This old barn goes way way back. Some dude named Ethan Allen slept in it one long-ago night, a small fact Mom used to tell all the guests until she realized none of them had heard of Ethan Allen. Just like me! But the point is that the old barn is empty and no one goes there. Mom has plans to knock it down, except that takes money. So it just sits there, getting older.

I headed across the moonlit meadow and straight for the old barn.

"He's onto something," Bro said, and he and Harmony hurried along beside me, walking quite fast to keep up.

Yes, I was onto something. Had I stopped to think, I might have realized that I was no longer picking up the slightest trace of Jimmy or Queenie scent. But I did not stop to think. I soldiered bravely on, which is what incorrigible heroes do.

"Good boy," Bro whispered.

"Good good boy," whispered Harmony.

I tried to pick up the pace and almost did. Was I a champ at following scents? Like you wouldn't believe! In my brain I had three scents mixing all together right now in a way that made total sense. I, Arthur, understood all.

We came to the barn door, a big door hanging loose at an angle from the rail. Harmony put her hand on my collar, and Bro went in first.

"Jimmy?" he called, a soft sort of call. No answer, of course. "Queenie?" No Queenie, either. But that didn't mean no one was in the barn. I moved past Bro, led the way across the uneven floor, the boards torn up in places, dead leaves scattered here and there, and cobwebs everywhere, some hanging all the way down from the beams above, silver in the moonlight, which came through glassless windows and holes in the walls and roof. There were stalls along one side, all empty. All empty except for the last one, where I stopped. My tail got going real good. It just couldn't stop itself.

The kids stood beside me, staring wide-eyed into the stall.

"Oh my god," Bro said. "Sweet Lady Em?"

"Got to be," said Harmony.

I, Arthur!

We gazed at Sweet Lady Em. She gazed back at us, chewing on whatever cows chew on. There was fresh hay on the floor and a few bales at the back of the stall.

"What's she doing here?" Bro said.

"It's pretty clever," said Harmony.

Bro nodded. "If whatever the plan was fell apart—"

"We'd get blamed for stealing Lady Em," Harmony said. "Let's get her out of here. She's proof."

Sweet Lady Em was roped to a hook. Bro untied the rope and then—and then I heard voices outside, voices I knew. My ears went straight up. Was barking the right move? I was wondering about that when Bro went still. "Harm?" he whispered. And then she heard the voices, too. Hard to miss at this stage. The huge bearded guy named Curly wasn't whispering, but speaking at normal volume or louder.

"I don't like this," he said.

We ducked into Lady Em's stall and stood still. She didn't seem to mind or even notice, just went on chewing.

"You don't have to like it," said Roscoe.

Their footsteps moved across the floor, coming closer. I heard the snick of a match being struck, then smelled cigar smoke.

"What kind of sensor?" Curly said.

"I don't know what kind of sensor," said Roscoe. "She just said it looks like a ball, a red ball. It was supposed to sink to the bottom or something, but yesterday it sent out a signal. They got a bead on it."

"Bead?"

"Coordinates—like on a map. The signal came from inside the inn."

"Why can't we check in, like we're guests?"

"The kid from the inn's already seen us. How dumb are you? We break in tonight when they're all asleep. I've got this little doodad that'll help. It lights up when it gets near the thing. Meanwhile we're supposed to let the cow go."

"Why?"

"The cow thing didn't work out. Isn't that obvious?"

"But—"

"Curly? Do you like the money?"

"Yeah."

"Then why all the questions?"

Curly had no answer. Neither did I. In fact, their conversation was a complete mystery to me. All I knew for sure were two things. First, Harmony and Bro were very scared. I could smell it. Second, Roscoe and Curly were coming our way.

These were not the kind of men who move quietly. Clomp clomp clomp went the hard soles of their boots. We got as far back in the stall as we could, not very far, since Lady Em didn't seem interested in sharing her space.

"One thing I won't miss," Curly said, "is taking care of this stupid animal. Like I'm some hick from—"

And then they were right in front of the stall, peering in. The moonlight seemed to brighten, a very bad moment for the moonlight to do that. For just an instant, Roscoe and Curly looked shocked, maybe even a little scared. But they recovered real quick.

"Well, well," Curly said. "What have we here?"

"Our year-end bonus," said Roscoe. "Come on out, kids. Recess is over."

Harmony's face got very hard, like it was made of stone. "You're going to jail," she said.

The kids didn't move. Neither did I. We stayed where we were, jammed all together beside Lady Em.

"Too bad you had to say that," said Roscoe. "This could have had a happy ending. Go on and pull them out."

"I don't know, Roscoe. They're just kids and—"

"Zip it," Roscoe said. "Or you can kiss this job goodbye." Roscoe got a real mean look on his face, shoved Lady Em to the side, at least slightly, and came striding into the stall. "Let's go," he said, and grabbed Harmony's arm.

Bro made a noise like I'd never heard before, at least not from a human. A growl, yes, but the sort of growl you'd hear from one of my kind. Bro growled that dog-type growl—the growl of a very big dog—and then rose up and threw a punch, a real hard punch, at least for a kid, that caught Roscoe right in the gut.

"Ooof," went Roscoe, and his cigar flew out from between his lips and into the straw. Then his eyes got wild and mad, and he threw a punch of his own, hitting Bro bang on the mouth. A tooth spun past me, catching the moonlight and vanishing. Then came blood, Bro's blood. Something happened inside me at that moment. I really don't want to remember. But the next thing I knew, I had Roscoe by the throat, down there in the straw. Straw, by the way, that now seemed to be on fire. Roscoe pounded on me, and now Curly, too, was in the stall, trying to corral Bro and Harmony. Lady Em began to moo, very loud moos that seemed to make the whole barn tremble. Flames started shooting up high, making lots of noise of their own.

That was enough for Lady Em. She bolted from the stall, not out the open front, the path most of us would have chosen, but through one of the walls. Somehow she didn't just take down the wall, but also a tall, thick post that rose up high into the shadows. She also ran right over Curly, who fell and seemed a little slow getting up. A moment later a whole big piece of the loft above, or maybe the roof, came plummeting down.

"Bro!" Harmony shouted. She was on her feet, reaching for Bro, pulling him out of the stall. Getting out seemed like a good idea to me, too. I let go of Roscoe and sprang—yes, all four paws off the ground at once—on out of there.

CRASH! Heavy flaming shapes tumbled down from above, like a whole fiery storm was going on in the barn. Roscoe and Curly were yelling things at the top of their lungs, but their voices sounded tiny. We ran from the storm, Harmony supporting Bro and me taking care of me, easy peasy for an incorrigible hero such as myself. Out the door we raced, and a moment later came an enormous blast and the whole barn caught fire, lighting up the night. Meanwhile Lady Em had taken off across the meadow, not headed for home, but in the opposite direction. Couldn't we just leave her here? I was very very hungry.

But no. We followed Lady Em, meaning I was still running, perhaps slightly behind Harmony and Bro, side by side, their legs churning in perfect unison.

"Won't she come back on her own?" Bro said.

"But what if she doesn't?" said Harmony. "Lady Em's the key to the whole case!"

So we ran and ran and ran some more. We were already past the longest run of my life and it didn't seem to be ending anytime soon. Then, from somewhere behind us, I heard a man calling, "Halt! Police!" the sound very faint, completely missed by Harmony and Bro. I looked back and saw we were far from the burning barn. Somewhere way back there, a white searchlight shone through the trees. Two silhouettes, one Curly-sized, one Roscoe-sized, went running through the white light. The distant man called again, his call barely reaching my ears.

"Halt!" This time he added, "Or we'll shoot."

The silhouettes stopped running; silhouette arms raised up high in the circle of white light. We ran on.

TWENTY-EIGHT
QUEENIE

SOME NIGHTS, ESPECIALLY WHEN the moon is bright, have a strange effect on me. They make me feel enormous and very powerful, like the moon itself. This was one of those nights.

We sat on the bank of Blackberry Creek, Jimmy and I, a very short distance upstream from Catastrophe Falls. The creek was flowing fast, black with silver sparkles from the moonlight, and where it reached the edge and rolled over for the long fall, it turned all silvery, bubbling and frothing. Like . . . like it was fighting not to go over. On the far side of the falls the downed tree that had saved Bro was still sticking into the water. Jimmy seemed to be staring at it, but when he finally spoke, I realized his mind was on something else.

"They say this is mine now, Queenie. Isn't that crazy? How can anybody own a waterfall?"

I didn't know. Neither was I interested. What interested me were Jimmy's troubles. What they were was a complete unknown to me, but I could see them clearly on his face and in his eyes. Jimmy was a loner. I was certain of that. It takes one to know one. Among my kind we're pretty much all loners, each and every one. Why? Because we're so in command of life. Surely you've noticed that by now. Maybe it makes you jealous. I don't care. And jealousy will get you nowhere, by the way. There's a free tip. Try to remember it.

Most humans are not loners, and with good reason. They don't do well on their own. I'm not judging them. Just sayin'. But it's hard not to judge them a little bit. Sometimes, wanting so much not to be loners, they get mixed up with the wrong people. That's bad. When they get mixed up with the right people, it's good. It can even be perfect, like with Mom, Harmony, and Bro. But that didn't happen often.

And here, not far from the BOOM BOOM BOOM, we had Jimmy, his troubles, and me. Jimmy picked up a twig and tossed it in the creek. It landed with a tiny splash and zoomed down the creek and over the falls, picking up speed the whole time, like it was getting sucked away by something mighty. Jimmy didn't take his eyes off that twig, and when it was gone he still kept his eyes on the blank spot where it had dropped from view.

"I saw this movie," he said. "Where this guy just jumped in his car, took off for New Mexico, started a new life."

Oh? That sounded pretty iffy to me. For one thing, Jimmy was a kid. Could I imagine Bro, say, doing any of that? Well, the jumping in the car part and taking a spin, yes—I'd already seen him doing that, a secret, I suppose—but the rest of it? Not a chance.

"What am I going to do, Queenie?" Jimmy shivered, although the night really wasn't that cold. It even might have been warming up. I sniffed the air and picked up the very faintest aroma of spring, still far far away but out there somewhere.

Jimmy tossed another twig into the creek. It went over the falls, just like the last one. I didn't like how Jimmy watched it go. Maybe we needed to be someplace else. I was trying to think where, when something stirred in the nearby bushes, and out into the open stepped a tall, lean figure dressed all in black, her hair and eyes the color of the moon. It was Ms. Pryor.

Jimmy scrambled to his feet. "Ms. Pryor?"

"Hello, Jimmy," she said, coming forward.

Jimmy backed away, right to the water's edge. "What are you doing here?"

"Don't worry," Ms. Pryor said. "I came looking for you, but not like the others. I want to help."

"What others?"

"All the others, really. Even that very nice family, the Reddys. None of them have your interests at heart."

"Sure they do," Jimmy said. "Bro and Harmony are my friends."

"I wish that were true," Ms. Pryor said. "But the truth is they don't want you to take advantage of your fantastic opportunity." She smiled, just a brief silver flash, maybe to herself. "The kind of opportunity that doesn't come along often, like taking off for the wide-open spaces, starting a new life."

Jimmy went still. "A new life?"

Ms. Pryor nodded. "You're young. It can happen."

Jimmy thought about that. I did not want him to think about it. I did not want to be near Ms. Pryor. I moved slightly away, upstream, seeing if Jimmy would follow. He did not.

"What's this fantastic opportunity?" Jimmy said.

"Let's sit down," Ms. Pryor said.

I did not want Jimmy to sit down, but he did, on the bank by the edge of the creek. Ms. Pryor sat beside him.

"Fantastic opportunities are all the same," she said. "They come down to a big bundle of money. All you have to do is tell Mrs. Reddy that you want to sell the farm." She took out a card, handed it to Jimmy. "Sell it to us," she added.

Jimmy read the card by moonlight. "Ottoline Pryor, Special Operations, Mellontic." He looked up. "Are you going to farm it?"

"In a manner of speaking, yes."

"I'd have to think," Jimmy said.

Ms. Pryor made her voice very gentle. But the effort part leaked into her tone and clashed with the gentle part in a way that was unpleasing to my ears. "Yes, Jimmy, think, by all means. But I already know what you're thinking. It goes like this. 'I'm eleven years old—what am I going to do with a pile of money?'"

"Well, kinda, I guess, but—"

"The good news," Ms. Pryor said, talking over him, "is that there are things you can do, really fun things. Did you know there's a school in Colorado where the desk part of the day lasts only two hours, and all the rest of the time is spent skiing and hiking in the mountains?"

"No."

"And there's another one in Hawaii that's all about surfing. Ever surfed, Jimmy?"

"No."

"You look like an athlete. I bet you'd be a great surfer. And the word is you've got real potential as a pitcher."

"Yeah?"

"News gets around in a small town. But I bring it up because out in LA there's another school that's all about grooming kids with baseball potential for the big leagues. I could help get you into any of these places."

"You could?"

"None of them cheap, of course. But the good news is you'll be able to afford it. All you have to do is sell the farm."

"The big leagues?"

"They sent a kid to the Red Sox last year. Ever watch the Red Sox on TV?"

"Almost every game, at least for an inning or two," Jimmy said. He faced the creek and gazed at all that water racing by. Ms. Pryor moved a little closer to him. The moonlight turned her face as white as the markers in the town graveyard but left her eyes in shadow.

At last Jimmy said, "All those schools sound great. But the farm's been in my family forever. It doesn't feel right."

Ms. Pryor's head snapped back, as though he'd hit her. "That's what your father said, and look what happened." The gentleness was all gone from her voice.

Jimmy turned to her. "What do you mean? You talked to my dad?"

"It's not important," said Ms. Pryor. "We're way off topic and time's running—"

Then came a boom, not the booming of the falls, but more like a thunderclap. Away from the creek, back toward the inn, the sky went red.

"What's that?" Jimmy said, looking alarmed.

Ms. Pryor glanced at the red sky. "People are so use-less." Sirens started up, distant but on the way. "Time is running out, Jimmy. That's the deputy with a whole squad of cops. He's a stupid man, and stupid men do stupid things when they're frustrated. Like shooting first and asking questions later."

Jimmy jumped up. "But I didn't do it! I didn't hit my dad!"

"I believe you," Ms. Pryor said. She rose and stood right beside him. "But lots of folks around here never will, no matter what happens."

Jimmy just sagged. I hated seeing that, and moved closer to him.

"That's why you need to get away." Ms. Pryor's voice got gentle again. "I've got a surprise for you. Do you know the lookout off old Route 99?"

Jimmy pointed across the creek. "It's on the other side of those woods."

"I've got a car waiting there for you. And guess who's driving."

"Who?"

"Your mom."

"My mom?" Jimmy stumbled, almost falling into the creek.

"She's cleaned herself up and wants to make a new start."

"But . . . but how . . . how did you find her?"

"Special operations. That's what I do."

The sirens got louder. I heard voices and also some strange bashing noise, coming closer.

"Swim to her, Jimmy. It's your only chance."

"But . . . but the falls." Poor Jimmy. He looked so scared.

Ms. Pryor took his hand and walked him a few steps upstream, coming closer to me. "The creek's much weaker up here. You're a strong kid. You can do it."

Sirens screamed in the night, closing in from different directions. Jimmy and Ms. Pryor stood side by side, eyeing the water. His eyes were full of fear. Hers were still deep in shadow. What could I do? Bite Ms. Pryor? Maybe biting Jimmy was smarter. I was leaning in that direction, when Jimmy said, "I don't know."

"Sure you do," said Ms. Pryor. She rested her hand on his back. "Don't be a coward."

"I'm not a coward!"

"Then go."

Ms. Pryor got her other hand on Jimmy's back, bent her knees, and—

And at that moment something huge and clumsy came blundering out of the woods. A cow? Cow! Yes, a cow, with terrified eyes, big and rolling, and Harmony and Bro running up behind her. The cow suddenly saw the creek and jammed on the brakes, coming to a juddering stop at the water's edge. But—but not before knocking into Ms. Pryor! Ms. Pryor cried out, pinwheeled her arms, and toppled into the water, the sound of the splash totally swallowed up in the BOOM BOOM BOOM. Blackberry Creek enfolded Ms. Pryor and swept her away, so fast.

"Oh my god!" Jimmy said.

Bro ripped off his jacket and stepped into the creek. Harmony grabbed him and held him back, held him with all her might. Meanwhile Ms. Pryor was trying with everything she had in her to swim across the creek.

"Swim!" Jimmy shouted. "Swim!"

And Ms. Pryor swam. She was a very strong swimmer, and while she didn't quite reach the other side—coming so close!—she was able to catch hold of the fallen tree, the same one Bro had latched onto.

"Hold on!" Jimmy shouted. "Hold on!" The kids all shouted, "Hold on! Hold on!"

But then: CRACK!

The tree split in two, and the part that Ms. Pryor was clinging to, clinging tight, shot toward the edge of the falls. She was looking our way. The expression on her face was one of complete surprise. Then it started to get much much darker. The moonlight finally shone on her eyes. They were terrified.

And then she was gone.

That was when Arthur arrived, panting heavily. We all gathered in a tight, little circle. Even me. The sky glowed red on the faces of the kids. I'll never forget how they looked under that red sky.

BOOM BOOM BOOM.

TWENTY-NINE

QUEENIE

WE HAD A PARTY IN THE BIG ROOM. Deputy Carstairs was not invited, but Emma was. She didn't come. Jimmy's uncle flew in from Dubai. He was going to stay at the farm with Jimmy for a while, but there were no solid plans for after that.

At least at the beginning, it was the quietest human party I'd ever attended, and therefore my favorite. Maxie Millipat was the big exception to the quiet part. He was jumping up and down. Not an expression: He really was. He'd found out all about Mellontic, a data-mining startup with plans to crunch all the information on everybody on the whole planet and sell it to whoever would pay. Mellontic was headed by a brilliant guy named Sergei—so brilliant he might be capable of appreciating Maxie. And Maxie was actually going to meet Sergei at the party. Maxie had invented a ball for the occasion, a ball that could do everything the red ball did, but "smaller, better, and blue," as Maxie told everyone who would listen and some who would not. Maxie was asking two million dollars for his blue ball, but he was willing to take one point nine mill.

Sergei did show up, in his skinny jeans and red sneaks, but he didn't meet Maxie, didn't get past the kitchen, where he had a private talk with Mom. Well, with me and Mom.

"Let's start with Curly and Roscoe," Mom said. "Now in lockup in the town jail. Among the worst of what they did was bribing Walter. He's going to juvie and he deserves it, but doesn't it leave a bad taste in your mouth?"

"If I'd been involved, of course it would," Sergei said. "But the fact is I heard all three names this morning for the very first time. You have to understand that Ottoline Pryor was a rogue employee—in fact, not even an employee but a contractor operating out of Menlo Park, on the other side of the country from headquarters."

"So her roguish secrets die with her?" Mom said.

Sergei blinked. "That's one way of putting it. I now believe she was unbalanced, Yvette. Mind me calling you Yvette?"

"Let's stick to Ms. Reddy," Mom said.

"Certainly. As you wish. I'm very sorry for what happened here. The truth is her conduct hurt me, too."

"You're one of the wounded parties?" Mom said.

"Not the most wounded, of course," Sergei said. "But as

a token of my—let's call it discomfort—I'd like you to accept this."

He handed Mom a check. Mom glanced at it.

"In return," Sergei said, taking an envelope from his pocket, "I'd like you to sign this little paper."

Mom didn't take the envelope. She handed back the check. "I'm sure you can find your own way out," she said.

Not long after that, back in the Big Room, Bertha handed a phone to Jimmy. "For you," she said.

Jimmy took the phone. "Hello?"

He listened. His face went through some changes, very hard to describe, but they were big.

"Thanks," he said at the end of the call. "Bye."

"Who was it?" Bro said.

"A nurse from the hospital," said Jimmy.

"What did she say?" Harmony said.

"My . . . my dad woke up for a few minutes. This was about an hour ago. He's not awake now, but he's not in a coma anymore. Just sleeping."

"That's great!" said Harmony and Bro.

"And while he was awake, he spoke," Jimmy said.

"Yeah?" said the kids.

"Only one word."

"What was it?"

"Jimmy," said Jimmy.

Things got noisier after that. Dancing started up, a clumsy spectacle I had no time for. I ended up back in the kitchen, specifically in the corner near the fridge. My special china saucer, white with the gold border, lay on the floor in that corner, filled to the brim with my cream, the best cream in the world, straight from Sweet Lady Em. I was just lowering my sweet little face to it when a certain party came ambling up, his tail wagging in that all-too-obvious way. His gaze went to the cream—my cream, my personal cream, the cream belonging to Queenie and no one but Queenie—and then to me. Our eyes met. Was he serious? Did he really imagine that wagging his ridiculous tail was going to persuade the likes of me? I did notice that he had Maxie's blue ball in his mouth. A certain party is not a complete loss.

I took a slow, delicate sip. Yes, he has some good qualities. For example, just by being here, watching, he made my sweet cream taste all the sweeter. I had no complaints. Life was good. And allow me to make one correction. Forget that phrase, "the likes of me." It's dishonest, and I'd never want that. The truth is there's no one like me, end of story.

ACKNOWLEDGMENTS

Many thanks to Mallory Kass, my smart, funny, and talented editor.

ABOUT THE AUTHOR

Spencer Quinn is the pen name of the Edgar Award–winning novelist Peter Abrahams. He has written many books for younger readers, including the *New York Times* bestselling Bowser and Birdie series, the Edgar-nominated Echo Falls series, *Ruff vs. Fluff*, *Paws vs. Claws*, and *Bark vs. Snark*. His novels for adults include *Oblivion*, *The Fan* (made into a movie starring Robert De Niro), *The Right Side*, and the *New York Times* bestselling Chet and Bernie mystery series. He lives with his wife, Diana, and dogs, Audrey and Pearl, on Cape Cod, Massachusetts.

KEEP READING FOR

A PEEK AT THE NEXT

QUEENIE AND ARTHUR

NOVEL, *BARK VS. SNARK!*

ARTHUR

GO, ARTHUR, GO!"

When Bro says go, I go, you better believe it. The green Frisbee soared into the sky, and I soared after it, my paws hardly touching down. Good luck, Mr. Frisbee, with ol' speedy-legs Arthur on the trail! Mr. Frisbee sailed over a park bench, curved around a tree, dipped down under a bridge, hitched a ride on a freight train, zipped into the open window of an office tower, and zoomed out through a window on the far side, but it was all for nothing, because I, Arthur, did all those things, too. And more! The look on Mr. Frisbee's face when he glanced back and saw me right on his tail? I was still enjoying that sight as I snatched him out of the air, spun on a dime, and charged back to Bro. By that time there was a huge crowd in Yankee Stadium, clapping and cheering. I trotted to the center of the field, letting everyone get a real good look at me. A chant rose up. "AR-THUR! AR-THUR! AR-THUR!" How nice of them! I pranced round and round the stadium, Mr. Frisbee securely between my teeth, my tail raised high.

"AR-THUR! AR-THUR! AR—"

Ding.

What was that?

Ding.

The crowd went silent.

Ding.

Ding? That ding reminded me of the bell on the front desk at the Blackberry Hill Inn. But I was nowhere near the inn. Wasn't I on the mound at Yankee Stadium? I tried to take a good look but saw nothing! Oh, no! What was happening to me? Then my eyes opened all by themselves.

And there I was, not exactly on the mound at Yankee Stadium. Much more like on the floor in the front hall of the Blackberry Hill Inn, curled up as though I'd been napping. Which I would certainly never do! Not in the middle of a busy day. Don't forget I'm in charge of security here at the inn. This was no time for play. I opened my mouth to let Mr. Frisbee drop out, but there was no Mr. Frisbee, although his plasticky taste lingered on my tongue for a moment or two.

Ding.

My gaze went to the desk, where a stranger with a suitcase was dinging the bell with the tip of his finger. Strangers are very much my business. I barked a low bark, not threatening, but just to make my presence known, the presence of someone you don't want to mess with. I could handle Mr. Frisbee and I could handle you, fella. But . . . but had I actually handled Mr. Frisbee? Or . . . or . . .

The stranger slowly turned my way. I've seen lots of humans, but never one who looked quite like this. An older sort of guy most likely, to judge from his shaggy white eyebrows and wild white hair, but his face didn't have much going on in the way of wrinkles, and his teeth were bright white.

He gazed down at me, then spoke in a deep, booming voice. "You won't get far on your looks."

That was baffling. I had no need for going far—or anywhere, for that matter. I was right here, at home. Poor guy, kind of out of it. I decided to put him in the picture. I rose, gave myself a quick head-clearing shake, and made my way over to my white-toothed friend. Hey! He was wearing tassel loafers. I hadn't seen tassel loafers in some time, but I had fond memories of the tassels themselves, especially their nubbly mouthfeel. I lowered my head, got my lips pulled back, and—

And the front door opened and Mom came in, a dirt smear on one cheek and a potted plant in both hands.

"Oh, hello," she said. "Is anyone helping you?"

"Not so you'd notice," said the man. All of a sudden he sounded kind of old, his voice thin and scratchy.

"Well, now I'm here, so—Arthur? What are you doing?"

Me? Why, nothing, nothing at all. I backed away from

those tassel loafers double-quick, my tongue possibly gliding over the toe of the shoe but completely missing out on
the tassel itself. Life is full of frustrations. You just have to
find a way to deal. I lay down in the nearest corner, and
found to my surprise that the tip of my tail was lying quite
close by. Almost saying, "Gnaw on me." What a stroke of
luck! Lucky strokes are how to deal, in my experience. I
got busy on my tail.

"Don't mind Arthur," Mom was saying to the white-
toothed guy. "He means well."

Of course I did! Many thanks to Mom for pointing
it out, but that didn't stop the man from shooting me a
glance that might have been a teensy bit on the unfriendly
side. There must have been some mistake. Doesn't everybody like ol' Arthur?

"So what can I—" Mom began.

"I want a room for five nights," the man said. "A quiet room,
far from"—he glanced my way again—"any disturbance."

"Do you have a reservation?" said Mom.

He gazed around the front hall and raised one of those
shaggy white eyebrows. "Do I need one?"

There was the tiniest pause before Mom spoke. She
pauses like that sometimes. I have no idea what it means,
but it always gets my attention.

"It's usually better," Mom said, "but in this case we do
have the Daffodil Room available."

"How much?"

Mom said some number I missed. Numbers are very missable in my experience, and maybe in yours, too. The man handed over his credit card. What is a credit card? I have no idea, but they always get passed back and forth when a guest checks in. I know the routine, better believe it! Could I run the front desk all by myself? Wow, what a thought!

"Welcome, Mr. Ware," Mom said, handing him a key. "I don't know if you have any interest in county fairs, but ours starts tomorrow."

"I have no interest in county fairs." He picked up his suitcase and headed toward the broad staircase that led to the guest rooms on the second floor. The suitcase gave off a very faint smell of cotton candy. I'd only come across cotton candy once before, and that was on my one and only visit to a Halloween party, sometime in the past. A very short visit, possibly because of an incident involving me, my nose, and a big vat of cotton candy. The point is I know the smell of cotton candy. Smells I know can sort of pull me along. For example, the smell of cotton candy was now pulling me to my feet, across the hall, and up the stairs, close behind Mr. Ware. When he came to the door of the Daffodil Room I was right behind him. He unlocked the door, went in, kicked the door closed with his heel, a heel that just missed my head. But who's luckier than me?

There I was in the Daffodil Room, hot on the cotton candy trail.

Meanwhile Mr. Ware didn't seem to be noticing me. He heaved his suitcase onto the bed in one easy motion— pretty good for an old guy—and then opened it and took out a black cloth bag, made, as I knew right away from the smell, of velvet. I forgot all about cotton candy and started concentrating on velvet, which is lovely for both licking and chewing, as you may know already. Also velvet doesn't stick to your nose like cotton candy. I made a big decision, then and there: velvet yes, cotton candy no.

Mr. Ware took the black velvet bag to a small table against the wall, the kind of table with a mirror for putting on makeup. He sat down and gazed at himself in the mirror, actually seemed to be staring into his own eyes. That gave me a bad feeling, so I was glad when he stopped doing it and reached up, maybe to pat his wild white hair into place.

Only that wasn't what happened! Instead he reached his fingers deep into the whole white mess and . . . and pulled it off! Oh, no! He'd pulled off all his hair? That must have hurt so bad! Once I'd had a little incident with my tail and a pot of superglue, so you can trust me on this.

But Mr. Ware did not seem to be in any pain. He sort of folded up his hair, still somehow in one piece, like the whole patch of skin underneath had come off, too—oh, how horrible!—and shoved it into the velvet bag. That was when I saw that Mr. Ware hadn't lost any skin from his head, now covered in dark hair, cut very short, and not bleeding or anything like that.

He went back to gazing at himself in the mirror. How strange he looked! Was he thinking the same thing? Was he about to say, "How strange I look," and put his hair back on?

Mr. Ware did neither of those things. Instead he reached out and pinched the end of one of his shaggy white eyebrows between his finger and his thumb and . . . and ripped it right off his face! Again no cry of pain, no blood. Underneath the shaggy white eyebrow lay another eyebrow, not shaggy, and brown in color. Was Mr. Ware going to rip that one off, too? At that moment I wanted to be out of there. I glanced at the door, but it was shut tight. Once Bro had tried to teach me how to turn a doorknob with my front paws, but that ended up being a little too hard—I had to stand on only my back paws at the same time!—even though he promised me a whole sausage the instant I got the knack. Should I mention that somehow that sausage found its way into my mouth later that same day? Life is good at the Blackberry Hill Inn.

Although maybe not in the Daffodil Room. This new Mr. Ware, again staring at himself in the mirror, was kind of scary. I wanted the old Mr. Ware back. The old Mr. Ware's face wasn't quite so hard. Was this a good time to sidle a little closer, let him know I was on the premises and now wanted out? I was just about to do that when Mr. Ware ripped off his other white eyebrow. He put both eyebrows in the black velvet bag. That was when I was hit by a memory, a sort of tremendous one: I'd see this dude before. I mean the younger one. He'd stayed at the inn some time ago. How long ago? That was a tough one, not the kind I'm good at answering, so I didn't even try. Why make yourself unhappy?

But the point was I'd seen him. I don't forget a face. And even if I do, I hadn't forgotten this one. And here was something amazing: He'd been wearing tassel loafers that time, too! Tassel loafers stick in the mind. Not only that, but a bunch of mountain bikers had been staying with us at the same time. Mr. Ware and Harmony and Bro watched them ride off early one morning, right on the front step, where I'd been at that moment, real close to those tassel loafers. Harmony had said, "Would I love a mountain bike or what?" And Bro had said, "Are they expensive?" "Oh, yeah," Harmony had told him.

Wow! What an interesting day I was having, just staying in my own mind. And then came an interesting question. How come he'd turned himself into the old Mr. Ware? I waited. No answer, meaning it was another tough one, and you already know how I handle tough ones.

Meanwhile he was fishing around in his velvet bag, and soon pulled out a small red squishy sort of ball. Balls are always interesting. You can play fetch with them, of course, which would be so much better if humans did the chasing, but there's also simply chewing on a ball to one's heart's content, always a good way to pass the time. Was there a chance Mr. Ware would now notice me, hand over the ball, and open the door so I could leave, taking the ball with me? Yes, there was every chance! It was about to happen for sure!

Instead something happened I'd never dreamed of. Most of my dreams are about food, although sometimes I dream about napping, but that's not the point. Mr. Ware took that soft squishy ball and stuck it on his nose!

A loud, high-pitched, possibly even frightened bark seemed to shake the walls of the Daffodil Room. Mr. Ware's head whipped around in my direction. He didn't appear to be barking so it had to be me. There you see a little something about how I roll. Even though I was possibly the slightest bit frightened—although fear is something that never ever gets into the heart of ol' Arthur, except if something really scary is going on—I could still keep a cool head and figure out who was doing the barking. Wow! I can be pretty impressive, as maybe you hadn't known. But now you do!

Mr. Ware rose from the stool he'd been sitting on and came toward me. "What are you doing in my room, you dirty dog?"

Whoa! First of all, I lived here! Maybe not in the Daffodil Room, but certainly in the inn, and the room was in the inn, so . . . I lost the trail of where I was heading, but then I remembered the second of all. Dirty dog? He'd called me a dirty dog! No way! We have a little pond in back of the old barn, and Bro and Harmony had shampooed me in it just the other day. I couldn't have been cleaner! Who likes to be called dirty when they're clean? Not me, my friends. I barked right in Mr. Ware's face, really let him have it.

Mr. Ware's eyes narrowed in a mean way. And then he reared back on one foot and . . . and kicked me with the other one! I leaped out of the way, lightning fast. Actually the lightning-fast part—and maybe the whole leap—happened only in my mind. But Mr. Ware's kick missed anyway. Was he expecting me to be lightning fast? Had I outthought him? Ha!

"Go on," he yelled. "Git."

He strode to the door and flung it open. I trotted out, in no particular hurry, the clear winner. But wouldn't you know? Mr. Ware tried to kick me again! This time he got me, although not squarely, more like his foot brushed my side. Which made his tassel loafer fly off! I ran toward it, but Mr. Ware, turning out to be pretty speedy himself, got to the loafer ahead of me and snatched it up. As he did that—a real quick bend and snatch—there was a big and possibly very nice surprise. His red nose ball fell off and bounced down the hall toward the stairs. Do you waste time thinking in a moment like that? You do not! You race after that ball, you grab it, and you take off for parts unknown.

Which was exactly what I did.

"Stop!" hissed Mr. Ware. "Get back here! Heel!"

Heel? Was that one of the commands I was supposed to know? Before I could get a handle on that, I heard Mom calling from downstairs.

"Arthur? What are you doing up there?"

Well, it was kind of complicated. I glanced back. Mr. Ware's face was not a pleasant sight. I had to admit to myself that he might not be a fan. Holding the tassel loafer in one hand, he backed into the Daffodil Room and closed the door. At the very same moment, Mom appeared at the top of the stairs.

"Arthur? What's in your mouth?"

Why, nothing! Nothing was in my mouth. That was my first reaction. And then my mouth sent me a message: It was holding a ball, namely Mr. Ware's red nose ball. What luck! I darted past Mom and down the stairs.

"Arthur!"

Down the stairs I went! From behind I heard Mom's knock. "Mr. Ware? Everything okay?"

"Yes," said Mr. Ware, now speaking in his scratchy old man voice.

"Has Arthur been bothering you? I think he has something in his mouth. I hope it wasn't yours."

"I'm fine. And busy at the moment."

"I won't bother you," Mom said. "Call the desk if you need anything."

No answer from Mr. Ware. By that time I was in the front hall, sprinting toward the door. It happened to be closed, and I was realizing that was going to be a problem, when suddenly it opened and in came Elrod, the handyman, carrying a surprising number of big paint cans in his huge hands. He saw me and I saw him, both of these sightings a little on the late side.

"Arggh!" Crash! Bang! Bangitty bang-bang, that bangitty bang-bang being the paint cans. Were the lids not quite securely fastened? This was no time to hang around. I ran out the door, headed for the backyard, zoomed past the shuffleboard courts, and finally came to a stop in the tomato garden, completely out of breath. But on my in-breaths, I took in the lovely smell from all the fat red tomatoes hanging on the vines. Hmm. Those tomatoes reminded me of something. What was it? I thought and thought, and just when my head was starting to hurt, it came to me: the red nose ball! And would you believe it? There it was, still in my mouth! Wow! Without another thought, I buried it nice and deep in the soft brown earth of the tomato patch.

READY FOR MORE ADVENTURE? GET YOUR PAWS ON THESE CAN'T-MISS MYSTERIES FROM SPENCER QUINN!